£4



# THE ADVENTURES OF NANA BARB

BOOK ONE

## LOST IN TIME

John Auckland

**The Adventures of Nana Barb**
**Book One : Lost in Time**

First published in 2012 by

**Ecademy Press**
48 St Vincent Drive, St Albans, Herts, AL1 5SJ
info@ecademy-press.com
www.ecademy-press.com

Printed and bound by Lightning Source in the UK and USA.
Cover illustration by Paul Tinker.
Book layout by Neil Coe.

Printed on acid-free paper from managed forests. This book is printed on demand, so no copies will be remaindered or pulped.

**ISBN 978-1-908746-41-2**



A CIP catalogue record for this book is available from the British Library.



This book is available online and all good bookstores.

To Mum, for making it a reality,
to Dad for your continued support,
and to Hayley for everything.

Most of all, thank you to Barbara
for providing the inspiration.

## Prologue

On your planet, which in English is called Earth, we are known by many names: the Norsemen call us the *Norns*; the Romans *Parcae*; and the Classical Greeks know us as the *Moirae*. We are classed as a singular entity and given the name *Fate* by the Christians and *Qismah* by the Persians. The classical Greeks understand us best, of course. We have unlimited power over the Universe, more so than the Gods – naturally, since we created (and continue to create) them.

To escape us is impossible, as you will discover in this story. I suppose the most appropriate name to call us in English would be the Web-spinners. We weave a web through time and space in which every conscious mind is inexorably linked. The humans of your age – the early computer age – try to understand this network of consciousness through the science of Quantum Mechanics, but the most successful proponents of our existence are philosophical minds, not scientific ones.

Web-spinners: there are three of us, each with our own characteristics and mannerisms, which are apt to change as fast as culture itself. The importance of this will manifest throughout this tale because we each take it in turns to narrate and our personalities will affect the events that occur within these pages.

I am telling you this so you better understand the story I am about to tell you. It is the tale of one of my favourite creations, a dear sweet lady called Nana Barb. She was the first human to experience 'temporal shifting' – the first if you put existence on a timeline, which is the way you Humans like to view it.

I hope you like the story but if you don't, I really won't mind. You don't enter any popularity contests when signing up as a Web-spinner.

## Prologue Part II

The room was dark. A light flickered on to reveal a solitary figure seated at a round table. The Timeseeker jumped.

"You're late," said the man at the table.

The Timeseeker held his nerve, despite his fluttering chest.

"Time is relative," he replied in his thick Southern drawl. "Of all people you should know that."

"Yes, but time is precious, *you* should know that. The speed at which the Universe is expanding beyond the critical point is speeding up, and if we don't restore balance soon then all existence will cease to, well, exist."

"I'm fully aware of the situation we're in, my liege. I have been visited by the messenger you told me about, which means we are on track."

"Which means the chosen one has been located and the prophecy is coming true."

"Indeed." The Timeseeker scratched his bearded chin thoughtfully. "There's been one teeny hiccup, well, more a surprise than a hiccup."

The man at the table sat up with interest, his shadowed face a picture of concern.

"What hiccup?" he replied.

"The chosen one is… " he hesitated, not sure how to say it.

"Spit it out man, the chosen one is what?" he demanded, hissing the words through tight lips.

"The chosen one is a lady. An old lady."

His eyebrow raised at the corner; the only hint of a reaction.

"Well I never. In my lifetime I've seen many thousands of cultures across countless eras, and still the Fates continue to surprise me."

"Ain't that the truth," the Timeseeker agreed.

# CONTENTS

# CONTENTS

# CHAPTER 1

## Temporal Shift

## 09:22hrs, June 15th 2013 C.E. - Nether Wallop, England

Over two thousand years earlier, and about twenty miles away, Dave slept. The window of the lounge of number 21 Freecock Gardens was slightly ajar, allowing a soft breeze to enter the stagnant room. This tiny wind marked the beginning of a series of events that could determine the fate of all mankind. Causality Physicists of your future will one day attempt to trace the origins of this minor meteorological occurrence, since never before can such a small event lay claim to starting off the most epic day in the history of the Universe. As it turns out, the original source of the wind was a poorly Border Collie that lived in New Jersey (he had got the squits from eating some mouldy chicken).[1] These same physicists were later heard to remark that this was by far the most exciting event to happen in New Jersey. Such was the importance of this incident that it caused a resonance throughout time, making New Jersey the everlasting butt of everyone's jokes, if you can forgive the pun.

The origins, however, are fairly trivial because, in Dave's mind at least, that breeze was the start to both the best and worst day of his life: June 15th 2013. The curtain in his grandmother's lounge flapped just enough to knock a glass of water on to the sofa he was sleeping on.

## Dave

Dave woke up annoyed. He was always angry in the morning since waking up is an aggravating event when you are eighteen and

1 Narrator's footnote – technically you could trace this back further to the owner, Jack Goldstein, an alcoholic who had a habit of leaving food around the house in places where the dog could reach. You could trace this back even further – and some of these physicists did just that – all the way back to the Big Bang. Causality Physics was deemed a pointless scientific endeavour when every single event in history was eventually linked back to the Big Bang, and so was soon disbanded as a legitimate scientific practice.

inclined towards laziness, but today he was particularly irritated. He hadn't slept long enough, had a sore neck because the sofa was too short for him, and now he was wet. Fully clothed and sweating because of it, he pulled at the neck of his t-shirt to let some air flow through. His blurry eyes slowly accepted the brightness of the room in front of him.

*Why am I asleep in the lounge?* He had a habit of falling asleep in front of the television, so the thought didn't stay with him for long. He stood up dozily and wandered into the corridor, intent on catching a few more hours of sleep before starting the day. He threw open the door to his bedroom, and was met with the sight of a single red high-heeled ladies' shoe looking vastly out-of-place in the middle of his messy bedroom floor. His eyes looked at the alien object for a while, trying to make sense of it. The night before came back to him partially, like a child's picture puzzle left half-assembled by a bored toddler. Just a short way away was a red hairband, and a short way from that a cream handbag. Like a trail of breadcrumbs, these strange objects led his eyes to his bed. It was occupied, and all memories of the evening came flooding back as he recognised who was in it. Sleeping in his bed was the most beautiful girl in his village: Stacey Dawson.

His traditional morning sulk all but dispersed, he gawked at her sleeping form as he contemplated the situation. He'd only been staying at his Nan's house for a month or so and didn't know how she'd react to finding a strange girl – Stacey Dawson, of all people – in his bedroom. In his *bed*. He fought off an uncontrollable urge to make a whooping noise, but decided it was best to be quiet in case he gave his Nan a shock. Or worse, woke Stacey up.

Dave had lost his job about a month ago and had to give up on his dreams of a luxury bachelor pad, with games consoles galore and a separate beer fridge. Staying at his Nan's place was easy on the bank balance, but he'd started to notice their arrangement negatively affecting his already negligible romantic life. Before the move he'd been on his, albeit small, share of dates with women who were actually quite good-looking. His best mate Simon wasn't particularly subtle in nature or in the way he judged the attractiveness of women, and had deemed his dates worthy on average of around five points out of ten. Normally he would shout it well within the poor girl's earshot, much to the embarrassment of everyone other than Simon. Nowadays, as soon as Dave admitted to his living arrangements (not being the lying type), even three-pointers would suddenly make trips to the toilet never to be seen again.

He knew he wasn't ugly. His light brown hair was a bit of a curly mop, but his eyes could light a smoky room when he smiled, or so he'd been told by a drunk, middle-aged woman in a cocktail bar last summer, during his first ever holiday abroad in Kavos. One major asset was his ability to make girls laugh, even if it was more often *at* him than with him. He had a frustrating tendency to be exceptionally nervous around beautiful women. For that reason he was amazed he'd had the courage to engage in conversation with Stacey Dawson, a clear-cut nine-and-a-half-pointer. She would have been a ten if she didn't have an annoying voice.

Dave looked at Stacey sleeping, and found his eyes wandering to a bare leg sticking out of the side of the duvet. Embarrassed, he looked away.

He would have to wake her up before his Nan wandered into his room with his morning tea. He wasn't exactly sure how she would react to having a girl over. They hadn't got around to defining the rules for female visitors. He wished he hadn't fallen asleep with all his clothes on, so that her first waking image wasn't of his sweat-soaked hair. But then what other choice did he have? The only pyjamas he owned were really childish so he wouldn't have worn those in front of her, and he sure as hell wouldn't have slept in just his underwear. He might have accidentally shown her his body, and he was too self-conscious to show it to new people, especially popular people like Stacey Dawson who might spread the word amongst other popular people that David Wilson had a hairy belly and a spotty back. In comparison, Stacey's leg seemed to go on for ever, with smooth, tanned-looking skin and with such a delicately petite foot it was a wonder she didn't struggle for balance.

Stacey's other leg still had a shoe on, which meant she was hopefully still clothed underneath the duvet. She rolled out of the covers to half confirm his suspicion, unknowingly showing Dave her secret tattoo of Superman. She was still wearing all her clothes, but her dress had ridden up in her sleep.

Dave didn't know where to look and was suddenly frozen like a rabbit in headlights. A girl, a fit one at that, was mooning his bedroom ceiling, and if she woke up he would seem like a pervert for looking at her. Worse than that, his Nan would be up and making his morning tea. No way on Earth could he allow his grandmother to barge in and make an unexpected acquaintance with Stacey's very own man on the moon.

He also didn't want to put Stacey in an embarrassing situation for any reason, in case it put her off seeing him again. Baring your backside to a boy wasn't exactly breaking the ice. He made a decision, so with sweating hands he walked into the room and put his arms out to cover her with the duvet. As he neared her, the door slammed shut behind him. Stacey woke up immediately, her head tilting upwards towards his. She stared sleepily at him with a confused look on her face. She looked behind her to where her dress had come up, and then back to Dave's raised arms.

Dave quickly dropped his arms and attempted a smile. "Morning." He tried to sound cheerful, but blasé. It came out like he'd just been caught trying to grab a sleeping girl's arse.

"Morning," she tried back at him as if surprised that she had been so lenient.

"Why do you have a wet patch on your trousers?" Stacey asked him as she hid the man of steel by pulling her dress down to an almost respectable level.

Dave felt his face turn bright red. "Don't worry, it was just a glass of water. I didn't wet myself or anything," said Dave inappropriately.

"Oh. Good," she replied, in a tone that suggested she was questioning her own sanity for being in the bed of a complete idiot.

"How did you sleep?" Dave asked, trying to get the conversation flowing despite feeling like he'd spent the evening licking Siberian Sand Toads.

Stacey pulled the duvet over what remained of her modesty. "Yeah, OK I guess," she replied, in a voice that sounded even more squeaky and annoying when hungover. He made a mental note to knock her down to nine points, which – if he was being honest – was actually an insurance policy on his pride.

"Me too. Like a baby," he croaked.

"Oh good," responded Stacey.

A silence followed. Stacey's sparkling blue eyes, now framed with smudged mascara and deep bags, looked everywhere except into his. His head throbbed as he thought of something to say. At least thirty seconds passed and he realised he had nothing. He couldn't remember anything they had talked about last night, any conversation topic or personal detail. He'd have to resort to small-talk.

Should he err on the side of caution and try the type of cliché blokes spun when making inane conversation with a girl? He tried to think of the witty lines from the magazines that he had taken the time to memorise, so he could one day unleash them like a veteran lothario. All that time he spent practising on the voice-recording function of his phone was apparently wasted, as the only thing he could think to say was, "So, do you come here often?" which was never going to be effective in a bar, let alone a bedroom in an elderly person's residence where he was quite certain she had never been before.

Whatever you do, Dave told himself, don't talk about the weather.

Tension was building as he tried to think of something that didn't sound ridiculous, which was particularly difficult since every blood vessel in his body had simultaneously decided to migrate to his face. It had to be a one-liner that sounded as if it were scripted for a Hollywood blockbuster, being spoken by a world-famous star with an ego surpassed in size only by their bank balance. It had to be clever, unexpected; it would make her fall out of bed with uncontrollable laughter.

Eventually, anticlimactically, he mumbled a really poor and unnecessarily crude joke about sleep and babies wetting themselves. Thankfully, he didn't say enough of it in comprehensible English.

Stacey looked at him blankly, so he covered his tracks: "It looks sunny outside. Probably won't be wet today."

Stacey clearly agreed that the weather wasn't a suitable subject because she responded by reaching for his bin and throwing up in it. As she retched on to half-eaten toast and thrown-away job applications, Dave tried not to look at the Stacey Dawson-shaped fake tan imprint on his bed.

As if an embarrassing situation couldn't get any worse, Nana Barb suddenly burst into the room.

"Mornin'," she announced, proudly clutching a cup of tea. "Oh," she said, baulking ever so slightly at the unexpected addition. "I s'pose I best make two."

Despite the promise of leaving the couple to their reluctant company, Nana Barb stayed perfectly still. Dave initially worried she was having a turn from the shock, until he saw a little movement on her lips suggestive of a smile. Stacey soundlessly swayed over the bin while his Nan stared blankly into space. Dave cleared his throat, not to spur his Nan rudely into action but because he didn't know what else to do. She's actually enjoying this, he thought. *Great, just bloody great.* Dave wasn't enjoying himself at all. He wished he could be teleported to another place completely, but that wouldn't happen for a few hours more at least.

"Right, I'll go put the kettle on then." Nana Barb took what seemed an eternity to place the cup on the bedside table (humans have an ingrained ability to bend time, but bizarrely they're only capable of initiating this power in embarrassing situations). She finally scurried out of the room with an excitable pace usually reserved for the Christmas holidays. *Oh well, that couldn't have gone any worse.*

"Morning Nan," Dave called weakly after her.

## Nana Barb

Barbara Janice Wilson, 85 years young, was affectionately known as Nana Barb to her seven grandchildren and her great granddaughter. Over the years she'd had many guests in the house, but never had she missed someone out on the tea rounds.

She dragged her short squat frame – much shorter now than it had been in her heyday – towards the kitchen so that she might partake in one of her favourite pastimes: the putting on of the kettle. Her close-cut grey hair was almost windswept from the speed she travelled, the excitement making her oblivious to the danger of another ankle incident like the one last July when she slipped on some experimental home-made peanut butter.

Fancy her cheeky grandson bringing such a pretty young lady home. She didn't realise he had it in him. His blonde guest reminded her of that girl who ran a lot in Baywatch, and Dave was no Hasselhoff. Has his grandfather's looks, she thought with a hint of nostalgia. Nana Barb came to the conclusion that Dave's young friend must have been drunk.

She went to take a mug from the tree and paused in mid-air. Perhaps she should avoid using the good china. It's not that she didn't trust her surprise guest, but she had been observant enough to notice her nail varnish was terribly chipped. *And was she being sick into Dave's bin*? She can have the old mug with the lilies on it, Nana Barb decided. She'd like that – all young girls like lilies.

Nana Barb looked for the milk and saw she only had enough left for one or two cups. After she had finished this round, she would have to collect the new bottles from the back of the garage, because they're bound to want more than one cup. It's lucky the milkman has been, she thought. Most days he would arrive an hour later and that poor girl would have been stuck with just the one cuppa. *And I'll bet she's built up such a thirst.* Nana Barb gurgled throatily as she stopped herself laughing out loud at her own joke.

She poured water into the teapot, the happiest she'd been since she beat Edna from number 38 at Heads Up Texas Hold-em Poker a couple of months ago.

## Stacey Dawson

Stacey, now dressed, found herself in the living room, sitting opposite the boy she had stupidly followed home last night. He looked a mess with his hair all straw-like, still dressed in the clothes he'd been wearing last night. She'd let him call her a taxi, despite offering a lift. It was never a good idea to let strange boys know where you live, just in case they turn out to be the chainsaw massacre type.

She thought she could remember his name... Dan, Dwayne, David, Dane. Can't be Dwayne, who's called Dwayne nowadays? It definitely started with a D. She decided that if the situation arose she would address him as Day, purposely trailing off so he couldn't hear the last bit.

She looked him over, making him blush for the fifth time since they'd woken up just fifteen minutes ago. What was she thinking? *The boy lives with his Grandma.* Had he told her as much? She realised it was quite likely, she was fairly tipsy last night. Oh well, at least he paid for the drinks.

Suddenly inspired by the memory of a moneybox in the boy's room that was shaped like a classic American car, she asked, "Have you got any cash on you?" She put on what she thought was a sweet voice, knowing she had ten pounds in her bag that she had managed to avoid breaking into.

"Oh yeah, of course," he said eagerly. He left the room at something close to a jog and returned with his hands clutched together, and as expected, rattling. "Don't worry about paying me back," he said as he poured the coins into her hands. Stacey pocketed over ten pounds worth of change, despite guessing the journey would cost no more than a fiver.

"So, it's a nice day. Have you got any plans?" the boy asked, trying to engage in conversation once more. Apparently he didn't appreciate a nice bit of peace and quiet.

"Yeah, I'm going shopping with my Mum," she replied, wondering why his face scrunched up after each time she spoke. She could have asked him what he was doing but simply didn't care, so once again she killed the conversation like a bad joke at a funeral.

Stacey was used to such situations so didn't consider it in the slightest bit awkward. It's not that she spent many mornings around the houses of boys with names that slipped her memory, more that she tried to avoid entering into discussions that required a response. Thinking of things to say would cause unnecessary stress lines across her forehead, an approach she would no doubt be grateful for taking when she reached her thirties.

Day...'s Nan came back in the room and put a cup in front of Stacey, which in her opinion was covered with the most grotesque looking floral pattern she had ever seen. She gave her a smile, but only with the lips. She'd seen the old bat looking her over in the bed, forming opinions. Who was she to judge?

Thankfully she didn't need to drink her tea. A loud beep sounded outside, which prompted Stacey to jump right up out of her seat. She couldn't get out of there quick enough.

Nana Barb asked, "Oh, is that your taxi, dear?"

*No it's the aliens who kidnapped me and forced me to pass out in your grandson's bed*, Stacey – fortunately – thought to herself. "Yes it is," she said brightly, with a smile worthy of a seasoned political campaigner.

"It's a shame your tea will be too hot. Never mind, I'm sure Dave will drink it for you."

Dave. That was it. "Oh, it's such a shame. I do like tea."

"That's nice, dear. Now, will we be seeing you again?"

Stacey glanced at the boy; the sixth time he'd blushed that morning. *He really is as wet as a drowning sponge.*

"Well you know what they say: you never know your luck in the big city." Hang on, that isn't the right phrase. Attempting to flick into clarity was a saying relating to the world being a small place. It failed to materialise, like a fluorescent light that doesn't quite make it on.

"So shall I call you later?" Dave asked her, obviously not comfortable bringing it up with his grandmother stood over his shoulder.

"Yeah, why not," she lied, wondering if she'd been stupid enough to give him her number. Before he had the chance to ask for it, she slammed shut the front door, glad to be free of that pathetic boy and his witch of a grandmother.

## Nana Barb

"What a nice girl," said Nana Barb.

"Sorry Nan, didn't mean to shock you this morning," Dave said with a huge grin on his face.

"No worries. How about some poached eggs?"

Dave clearly wanted some eggs. His eyes opened wide and Nana Barb was reminded of her old dog when he had caught the clang of his food bowl.

She walked to the kitchen and put the kettle on to boil. Upon opening the fridge to retrieve the milk, she cursed her memory for forgetting she'd already run out. Putting on her slippers, she prepared herself for the walk outside, completely unaware of the events that were about to take place.

In the house next door a clever young woman called Louise was, with disastrous consequences, about to make a scientific breakthrough in the field of time travelling. A strange device, called a Quantum Consciousness Retagging Device – which was a working title since it couldn't be turned into an acceptable acronym – was pointing through a window in the opposing residence, and was about to be accidentally switched on. It was facing precisely the same direction in which the old lady was scuttling.

The most adventurous occurrence in Nana Barb's life since the War had been a power-cut in her local Tesco. All was about to change however, as we Web-spinners have a rather interesting plan in store for the lovable old lady. Without entering into too much detail at this early stage, the Quantum Consciousness Retagging Device alters the state of a consciousness until it exists in another time and place completely. Were you to happen across its beam, Louise theorised at least, you would very likely be propelled into the past, the future, or another dimension entirely.

Nana Barb walked out of the back door and over to the milk bottle holder, which she leant over to pick up. At the same time Louise was bending down to plug in her hair straighteners. As she went to flick the wrong switch, she had no idea this simple action might affect the fate of all existence.

Nana Barb's back clicked unpleasantly and she swayed on the spot, trying to cope with the pain. A high-pitched noise suddenly appeared from behind her, quickly intensifying as it got closer. Before Barbara had time to look around, there was an amazing flash of light and the world around her changed in an instant.

It was only an instant, but in the same way your life flashes before your eyes upon your moment of death[2*], the thoughts that occurred

2 * This was a concept we devised in an attempt to make conscious life last twice as long. Humans say it's only a flash but really it lasts as long as your first life.

during this time seemed to be vast. Nana Barb saw her body melting away from her as its atoms were poured into the immensity of the Universe. Time and space were being manipulated in Nana Barb's mind and the particles that formed her aged body were being encouraged to reform in a new place: the distant past. Nana Barb, never one for strong analogies, later likened it to watching her egg timer when she was hungry for boiled eggs. The sand seems to pass through the glass really quickly, yet the amount at the top hardly moves. *Amazing*.

In that instant, that nanosecond of the human perception of time that passed while the very perplexed Nana Barb was hurtling into the past, the Universe stood still. She wouldn't have considered herself an intelligent lady, not even before her memory had started to fail her, but with that snapshot of the entire network of consciousness came an understanding of everything that had passed before, and everything that would happen in the future. If Nana Barb even knew what a Theory of Everything was, she would have realised that in that moment she knew more than Einstein had taken a genius' lifetime to come close to comprehending.

The light faded and with a dazed look of a kitten on catnip, the still bent-over Nana Barb took stock of her surroundings. She was able to stand again and the pain in her back had gone completely, her only grievance now was the tinnitus piercing through her ears. Looking around she could only assume she was still in England somewhere – those rolling hills and indigenous oak trees made it a fairly safe bet. She just couldn't work out where the houses had gone, or where all the trees had come from.

More importantly, Nana Barb was furious with herself. She was absolutely certain she had just been given access to unlimited knowledge, yet she couldn't remember a bloody thing.

At precisely the moment of Barbara's disappearance, a rather confused horsefly suddenly materialised in a field at the back of

Freecock Gardens. This horsefly, acutely aware of its own existence and in a heightened state of consciousness, was now contemplating the meaning of life. He found he was able to explain his predicament to a passing pony, who was utterly flabbergasted that she could understand her nemesis, and further incensed that this creature was now biting a chunk out of her flesh.

This horsefly would have been happy to know that his place in history was elevated above any other insect, since without him the epic aftermath of Nana Barb's time travelling would never have occurred. Unfortunately no one took the time to explain this to the fly, especially the pony who, to be honest, was too angry to offer a dignified response. And so the poor fly continued the rest of his short life – fifty-eight seconds – miserable and dissatisfied.

The pony soon got her revenge when the annoying insect flew too close to her tail – by whipping one of his wings clean off. As the fly spun in a circle on the floor, wondering if his day could get any worse, he was stepped on by an enormous hoof.

# CHAPTER 2
# Missing Nan

## The Hyper-real Universe, Dimension Alpha $2^{-32}$

After that momentary excursion to the past, the story must return to your present and to our protagonist, the hapless Dave. At this point in the tale, however, your current narrator must take a short interlude. The beautiful thing about reality is that all existence is created by consciousness, yet all consciousness is created by us, the Web-spinners. There is effectively a feedback loop between the material world and hyper-reality, the alternative Universe where we pen the eternal narrative of your existence. So we create you, and yet we exist in your image. In effect this is because you need to visualise us if we are to exist.

In a roundabout way, what I'm trying to say is that I am an old man. Your patriarchal culture deems old men to be wise and the wisest person imaginable is a withered old magus with a wrinkled, stooped frame. Thc unfortunate side effect of this amazing fact of science is my pathetically weak bladder. So, I must excuse myself while I attempt to pass my kidneys through my urinary tract. Do not fear because the tale itself does not end, instead the focus of attention momentarily shifts from our aged heroine. You are hopefully all keen to find out what has happened to Nana Barb, but this small toilet break has its own place within the grand scheme of things.

I don't know if you have noticed, but characters rarely visit the toilet during stories. It is as if storytellers like to pretend natural functions do not occur in their ideological fictions. Well they do, so go and make yourself some form of refreshment, bookmark the page while you release some bodily fluids of your own, or if you prefer you can continue to read, because in my absence you will be left in the capable but malicious hands of Craag, who is renowned for his dislike of Virgos.

Unfortunately for him, Dave is a Virgo.

## 12:05hrs, June 15th 2013 C.E. - Nether Wallop, England

### Dave

Dave continued to watch Saturday morning reruns until his stomach let out an audacious rumble. He realised it had been about an hour since his Nan had gone to poach him some eggs, and due to his decreased brain activity he had failed to notice the lack of noise coming from the kitchen.

He hit the mute button on the remote and listened out for sounds from other parts of the house.

"Nan? Nan, are you OK?"

Silence.

"Nan, are my eggs done yet?" That's strange. Usually Nana Barb's instinctive longing to please her grandchildren outweighed any personal injuries that had occurred. There was definitely something amiss. She could have been kidnapped, or she might have finally succumbed to senility and wandered down the shops looking for some cats to scream at, or whatever else crazy old senile women stereotypically do. Dave decided this required drastic action. He was going to have to get out of the comfy chair.

He walked into the kitchen, immediately spotting the lack of activity. The pan hadn't yet been removed from the cupboard. An empty milk bottle was the only item out of place, a clue perhaps. Dave's attention lifted and, inspired by the American forensic detective programmes he'd been watching, he decided to approach the situation *à la* C.S.I.

He opened the fridge. No milk. Two bottles of milk were delivered on a Thursday morning and there was no way the three cups of tea they had drunk between them accounted for two whole bottles, even if Nana Barb had made herself porridge before he and Stacey had woken up. Something had happened between here and the milk bottle drop-zone. The answer might be something simple, like a failed delivery. She might simply have gone to the shop instead. At this stage of the investigation, Dave was taking no chances.

Our young would-be detective walked to the side door of the house, noticing it was on its latch. He flicked it off and stepped outside. The milk bottles, as he expected, were there. That meant she hadn't gone to the shops to get some more. Maybe they had run out of eggs. Dave hadn't thought of checking the egg carton at the time.

Any mental image Dave had created linking him to that famous American series was gone in an instant as the side door slammed shut behind him. He tried the handle even though he knew in a moment of pure insanity he had taken the latch off. Sure enough, it was locked.

He went to the front door to try his (currently non-existent) luck there, despite knowing it hadn't been used for a number of years. He twisted the knob and thought he felt it give a little bit, so took a few steps back and threw all of his weight into it. The door responded with a sound of cracking wood, but stubbornly remained shut.

He turned round and caught sight of an old man staring at him through the window of the opposing residence. Before sitting down to watch the tele, Dave had put on the pyjamas his Nan had given him for Christmas, hoping it might soften the blow of the embarrassing episode. Now the full horror of locking himself outside in his pyjamas dawned on him.

Trying to communicate all of this information by waving was quite a difficult task, and pretty soon the old man closed his curtains to the crazy youth with the racing car pyjama bottoms. Dave sat down on the step in resignation. The paranoid old bloke living across the road had no doubt forgotten he was the grandson of Mrs Wilson, and Dave was certain the snooping halfwit was doing his nosey neighbourly duty in calling the relevant authorities. He had once called the local police station after Nana Barb had her great-granddaughter's friends over for the day, insisting they implement the dispersal order under the Anti-social Behaviour Act of 2003. The very serious, but extremely friendly police sergeant, who was called in all the way from Salisbury twenty miles away, had insisted on rounding up the unruly youths in Mrs Wilson's back garden. Still, he was extremely apologetic for his part in breaking up the toddler garden party.

At least Dave was saved the trouble of reporting his missing Nan.

On another day, Dave might have had that same friendly police sergeant turn up to investigate the attempted break-in at 21 Freecock Gardens. Unfortunately for Dave, this wasn't another day. Soon afterwards, a police car turned up, and an angry-looking constable with dark greasy hair and a severe mono-brow stepped out. He immediately set about questioning him.

"What do you think you're doing, lad? I hear you've been disturbing the peace," he said.

Dave had a hangover and dangerously felt the urge to adopt a sarcastic stance with his accuser. "Who would be disturbed by someone banging on a door? The woodlice that live in the doorframe might be a bit put out I guess," he replied.

"The gentleman over the road tells me you were disturbing his peace."

"Are you sure he wasn't telling you he's mentally disturbed?" Dave retorted.

"Watch it – don't get smart with me. What are you doing trying to get in this house?"

"I live here. I accidentally locked myself out."

"I've been informed that an elderly person lives here alone. I don't believe you," said the obstinate officer.

"Well you can tell your informant to mind his own nosey business and get his facts straight."

"That's quite enough, thank you. Now, I'm going to ask some simple questions and I would like you to answer honestly. Is that simple enough?"

"Yes."

"What is your name?"

"David Wilson."

"Age?"

"Twenty-one."

"Address?"

"Uh, this house, 21 Freecock Gardens, Nether Wallop, Wiltshire."

"What's the postcode?"

"I can't remember. I haven't lived here that long."

The policeman frowned. "I see," he said as he wrote something in his notepad.

"Oh come on, loads of people forget their postcode. Is that a crime?" Dave asked, a bit too aggressively.

"I don't like your tone of voice. May I remind you that you're talking to a police constable? What is your relationship to the elderly resident?"

"She's my grandmother," explained Dave. "I don't know where she is; she must have popped out somewhere."

"Quite convenient don't you think? How do I know you're not trying to rob the place?"

"Because I'm wearing my pyjamas," Dave suggested.

"That could be a cunning disguise."

That was the gnat's breath that blew down the house. He was cold and hungover, and so offered his unwanted opinion, "Well it wouldn't take much cunning to fool the local police if they all display the same level of intelligence as you."

He was promptly taken down to the station and arrested for attempted breaking and entering *and* suspicion of assisting in a kidnapping.

## Dave

Lying on the bed in his cell, Dave drifted in and out of sleep. He was having a lucid dream that involved being eaten by a room made entirely of skin. His grandmother's face became a recurring motif, which he supposed must have been a visual manifestation of his concern for her. And yet he irrationally felt connected to this dream somehow, and that it was more premonition than ideas from his own imagination. He wanted to stay asleep, to find out how it would end, but the background noise and uncomfortable bed kept waking him.

Eventually he was dragged back to reality by the sound of a hand knocking on the cell door. The owner of this hand turned out to be a spotty young desk clerk, who helpfully informed Dave he was free to leave, as fortunately for him his story 'checked out'. During the past hour, the clerk explained, the police had attempted to reach his grandmother, but the phone in her house remained unanswered.

The forgotten items of Dave's pyjama bottoms were humiliatingly relayed to him for the second time that day: "One tissue, presumed unused; one paperclip; one one-pound coin. There you go sir, if you can just sign there please." A well-chewed black ballpoint was thrust into Dave's hand.

"I can understand you wouldn't let me take in a pound coin in case I choke on it or something," Dave reflected as he signed his name in three places, "but why can't I take a tissue into a police cell?"

"Well sir, that's a good question. The answer is quite simple: drugs."

"Drugs?"

"Yes sir. Smuggling them in by all sorts of means nowadays. Just last week I noticed this old-timer with a funny limp. Turned out he'd hollowed out his false leg and hidden some Temazepam in the hole."

"Temazepam? Isn't that a sleeping tablet?"

"Yeah, who'd have thought it?"

"Why would you smuggle prescription drugs into a police cell?"

"Beats me sir. You get all sorts nowadays." The spotty clerk smiled inanely, as if expecting Dave to copy him.

"And how exactly do you conceal drugs inside a single man-size tissue?"

"Where there's a will there's way, sir. These drugs barons are getting craftier by the minute."

"I don't exactly think I'd fall under the drug baron category for having a single drug-laced tissue. Although I have to agree with your line of thinking, it would have countless uses when you're trying to break into a house." *That short sleep obviously hadn't helped clear my acerbic mood*, thought Dave.

"In your statement you said you weren't trying to break into that house."

"I was being sarcastic – never mind. We're clearly not on the same wavelength. And do I dare ask why I'm not allowed a paperclip?"

"Oh ho ho," came the bizarrely festive reply. "That, sir, has two reasons. You see, a paperclip can become quite an effective tool for an illegal locksmith. And, if you bend it just right, you could take someone's eye out with a paperclip. Health and safety laws restrict us from having anyone's eye out while under our care. We'd be liable you see."

"Of course you would. So at what stage did you decide that someone who'd managed to lock himself out of his own house would be well trained in the art of lock-picking?"

"Good question. Well, the drugs could have affected your hand-eye coordination."

"But I didn't have any drugs."

"We didn't know that at the time and we've got to be extra careful nowadays."

Dave stared at the man, judging whether he was playing the fool intentionally, or whether he was a wholeheartedly genuine, prizewinning idiot. He decided it was the latter.

"This conversation is going nowhere. So what do I do about my missing Nan? When do you start looking for her?" Dave asked, knowing that it was probably a futile question if the current logic were to continue.

"We can't do anything about that until she's been missing for twenty-four hours," came the reply, confirming that it was in fact a futile question.

"So I can be arrested for apparently kidnapping her, but you won't start a search if presumed missing until a full day has passed?"

"Quite right sir, that's standard procedure."

Dave sighed. "Fair enough, so I suppose I need to look for her myself then."

"May I suggest a change of clothes before you do, sir?"

"I would do if I could get into my bloody house!"

"Quite right sir. Good luck with that."

Dave felt like screaming, but sensibly decided against it in case he was arrested again. He was shown out by a full-time officer, who was grinning ear to ear. "You met Roger then?" he asked.

"I assume that imbecile behind the desk was Roger." Why did he feel compelled to say things that could get him into trouble?

"Careful, that's the tone that got you in here in the first place. Roger can be a bit excitable, but he's a volunteer and gets carried away with ideas above his station."

"A volunteer?"

"Indeed. There was a strange accident on the A338 blocking most of the change of shifts from getting to the station. Some sort of UFO sighting apparently. Roger there just lives around the corner and pops in to help from time to time. We try our best with him, but he models himself on the television detectives rather than the real ones."

Dave refrained from mentioning that it was similar behaviour that landed him here in the first place. "Hang on a minute, did you say UFO sighting?" he asked, suddenly realising what the officer had just said.

"Load of old rubbish if you ask me. The driver was clearly drunk, even if he did pass his breath test. Anyway, sorry about your grandmother, I would help if I could. Because of her age I'll give the hospitals a quick call to see if she's turned up. Other than that there's not a lot I can do."

Dave thanked the officer then walked out of the station. On his way out of the front door he slipped on the step, falling face first into the door.

## The Hyper-real Universe, Dimension Alpha $2^{-32}$

I have returned from my intermission, and so your aged narrator will once again pick up the storytelling from my ugly cousin – no hard feelings, Craag. He is young and somewhat ruthless, but then even the fates need the influence of youth sometimes to keep us in touch with the younger generation. It's amazing really, he has existed in various guises since the dawn of consciousness and yet has the permanent mental state of a five-year-old that has just fallen off his new bike.

The Universe is such a strange place.

## 14:22hrs, June 15th 2013 C.E. – Salisbury, England

## Dave

Craag must have been in a particularly good mood, as the pound Dave couldn't remember putting in his pyjama pocket served two useful purposes. He managed to make one phone call to his friend Simon to come and collect him from the station, and another to his aunt to confirm she had a spare set of keys and that he could come and collect them from her at four o'clock when she was back from work. He left Simon's mobile number, just in case, and nonchalantly asked his aunt if his Nan had been in touch. He felt a small pang of concern when she said she hadn't heard from her since Monday. Dave walked outside the police station rubbing his blackening eye, hoping his luck would improve. It undoubtedly now would.

After waiting outside the station for about half an hour, a bright pink Cadillac drove around the corner, with an Alabama number plate stating GR8 SCOT. Unexpectedly, the car pulled up next to him. The front window wound down revealing Simon's slightly plump face, which was looking extremely pleased with itself. "Jump in," he said in a broad Wiltshire accent.

Dave wondered why strange things always seemed to happen with a hangover. He couldn't decide if it was due to the perverted way you viewed otherwise normal events, or whether reality itself warped if your mind wasn't quite right. (It happens to be neither. Quite simply, Web-spinners find it hilarious to pick on people when they're feeling sensitive.)

Dave dumped himself on to the passenger seat, which would normally be the driver's seat. "Nice car. Series 62, right?" he asked.

"You know your cars, my friend."

"What's that smell though?"

"Probably the dead deer I just picked up," Simon replied without a suggestion of sarcasm.

"Fair enough." Dave allowed a few seconds to let the statement sink in. Or perhaps he was waiting for further elaboration. None came. "What dead deer?"

"There's a dead deer in the trunk."

"Of course there is." Dave would have held his head in his hands, but decided it was too cliché. "Simon, where in hell's name did you pick up a dead deer?"

"I was driving through the forest; this posh bloke with a brand new Range Rover was stood next to it scratching his head. I figured he was the one who hit the poor thing, so by the rules of the land he couldn't take it home."

"What rules of the land? Did you just make up a law up to satisfy your insatiable desire for a free lunch?"

"No it's definitely true. I saw it on an episode of *Top Gear* once."

"And the content of *Top Gear* is completely infallible is it?"

"Yes."

"Do you even know what infallible means?"

Dave knew it wound Simon up when he used words he didn't understand. As expected, Simon began to sulk.

Dave wanted to let him brood as he usually did when he became moody, which happened quite a lot. But he was stuck with him until four and Simon would be a horrible companion if he couldn't make him forget the deliberate insult. "OK, so where did you get the car?" he asked with reluctant concession.

A faint smile appeared on the edge of Simon's lips.

"The pink definitely makes you stand out," Dave threw in for good measure.

That opened him up, and before long Simon was relaying the story. Dave knew immediately it was going to be one hell of a monologue so he sank back in the seat and made himself comfortable.

## Simon

Simon loved telling a good story and this was the best he had had in a long time. If there was one aspect of his character that made him stand out, it was his ability to spin a good yawn (Simon's aphasia, so please don't condemn your Web-spinning narrator for his periodic linguistic mistakes). He put on his storytelling voice – which was in no way distinguishable from his usual voice, but Simon fancied it made him sound more important – and began to tell Dave about the previous evening.

"I met this bloke called Sue in the pub last night. And before you say it, he isn't one of them types of blokes – not that I've got a problem with shirt-lifters. My mate Dan's sister is one of them lesbos, and I'm not racist or anything so I haven't got a problem with gays, just so long as they don't try and convert me, or whatever it is those Irish priests do to them young boys.

"Anyway, I'm digesting. The point I'm trying to make is, this bloke was called Sue and he has a bandana and big tattoos all down his arms, which were the size of turkeys – no not turkeys, hams, they're more the same shape. Anyway, as you can imagine, he had a tough time of growing up with a name like Sue, so he started go'n to the gym to beef himself up a bit. Needless to say this chap's built like a brick sh... oy!" Simon suddenly beeped his horn as hard as he could, which shocked open Dave's drooping eyelids. "Get in your own bloody lane!" He tutted his disagreement and said with all sincerity, "Bloody Thursday drivers."

Before Dave had time to comment or interrupt, therefore ruining his flow, Simon picked up from where he had left off. "Anyway, back to last night and the pub. This Sue bloke rocks in while I'm on the pool table, winner stays on and I'm on a seven game streak, which was lucky 'cos I only had a tenner to my name, and puts his quid down on the side. So I finish beating Norman, the old pisshead who sits in the corner, and goes to introduce myself to my next opponent. So I says to this bloke, 'All right, the name's Simon,' and he looks me up and down and in this Tom Cruise from *Top Gun* accent goes," – Simon attempted an American accent – "'Howdy, my name is Sue'. That was it then. It was all I could do to stop myself from laughin' in his face. I was expecting a beating, laughin' at him and that, but all he did was give me a great big grin. He said, 'Boy, I like you. You're honest'. That's what he said! Can you believe it?"

Dave snored.

"Oy, don't be so bloody inconsiderate." He tapped him on the side of his head. "Dave, open your eyes," Simon insisted, throwing in a quick flick for good measure.

"What? Don't flick me, it's irritating."

"Don't fall asleep on me then. I said, can you believe it?"

"Oh, yes. Err, no I can believe it," Dave speculated.

"Anyways, turned out the bloke was a shark."

"A shark?"

"Yeah, he let me win twice then bet a fiver on it for the last game. Bloody beat me an' all."

"So how did that result in you getting this pretty garish looking automobile?"

Simon beamed. "Thanks, I think so too – although it's Salmon Pink, not Garish."

Dave snapped, "Can you not just tell me why this bloke gave you the car?"

"All right, hold your horses. Sue let me drive it, didn't he? After three pints I only had a couple of quid left so I couldn't afford the fiver I owed him for the game. I only agreed to the bet because I thought I had him whipped. When he wanted paying I had to admit I was skint, so he came up with an alternative option. He let me clean his car instead."

"And now you've stolen it."

"I've not stolen it. I just borrowed it to come pick you up."

"What's wrong with the Micra?"

"What's wrong with the Micra? Don't insult my intelligence please. My Mum's Micra is not an automobile to be seen driving through Salisbury town centre in."

"You normally do."

"It's broken if you really must know. Starter motor's gone apparently."

"What's with all the Americanisms anyway?" Dave asked. "It's a boot, not a trunk, and a car, not an automobile."

Dave was always doing this, Simon thought. He's always such a bloody nitpicker. It was infuriating. Simon didn't have a posh education like his best mate. Dave had spent six months at grammar school before being expelled for drinking peach schnapps in the boys' shitter, which practically put him on a level with that wheelchair bloke who shagged his nurse. Simon could never compete with that. "What's wrong with you today? You're acting all disgrumpy."

Dave laughed. "Don't you mean disgruntled?"

"Leave me alone." Simon retaliated the only way he knew how, by sticking his bottom lip out and frowning like a sulky schoolboy.

Simon would happily sit in a mood for hours, but he knew Dave couldn't stand it. He would always be the first to apologise.

"Simon, look I'm sorry. It's just this whole mess about my Nan being missing."

*That's beside the point.*

"I really need your help today, mate."

Perhaps his Nan really was missing. Dave wasn't usually like this, and wasn't the type to overreact. He stayed silent a few moments longer, so he didn't appear soft, then reluctantly decided to go against every instinct telling him to be childish. "Oh yeah, I forgot about that. That's why you can't get in your house."

"And why I got put in a cell for two hours."

"Yeah, that too. Don't worry, it'll be fine. We'll get back to yours and she'll be there in the kitchen ready to rustle up some of her scrumptious bacon sandwiches." Simon's mouth watered.

"Maybe." Dave didn't sound so convinced. "The police apparently tried calling her a few times, so she could verify my identity, but I don't imagine they put much effort into it. Her hearing is getting worse; she could have been in the garden I guess."

"Well, we're nearly there so we'll find out pretty soon. If there's no sign of her we'll look around further – the usual haunts: post office, village shop, maybe the pub." Simon tried to flash Dave a reassuring smile, even though he wasn't convinced himself. Nana Barb never did anything without telling someone first. She was the kind of person who left you a note to say she was just popping next door to borrow some sugar. They arrived at the house to find it as empty as before, obviously since Nana Barb had been teleported to the Stone Age.

Dave looked worried. Simon realised he wouldn't get that bacon sandwich.

## The Hyper-real Universe, Dimension Alpha $2^{-32}$

For now we must part company with simple Simon's internal monologue. We can leave these two friends to their fruitless search of Nether Wallop and the surrounding area so that I can introduce you to the rest of the characters in our hyper-real Universe.

First, for those of you who are interested, hyper-real is a name first penned by Jean Baudrillard, a twentieth century French cultural theorist. It refers to an event influenced by popular culture, its effect on (your) modern society being that an individual cannot distinguish between true events and the proposed reality of art. He uses the example of the public subconsciously reacting to the Gulf war as if it were a staged event, because of its regular appearance on a medium that is more often attributed to Hollywood war movies. In turn, the soldiers who then go on to fight subsequent wars in the future will increasingly begin to act like the war heroes they see on TV, which creates a reality that is transformed by art, a feedback loop of sorts. Its definition draws similarities to the reason behind our existence, so we have decided to adopt it as the name of our Universe.

Your main narrator goes by the name of Hector. I am male, despite the parallels I might otherwise draw with one or two classical protagonists: Hecate is a Goddess of Mycenaean Greece, popularised in Western society by Shakespeare in *Macbeth*; Hector a veteran of the Trojan wars, immortalised in Homer's *Iliad*. My name extends from these foundations, but other than religion, history and literature are the two primary sources of name origins, so Hector seems an appropriate name to call me for now. I am not a leader as such, although I am leading this particular narrative.

Ogg you haven't met. He is also male, although his namesake happens to be a witch in a popular fantasy novel from the end of the twentieth Gregorian century. It is also a phonetically similar, almost childlike allusion to the English word God.

Craag you have met. His name sounds a bit like Craig, which is a nice enough name.

Our appearances as well as our names change regularly as the cultures that create us are given new narratives to follow and new Gods to worship. In the 80s we looked surprisingly like a Human League cover band.

We are all male for now, but in your future we will gradually all become female. That is a long way off as a Matriarchal culture, a society ruled by women, takes some time to form. Ogg will be the first to turn, hence his name currently being the same as a fictional female. Plus he has a particular love of floral dresses.

Before this wholesale change occurs, the attraction of sport will become so great that politics and war seem demeaning, mere child's play. Unwavering male pride in a sporting team eventually overcomes any patriotism they might have felt for their place of birth and so the only people left caring about the state of the country will be women. The most successful sporting nations adopted this policy first. Unsurprisingly, the idea took some time to catch on in England.

It is very difficult to say what came first: the Web-spinners, or self-aware minds. We don't really have memories, just an endless knowledge of the mechanics of the Universe, which if understood fully gives you the knowledge of all that has been and passed. To further comprehend this idea you need to imagine the birth of the Universe as such: picture – if you can – your first ever memory. Now remember the last time you were pissed as a fart. Finally imagine yourself becoming disorientated via some form of activity, be it getting washed up on the shore by a wave, a vehicle you are driving spinning out of control on some ice, or learning to skateboard when blindfolded. This bit is the hard bit. Now visualise all three situations occurring simultaneously, but lasting for a hundred million years. That was how it felt at the dawn of the Universe.

You might be thinking now that we are contradicting ourselves by implying we have existed since the birth of the Universe. Quite the contrary, we don't even exist now – not in any reality you'd be familiar with. We are quite simply aware of all the events that led up to our appearance, and all the events that occur after we are gone. Our thoughts aren't linear like yours, which Nana Barb had a short experience of during her Temporal Shift.

Anyway, I'm sure this has been a touch on the heavy side. Don't worry – we'll go straight back to Simon and Dave and the ridiculous situations they find themselves in. If you are keen to find out more about philosophy then I suggest you do what normal people do and look it up in their local library or on the internet. If you prefer the excitement of people making a mess of their, and others', lives, then I invite you to read on.

# CHAPTER 3

# The Search party

## 15:05hrs, June 15th 2013 C.E. - Nether Wallop, England

### Dave

It didn't take long to establish the old girl was well and truly missing. After kicking their heels on Nana Barb's driveway for a short while, they made a move towards Simon's house to make some Missing posters. Dave was appreciative of his friend's newfound helpfulness, although he wouldn't tell him as much.

Five minutes into the drive Dave turned the radio on to be greeted with a low voice singing about a boy named Sue. It took a minute to register, but eventually Simon pointed out, "Dave, listen to that! It's a song about the bloke who owns this car."

"Sorry to disappoint you Simon, but this is a Johnny Cash song from years ago."

Simon looked dejected. "Oh," he said, "still it's a bit of a coincidence, isn't it? Can't be that many blokes called Sue."

"I guess not."

"What happened to you last night anyway? I thought you were gonna meet me at the snooker club?"

"Sorry, I got distracted," Dave replied. "I ended up going home with a girl."

"Bull. I don't believe you." He eyed Dave up, as if expecting him to be stifling a laugh. "Quite the dark horse, aren't you? Who was it then?"

"Stacey Dawson."

"Oh dear David, stop talkin' through your fudge maker. Stacey Dawson is a nine-and-ha'f pointer. That'd be punching well above your weight, even if she was completely gazeboed."

"I'm not lying Simon. She really stayed at mine last night and she wants me to give her a call later. Oh, and I've knocked her down to nine because her voice is even more annoying when you have to spend any longer than five minutes with her."

"Stacey Dawson sleeping at Nana Barb's house, who'd ever believe that? Bloody next thing we'll have pigs flyin'."

A few moments later they arrived at Simon's mother's house, slamming shut the doors of the Cadillac as they jumped out. Dave noticed Simon give the paintwork a quick rub where his hand had left a greasy smudge, felt like questioning the benefit of doing this when he had a decomposing animal in the boot, but decided to maintain the temporary truce.

Dave wondered what condition Simon's mother would be in today. She was known for being a little crazy – not Norman Bates crazy, she certainly hadn't ever killed anyone before, at least to Dave's knowledge; she is perhaps more Winona Ryder crazy, seeming perfectly normal when you first meet her, until you discover she'd been secretly working out how to steal your watch, or when you receive the hand-knitted bib for the baby you don't have. (I would like to point out that Winona Ryder has never actually publicly been accused or discovered doing either of these things; as far as we know she isn't even very good at knitting. Even Web-spinners aren't immune from the lawyers of the twenty-first century and their vigorous approach to litigation.) Dave had always found it difficult to hear all the kids in town poking fun at his best mate's Mum. She was a lovely lady if you looked past all the crazy ramblings and embarrassing episodes of nakedness.

"Hi Mum," Simon shouted as he entered.

"Hi Mrs Ellis," Dave called as they ran into the house, heading straight up the stairs and into Simon's room. They spent a few minutes making a flyer on Simon's computer, and after messing around with the fonts and layout of their hastily-constructed document, they sent it to print.

Dave, as ever, felt worried. "Do you think this will work? It's not like we're looking for a lost kitten."

"Of course it will work," Simon replied confidently. "It works in the movies."

One of the many things about Simon that infuriated Dave was his friend's delusion that his life was one long film script. "That's your answer to every crazy plan you come up with. And in what movie did they ever search for a missing grandmother by using printouts of a dodgy picture taken on a mobile phone?"

"That's not important now. Finding Nana Barb is. If you've got any better ideas then let them out, free them from your moody brain. You've still got sixteen hours or so before the fuzz even start looking. She could be outside all night. Worse, she could have been picked up by a passing Alganian and sold into the West's budding sex trade. I hear granny fetish is gettin' all the more popular."

Dave reeled. "That was a bit much, Simon. I know it's your belief that shocking equates to funny, but leave it out when it comes to my family, OK? I'm paranoid already. And where exactly does an Alganian come from?"

"Algania, of course," replied Simon.

The sound of the printer spraying ink interrupted their inane exchange as the first test copies started to print off.

"I'm gonna make us a cuppa," Simon offered. "Four sugars?"

"Yeah, cheers mate."

Dave picked up the first sheet of A4 and shook it a bit, presumably forgetting it wasn't a Polaroid picture. He looked at the hastily-made flyer to see his Nan's face staring back at him disapprovingly through a fisheye lens, as if accusing him of both losing her and being a terrible shot with a camera phone. If he wasn't living with his Nan, Dave realised, he would have been oblivious to her disappearance. Even before this incident he had felt guilty for all the years he had allowed their relationship to become so distant. Right up until his grandfather died, Dave had only spent time with his Nan during the usual family occasions, for which he had no excuse other than being a useless grandson.

Under normal circumstances, Dave's aunt would visit Nana Barb every day, so would have been the first to discover her missing. That responsibility was his now and he had failed to respond effectively. He wondered if he was overreacting, that maybe she had just found a new sense of adventure and caught the bus into Salisbury to buy a new pair of shoes. However, deep down he knew his Nan wasn't so spontaneous. More than that, he had a sense of impending doom annoyingly etched into the back of his head, a feeling that wouldn't budge regardless of the amount of rational logic he tried to throw at it.

"Are you happy with that then, Dave?" Simon asked as he put a cup of tea down in front of him.

Dave stirred from his thoughts. "It will have to do," he said.

"What's with all the sore grapes? I think it looks pretty good."

"Simon, it's sour."

"Sorry, the milk was a bit off."

Dave bit his tongue until it nearly bled. He would maintain this peace if it killed him.

He printed off a hundred copies while Simon went in search of some Blu-tack. About fifty pages into the printing process, Dave heard a knock at the bedroom door. An untidy, leaf-ridden mess of hair appeared round the corner of the door as Simon's Mum poked her head into the room.

"Hello Dave. How are you, my love?"

"Hello Mrs Ellis. I'm fine thanks. How are you?"

"I'm OK. But don't try passing yourself off as fine. You're a terrible liar, David."

"How did…?"

"It's written all over your face, dear. And that flyer you're holding."

Dave looked at the paper in his hand with the word MISSING written in a delightful font known as Old Dreadful, which Simon had insisted set the tone for the piece nicely.

"It's nothing, Mrs Ellis. We're just a bit worried because we haven't seen her for a few hours. I'm sure she'll turn up."

"I'm sure she will, dear. Do you really think posters are such a good idea though? I can see your logic in asking around after her, but if she's suffering a spot of memory loss, or has a genuine reason for going missing, seeing her own face plastered about the town might come as a bit of a shock."

She had a point. He had to do something though. "What else would you suggest?"

"You can go door to door, ask around that way. Enough people know her from your street, and that way you can avoid letting certain people know you are looking for her."

Dave didn't know what she meant. "Why wouldn't I want someone to know I was looking for her?"

She paused as if thinking of a suitable response then answered dismissively, "I just meant if you had any nosey neighbours." She changed the subject. "Anyway, love, would you like a cuppa before your big search? I'll give you a hand looking if you like."

"Thanks, I'd really appreciate that."

With that sorted, Mrs Ellis wandered off, muttering to herself in what sounded like German.

# CHAPTER 4

## A Tribal Encounter

## B.C.E. 3071 - Salisbury Plain, England

## Nana barb

Barbara was worried. Something very strange had just happened, and she never had the chance to finish her cup of tea.

What in blazes just happened to her? She had a strange feeling of déjà vu, as if she had been in this situation before.

She looked around in disbelief. The adjacent hills looked as if they could belong to Salisbury Plain, but in place of the fields near which she had lived all her life, she found herself surrounded by heathland and forest. Despite the different appearance, it still felt as though she was close to home. She could just be going crazy, clinging on to a false hope that she recognised a familiar pattern in the local geometry. She felt perfectly sane, but then what rational person ever admitted to being beam-me-up-Scottied to another time completely?

Her heart was in her mouth and her head was spinning, but she tried to think clearly nonetheless. She needed to find out where she was, that was clearly the first move she needed to make. She studied her surroundings, looking for a familiar pattern. Following nothing other than intuition and luck (or so she thought), she estimated her position to be about fifteen or so miles from her village, slightly north of Salisbury. However, rather than being in the middle of a forest, by her reckoning she should be standing on the A303 from Andover to Yeovil.

She came to the conclusion she needed a landmark, a point of reference. Something very unusual had just transpired, of that she was fully aware. There was a strong feeling that civilisation had either been destroyed, or had yet to develop – at least in this part of the world. Neither option was particularly reassuring.

She wondered if she would find new species developed from years of evolution, or even animals that had been long extinct. She also wondered why she was so sure she had travelled through time, but wasn't really scared or surprised at the thought. The only thing that was scaring her was the feeling of being lost.

She didn't feel her usual self. Her senses were all rather heightened somehow, more aware.

Barbara was in fact experiencing time sickness, a condition quite disorientating, but at the same time enlightening. Sickness is perhaps an inappropriate word, since the effects can actually be quite beneficial. The sufferer of time sickness experiences temporary improvement in brain activity, increased ability to think logically and an inexplicable capability of speaking and understanding any language. The only side effect is a disorientating sense of self.

Nana Barb realised that if for some reason her wild presumptions were correct, she would be within walking distance of a very recognisable landmark, one that would immediately tell her if she'd travelled backwards or forwards through time.

Potentially, she was only a mile or two from Stonehenge.

Having a sense of her location gave her a new sense of resolve. Getting her bearings, she marched up the hill in the direction she hoped to find the prehistoric landmark – pre my own history anyway, she thought. She found a surprising pace in her legs and no pain in her previously arthritic knees. In fact she made such good time she covered the good half a mile to the brow of the hill in about twenty minutes. As Nana Barb reached a clearing at the top of the hill, she paused and caught her breath. It became obvious she was in the distant past.

Below her a monument was being prepared for a ceremony. There was a hive of activity in a large clearing in the woods, which was centred on a circle of upright wooden poles. Dirty people with animal skin clothing were busy digging a large ditch to the left of this primitive temple. Stonehenge was missing; in its place was a wooden equivalent. It was outlined by a bright circle of white chalk, which she had to admit made it look quite beautiful.

Barbara seemed to remember watching a documentary about the early Stonehenge being built from large wooden posts that were dug into the Wiltshire soil. She couldn't remember when the change from wood to stone took place, so couldn't pinpoint exactly when it was.

Overwhelmed with what she was seeing, she had a pulling desire to find out more. She decided to approach them and have a good old chat, hopefully over a hot beverage. Perhaps they would see something that might explain her time travelling and even how she might get back to the right century. They could even know of a sorcerer, or warlock, or someone who could magic her back to her own time. She'd got here by some unknown hocus-pocus, so perhaps that was her way back too. Bit of a long-shot, she admitted to herself, but she couldn't think of anything better to do. Despite the heightened brain activity, it never crossed her mind that with her strange clothing and sudden appearance she might be the one taken for a sorcerer.

She walked confidently down the hill, preparing herself for her conversation with the indigenous people of her homeland. As she wandered down, thinking of things to say, it dawned on her that she'd have no way of communicating with them. She came to a stop as if she suddenly remembered she was a mime artist who was trapped in a box. She cursed her brazenness, but it was too late to change her mind.

A topless woman with animal bones in her hair and fur covering her waist looked up from her task of crushing pebbles into a white powder. She looked Nana Barb directly in the eyes, dropping her bowl with a small gasp of surprise. Barbara felt the urge to turn and run, but doubted her legs were capable of this long-forgotten ability. Her feet locked to the ground, her body feeling like it had lost all strength. Before Nana Barb had the chance to think, the woman fell to her knees and started chanting.

The whole tribe stopped what they were doing. They all turned to see the cause of this interruption and amazingly, one by one, took up the chanting. As it got louder, Nana Barb realised she could understand what they were saying:

*Maiden who is blessed we love you in mind and spirit*
*Maiden of the night who lights our dark way*
*You will come to us with wolf and full moon*
*And we will dance with joy and happiness*

They repeated this over a few times, clearly directing the words towards the dumbfounded Barbara. She looked over her shoulder to check if there was anyone there. There was no one else they could have been talking to. Nana Barb blushed for the first time in years. It had been a long time since she'd been called a maiden.

The language they spoke was guttural and gruff, and yet the words came to her in perfect English. They didn't exactly rhyme, but were quite alliterative and not displeasing to the ear.

Eventually the chanting stopped. As if rehearsed, the tribe brought it to an end simultaneously. An extremely ugly man, who was slightly taller and had more animal bones in his hair than anyone else, stepped forward to address Nana Barb. "You are older than we thought," he said.

Nana Barb admitted she was old, but wasn't sure why she might have been expected. "How old did you presume I would be then?" was all she could think to reply. Amazingly the words coming from her lips were in the same language as the tribe were speaking, and yet she had never even contemplated such sounds before. She'd heard of people awaking from comas speaking fluent French; was she experiencing something similar?

The man's eyes flicked downwards. "Younger," he replied.

"Well that's a fine thing to say to a lady you've just met," she retorted.

A rib and a femur swung over the man's head as he dipped it down abruptly. "I did not mean to cause offence, oh revered one. We just assumed with a name like maiden you would be younger."

"How are you so sure this maiden you're talking about is me?" Nana Barb asked, realising she was quite enjoying the control she had over this man.

"Because you are wearing the picture of the wolf and the full moon on your breast and this is how it was prophesied."

Nana Barb looked down at the jumper she'd bought herself from the shopping channel.

"No such artwork is possible by a human hand. This must be a trick of the Gods."

"Yes it is a nice jumper. Thank you for saying so. I am terribly sorry, but we haven't even introduced ourselves. I'm Nana Barb." Her name came out perfectly normal. It was like hearing one of those tourists on public transport talking their own language, but saying the place names in English.

"You cannot believe how long we have waited to hear your true name." He tried the words: "Na-noo Baarp."

"It's Nana Barb, try again."

"Nanah Barp."

"Well done, that was nearly it!"

The man smiled from animal bone to animal bone. "And my name," he said very grandly, "is Oc-ri Dér. It means one who sees far."

"That is a lovely name. If you'd have been the first to spot me it would have been a very appropriate name too," said Nana Barb

"Thank you," his smile was close to joining up around the back of his head. Apparently the founding race of the British Isles didn't quite grasp the concept of sarcasm. "You can call me Oc if it is easier," he said humbly.

"So is this ritual you're about to perform in aid of me?" Nana Barb asked.

"Oh no, it's the preparations for the midsummer festival," Oc replied shyly. In fact he looked thoroughly embarrassed, which was understandable since he had just told a God she'd turned up a week early and to the wrong party.

"And you're completely convinced I'm this maiden you've been waiting for?"

He turned to his tribe for support. A grubby-looking old man shrugged his shoulders nonchalantly. "Yes, we are unanimous in this belief," Oc announced proudly. There were a few nodding heads from the crowd behind him.

"And what if it turns out I'm not who you think I am, that I'm an imposter of sorts?" Nana Barb asked, aware of the sharp flint-headed hunting spears lying on the ground behind the tribe members.

"Then you will be killed for mocking our beliefs," shouted someone from the crowd.

Nana Barb made a decision. Today, she was going to be a Goddess.

## 15:48hrs, June 15th 2013 C.E. - Nether Wallop, England

### Mrs Ellis

Mrs Ellis insisted on sticking with her lad Simon and his friend Dave to make sure they only asked *certain* people if they had seen Barbara Wilson. She'd had a dream, and if life had taught her anything, it had taught her to listen to dreams. (Sound advice really, since we often leave handy messages amongst all the useless drivel transmitted into your heads during sleep.)

She hadn't a clue who might know where Mrs Wilson had gone, but she was fully aware some nasty-looking men would come looking for her. It made her shiver to remember their cold soulless eyes, which shouldn't have been that scary really since humans don't even have souls, only butterflies do.[3]

It was a good job she'd stopped the lads from putting up those posters. Those two suits would have known Barbara was missing straight away. Two houses on that street were empty and another two had gone on holiday. She could only hope that when those two men visited the street later today, the search would hold them up long enough for Barbara to get as far away as possible.

She had no idea what organisation the men belonged to – could be CIA, MI5 or even some other acronym she didn't know the spelling of. Whoever they were, it seemed they knew someone had gone missing, but they didn't have a name for them. Mrs Ellis was damned sure that as soon as they had her name, they would waste no time in trying to track her down. When they eventually found her, it could spell the end of the world.

Mrs Ellis wasn't about to let that happen.

## Dave

Dave was getting frustrated. They'd been round at least fifteen houses and nobody had seen her. A couple complained of a minor earthquake that seemed to have taken place earlier that day, but agreed they couldn't envisage any relevance that might have had in relation to her whereabouts. The whole situation was made worse by Mrs Ellis acting up, but thankfully she didn't stay around too long as she had to meet a friend for coffee.

His neighbour was the most likely candidate on his street to have seen her wander off, but she was nowhere to be seen. He was desperate to talk to her – more so than usual (she was extremely

3 King Darthad the Third, ruler of the planet Ventricon, which exists in a dimension more suited to sentient life than yours, deemed Butterflies the most beautiful insect in any existence and so commissioned a device that made a copy of them the moment they died on Earth, so that they may live in eternity in the skies above his own planet (which is now barren from the lack of sunlight). Although not souls in the traditional sense, this is the closest example of the English definition.

attractive).

His aunt called Simon's mobile to say she was running late and he made the decision to break the news that he'd lost his Nan. He felt it was easier to tell her over the phone than it would have been face to face. When his aunt shouted it sounded like a magpie having its feathers torn out, Dave thought, fortunately realising it was probably an inopportune moment to tell her this.

All they could do was sit in the Cadillac and wait for Dave's aunt to arrive. The stench of the dead deer was becoming almost unbearable. As Simon wound down all the windows and tried to clear the smell, Dave made a quick call to the police station, which confirmed she wasn't in any of the local hospitals. As he hung up the phone a car pulled into the drive next door, indicating the return of his neighbour and his best chance of a witness to his grandmother's disappearance.

"Yeah, you're right," said Simon. "She's definitely an eight-pointer. Although, if it was out of two, I'd have to give her one. D'you get it? I said I'd give her one." Simon chuckled at his own wit, oblivious to the fact that Dave wasn't contributing, which he never did when Simon made that 'joke'.

Dave checked his hair in the rear-view mirror before leaving the car, without it crossing his mind that his unfortunate attire had probably already spoiled his chances.

## B.C.E. 3071 - Salisbury Plain, England

### Oc-ri Dér

Oc had witnessed many miracles in a very short space of time. The Goddess had a magical device on her wrist that tracked the movements of the sun God *Phaal*. If that wasn't amazing enough, she impressed her awestruck subjects by capturing their souls with a miniature demon. Thankfully the Goddess was gracious and returned them to their owners soon after.

The tribe were fascinated with their guest and Oc hadn't seen them so excited since their great warrior, *Arun Gaa*, returned with the head of a warrior from a neighbouring tribe from the Sunrise Plains. They had seen many years of peace since, which had degenerated into something close to boredom. He had since seen a gradual decline in the belief of his subjects and their interest in his ceremonies. He needed a good war to reignite their interest in the afterlife, or so he had thought. A visit by a genuine Goddess appeared to have lifted the mood sufficiently.

A few hours after *Phaal* was at his peak, they walked back to their settlement. The tribe had left him alone to walk with the Goddess, for he was the high priest.

They ducked into his tent, which was the biggest of all the tribe, and sat down on a mat of weaved reeds. He gestured to the Goddess to sit opposite him on an ornate carved wooden chair – his own seat usually but under the circumstances he was willing to submit. He had taken her to his tent for some privacy, and despite the hundreds of questions he wanted to ask, he found he was stuck for things to say, what with his lack of experience talking to real Gods; he had prayed to plenty of them in his time, but didn't think he'd ever actually meet any. Deep down he was sceptical they even existed, and mostly just used them as a means to control his subjects. He hoped the Goddess wasn't here by way of warning because she had noticed the insincerity of his worship. To make matters worse, he didn't have any *Tee*, whatever that was.

She seemed fascinated by his living space, looking around with awe. She would gasp with wonder as she spotted everyday things, like the animal skeletons hanging from the rafters or vessels full of the body parts of tribes they had once warred with. He wondered absently why she covered her top half in a cloak, even though the temperature was warm.

After a few minutes of intermittent small talk, Oc decided he would use the opportunity to ask about the afterlife. However, the Goddess kept trying to avoid the subject. Supposedly there were some things she could not say, but he pressed anyway. How many other chances would he get in his lifetime?

When he asked her what it was like where she came from she replied, "Quite nice. The locals" – presumably the other Gods – "are a bit nosey, but they mean well of course and keep the neighbourhood watch going strong." Not being something that directly translated, Oc could only assume that this 'neighbourhood watch' was something beyond the limits of understanding for mere mortals (which is an incorrect assumption, because we immortals haven't got the foggiest either).

Oc was fascinated by her age. He had never seen someone so old, and it struck him as odd that a God would choose to appear as someone past their prime. He asked her, "I hope you do not take offence from me asking, but why would you choose to appear so old?"

"Where I come from I'm not as old as some," she replied. "And I don't choose to appear old; age is something that catches up with all of us."

Her answer made Oc suspicious. This God was starting to appear more mortal than she should be. Her incredible age was clearly an indicator of her other-worldliness, but to be a God she surely had to live for ever. "I thought Gods never died? Do you just keep getting old until you're a ball of wrinkled skin and white hair?"

The Goddess looked worried, as if the answers to his questions were evading her. Eventually she said, "Well if you're going to ask questions like that I'd better make sure there's no misunderstanding. I suppose my body is just temporary and it allows my... my thoughts and memories... to be here on earth. When my human body dies, my, how do you say, Godly spirit will rise to heaven once again."

Despite the Goddess's hesitation, her answer made some sense.

Oc was satisfied; of course she would choose to inhabit a human body during her time on earth. And the older she appeared, the more they would respect her. Besides, they'd have run away in fear before she had the chance to talk to them if she had appeared as a spirit, or some similarly supernatural apparition. Looking like she does now she'd have trouble scaring a newborn fawn.

As soon as the thought came into his head he wondered if the Goddess had heard it. There were so many things to take into consideration when talking to a God. He could think something dangerous and end with her striking him down with lightening. "Can you hear inside my head?" he asked her.

She looked at him as though he was a madman. "I'm sorry, what did you say?" she replied.

"Do Gods know what you're thinking?" He was sweating now. He often had some extremely disturbing thoughts. If she was capable of accessing them he was in quite some trouble.

Fortunately she replied, "No I, er, we can't. Privacy should be respected." Oc smiled in relief.

Something that always concerned him was their religious practices. He had prayed the way his father had prayed and as his father had done before that. But who had told them how they should pray? Had they been as fortunate as him to be visited by a Goddess? "Are we worshipping you in the right way?" he probed. "Sometimes I think that our rituals have been created by power hungry priests." And he should know.

She didn't reply immediately. Oc wiped away a bead of sweat that threatened to drip into his eye. After some concentrating she said, "Religion really comes down to faith. It doesn't much matter who you believe in, but any way you decide to show your faith is fine by me, so long as you feel like it's the right thing to do."

"So is it a good thing to sacrifice beautiful virgins then?" Oc licked his cracked lips. He liked this part of religion very much; he didn't have a lot of luck with any women who still had most of their teeth, which made him particularly bitter.

Nana Barb looked shocked. "Goodness me, no! It's never right to kill someone. That's a barbaric thought, and you are too well-spoken to be a barbarian. I think I might have missed a bit out so I'll try again shall I? It doesn't much matter who you believe in, and any way you choose to show your faith is fine *as long as* you're not hurting anyone else in the process. There is the odd occasion when someone wants to be put out of misery because they are in horrible pain or some such, but I imagine a young virgin wouldn't have such cause."

Oc didn't like having his belief system questioned, even by a God. He decided he was going to creatively interpret her reply. She had said if they *wanted* to be killed, and most of his virgins willingly took the guaranteed path to the Kingdom of the Gods. And besides, once they had started to burn they probably did want to die, and quickly.

He changed the subject. "So, did you like our temple?"

"It was lovely. Really artistic."

Oc beamed. "Is there anything we can do to, you know, make it more suitable?"

"Well since you ask..."

"Yes?"

"Oh no, I'd better not."

"Please, I would like to know. I won't be offended."

"Well, it's not that it isn't lovely, but there are monuments in Egypt that are much bigger."

Oc thought about this then asked her, "How do they make them bigger? The higher we build the wood, the more often it falls down."

"Well they make them out of stone," she replied. "Big blocks of stone."

"How big?" He didn't like her answer.

"Really quite big – almost as big as a mountain."

"And if we were to build a rock monument of our own, where could we find the materials?"

"Well," she replied, "I seem to remember hearing about the stones in Wales being quite good for building."

"Wales? What is that?"

"It's a separate country that sticks out of the side of England. You just follow the river Avon and it takes you right there."

As Oc pondered these revelations, he offered the Goddess some of the tribe's rarest delicacy: matured raw bear steak. She declined his offer, quite rudely he thought. That's the problem with all deities, he decided, their conviction that they are so much better than everyone else.

However, it wasn't the time to feel bitter about his inferiority. He had just been given instructions from a God to build the greatest monument in history. The river Avon (although not called that in his own language) was a place he knew of, and so he could perhaps find the rocks of which she spoke. He would have to get her to repeat herself to the rest of the tribe otherwise they'd never be happy to move enormous rocks from this Wales place. Rocks are really heavy. He would need manpower, and such that his tribe could not possibly handle the task alone. He would have to gather the neighbouring tribes in council and together they could build this great temple.

He decided he would need to arrange a meeting with the town elders immediately to tell them of his plans. If he was ever to accomplish anything in life that could propel him to greatness, this would be it. It would perhaps elevate him to a position worthy of sitting alongside the Gods in the afterlife.

He had to act now. He had no idea how long she would stay with them. Gathering the other tribes would take time, a few days at least. Before he disappeared to find the tribe elders, he explained to the Goddess that he would be leaving for a few moments to gather everyone for an important announcement. Her reaction was very strange. She mumbled something in a tongue completely alien to him.

He was initially confused, until it dawned on him that she was speaking her own language: the language of the Gods. Oc was honoured. He smiled to her and grunted his appreciation, then cursed his obvious mistake. Gods clearly don't eat unless it's a *freshly* sacrificed animal. He exited his tent with a deep bow, leaving the confused-looking Nana Barb speaking that ethereal tongue and wondering where he might find a newly captured bear fit for a God.

## Nana Barb

Nana Barb was terrified. She had been talking to that smelly man about Stonehenge as if she had been possessed. She had practically begged him to build the monument out of stone, and had no idea why she was acting like that. To make matters worse, his wart-covered face had been spouting words and her brain had been translating into perfect English, but then all of a sudden he'd turned into this beastly savage, speaking a primitive tongue she didn't understand. All the while she could make sense of what he was saying, she had subconsciously pretended she was on a movie set with an Oscar-winning costume department, or something of the sort. As soon as she couldn't understand him any more, the reality of the situation hit like a sports car squashing a surprised fly.

She tried talking to herself but it came out in a mixture of the two languages.

Fear took over. She was lost in time and if she could no longer understand the locals she was in for some serious trouble. Gods would at least be expected to understand the language of their subjects, let alone speak it. The last way she thought she would pop her clogs was from a prehistoric tribe using their spears to turn her into a pincushion.

For the first time, she contemplated the reason behind her strange excursion to the past. Very little memory of the event remained, other than the strange high-pitched noise that suddenly appeared when she went to collect the milk bottles. Had someone done this to her on purpose? Was she some sort of experiment, or was time travel a fairly common thing nowadays? The world around her was progressing so quickly and she never really felt the inclination to keep up with all these new-fangled gadgets they were convincing young people to buy with their credit cards. She only got a camera phone so she could take pictures of the grandkids. Out of principle she refused outright to get an email address, and she wouldn't even know where to *begin* writing to a twit on tweeter.

Pushing all these thoughts from her mind, she tried to focus on the present, whatever that meant. One option was to run away, but she feared she wouldn't get very far before they caught her up. She ventured cautiously out of the tent to see if there was someone she could attempt to communicate with. Perhaps she could get some message through to them before her ability to speak their language failed completely. She spotted a young Mum with a small child attached to her ample naked bosom, while she was stirring a large pot of food at the same time. Not wanting to cause her alarm and scare her off, Nana Barb approached her as slowly as her dangerously fast heartbeat would allow.

"Hello," she ventured.

The young woman smiled at her. "Hello," she replied. Then she said something incomprehensible followed by, "is that you?"

"Yes that's me," she quickly responded. She had to try and get a message across as best she could before it was too late, one that would allow her to escape without pursuit. "I have to leave right away. I'm going back over that hill to go home, but you can't follow me otherwise you'll die a horrible death and burn in hell. Zeus and Apollo are, um, cooking me dinner and I don't want it to spoil."

The young lady looked shocked. "Oh, *urff grr dittok*."

Nana Barb hoped the young mother had understood enough of her statement. She turned around grandly and walked off towards the woods with a confidence she didn't feel. She could hear the girl run off behind her, hopefully to pass on the warning about burning in hell.

## Oc-ri Dér

There was quite a commotion down in the village, since word of the Goddess's visit had already begun to spread to some of the neighbouring tribes. Oc spotted visitors from two different clans, who must have travelled over two thousand paces from their own settlements to see if the news was true. They had left their weapons at the village edge to show their peaceful intent and were now eagerly mingling with his own tribesmen. He had no need to call the elders to council, for they were already gathered in excited discussion.

He offered his greetings and started to explain the instructions from their Goddess. The visitors were keen to see proof of this Goddess and so interrupted him, "Where is this Goddess? We need to see her with our own eyes."

"You will see her in due course," Oc snapped.

He had barely got to telling them about the temple when he saw the young girl Lilak running down the hill towards them. "What is it, Lilak?" he said, "can't you see I'm in the middle of something?" She was quite a pretty girl. Shame she wasn't a virgin.

"The Goddess, she mentioned something about going home. I thought you'd want to know."

Oc gasped. He wasn't about to see his ambitious plan to build the greatest monument in history spoilt, simply because the God to whom it would be dedicated was starting to feel homesick. "Yes, very good. Did she tell you where she was going?"

"It was difficult to tell. It was mostly sounds I didn't recognise, but I could understand some of it."

Oc thought about this. A God in human form would have a natural ability to understand her subjects. Perhaps that meant the Goddess was indeed nearing her return to her kingdom, and as that time approached her ability to communicate with them was fading. "Try and remember, what exactly did she say that you could understand?" he asked, trying to hide his concern that his grand plan for a place in history might be falling apart so soon after it had been made.

"Well, it was something along the lines of mumble mumble *want* blah blah *home* something something *death* mumble *burn*. After that it didn't make any sense at all, as if she had forgotten how to speak."

"In what direction did she run?" he asked Lilak.

"Towards the temple," she replied.

The neighbouring tribes were restless and he could see he needed to rescue the situation, and there was his opportunity. He had a witness, and the Goddess had used her last words to pass the message that he was to perform the only known ritual that guarantees entry to the Kingdom of the Gods, so that she might return home. She had asked him to burn her to death on the sacrificial stake.

"We must track her down. She wishes to return to her own land, and who are we to defy the wishes of a God?"

After the miracles that had taken place today, the group were quick to agree with their priest and so dispersed to search for their Goddess. Their sceptical guests were clearly interested and so stated their intention to join their pursuit. Oc ordered a boy to grab rope, straw and flint from his tent before running on ahead. God or no God she probably still felt pain in her human body, so he'd have to stop her from wriggling.

He needed to get to her first so he could ask her some questions. He was a cautious man, and wanted to make sure he was as prepared as he could be. He ran far ahead of the others, and quickly found her hiding amongst the trees en route to the temple. She looked so weak and pathetic cowering away from him and in that moment he realised how truly feeble the human frame is, even when inhabited by a Goddess. The sooner his Godly spirit could be free from his pathetic vessel the better.

Before he announced his find he stared her in the eyes and asked her, "Do you understand me? Can you still speak our language?" As an afterthought adding, "Oh revered one."

Nothing. Not the slightest suggestion she understood him. His plans were falling apart around him and he feared he would be ridiculed in front of the visiting tribe members. If she couldn't speak, how could he force her to tell the world about his temple? *Her* temple – he corrected.

The tribe had seen him talking to the Goddess and so were now gathered around them in expectation. The word had spread that the Goddess had stated her aim to return home, and everyone was jostling for a clear view in case it was their last chance to see her in the flesh.

His bladder felt fuller than it was at the expectation of the fraud he was about to commit. He would have to pretend he could understand the language of the Gods. He announced his discovery to the other elders and stood himself in front of the Goddess to proclaim, "I, Oc-ri Dér, summon the power to speak the divine language of the Gods." He made some wild movements with his arms, hoping it made him look suitably spiritual. "Nano Barr," he continued, "who is the holiest priest of them all?" She looked at him defiantly, refusing to speak.

He hadn't thought about what he would do if she didn't say anything. How could he falsify the translation if she refused to speak? He tried asking her a few questions, but it was obvious she was no longer going to talk to them.

Oc grunted to himself as he thought through his options. He decided to improvise: "Her powers must weaken as her time away from the Kingdom of the Gods lengthens," he suggested weakly to the watching tribe. "She has made a request, so we must return her before it is too late."

"But how do we trust the word of young Lilak?" the more cerebral of the town elders asked. "The Goddess could be in some sort of trance. Maybe we are being too brash."

"How do we even know she is a Goddess?" asked a big balding man from the *Phaal*-bound Hillock tribe. "So far she has demonstrated nothing except for an amazing ability to draw on her clothes."

Oc grumbled in frustration. He was starting to regret the day those two strangely-dressed prophets preordained her arrival, which occurred over twenty summers past. His guaranteed chance of eternal life was slipping away from him because that stupid Goddess refused to speak, and now his authority was being questioned by those to whom he could not show weakness.

He simply couldn't run the risk of being undermined. He had to try and communicate with the Goddess, to get her to say something in her own language at least. He picked up a stone from the ground nearby, causing the Goddess to shy away from him. Waving in the direction of the temple, he pointed at the stone encouragingly. He smiled at her. She smiled back timidly. He seemed to have the attention of the elders.

"Did you prophesy the building of a new temple, one made of rock?" He pointed at his rock again then back in the direction of the temple. Oc nodded enthusiastically, to which the Goddess nodded back tentatively. She spoke a few words in her language then immediately covered her mouth with her hand. One of the elders let out a small gasp of surprise.

Oc turned to the tribe and said, "She replied 'Yes I did'." He turned back to Nana Barb. "Did you say we would make the long journey to Wales, found at the end of the Earth, somewhere over there..." he pointed behind him, "to collect great big rocks to build a new temple?"

Nana Barb looked at him blankly.

He picked a stick off the ground and drew a squiggly line to represent a river. To emphasise his point he wiggled his hands in a fluid motion. That seemed to help and very soon she was nodding like an eager young pup in hunting lessons. She spoke a few more words in her own language; she seemed to be relaxing.

Oc translated creatively: "She said that the sacred place known as Wales can be found that way, and we are to dig some big stones for her monument."

One of the elders groaned. "But rocks are really heavy! What's wrong with wooden posts?"

Finally, Oc took his stick and drew a crude copy of his tent in the dusty ground. He pointed at the tent then to the Goddess. "And you wish for me, Oc-ri Dér, who you proclaimed to be the greatest priest in history, and who alone you allowed the privilege of speaking your Godly language, to return you home? *Nanoo Barp* return home?"

The Goddess looked a little unsure, but nodded all the same.

"Grab her and tie back her arms. We must quickly build a pyre fit for a Goddess."

Two of the younger tribe members rushed on her, pinning her arms back. The Goddess whimpered in expectation of the pain. The poor woman, thought Oc. The fire will burn quickly, so she will soon be back where she belongs.

# CHAPTER 5

## The Scientist Next Door

## 16:10hrs, June 15th 2013 C.E. - Nether Wallop, England

### Louise

As her weird neighbour relayed his story, Louise started to feel a wave of panic. At first she thought it was a joke, that her one time Oxford lecturer, Professor Armitage, had discovered a sense of humour, deciding to act on his threats to humiliate her if she continued to pursue her wild fantasies of matter transportation. However, she realised the time he claimed his grandmother went missing coincided with her accidental test run of the machine, and so she decided to take him seriously, as difficult as that was when he was wearing pyjama bottoms covered with Formula 1 cars.

The hardest thing to accept was that the beam of her device might work over such a great distance. It was a terrifying thought to realise her machine could cause people to disappear spontaneously. In the wrong hands it could be put to deadly use. Worse still, if she had sent this old lady on a trip through time, since the individual in question was so far away from the source of the beam, Louise would have no idea where or when she had sent her. If she had accidently lost an elderly neighbour in the immensity of space-time then she would be getting that Nobel Prize she'd always dreamed of, but she was damned sure she didn't want to be collecting it in a prison cell.

"So you say she would have popped outside to collect the milk; where does the milkman drop it?" she asked, trying to sound as casual as possible.

He was distracted and didn't seem to register the slight tremble in her voice. "By the side door of our house," he answered.

"The side door just above my basement window?"

"Yes, next to the one you always have the curtains drawn across." Her neighbour blushed at his admission of knowing this detail, but Louise barely noticed.

"Are you sure she hasn't just popped into town to treat herself to some new shoes?" Louise suggested hopefully.

"No, absolutely not. She doesn't even leave the house for five minutes without prior announcement. She is perfectly sane too, before you think she might be losing her marbles."

"I wasn't suggesting anything of the sort. Have you tried telling the police?"

"Yes I tried, but they won't start looking for her until twenty-four hours have passed. They said if I saw something remotely suspicious that they could change the case from a missing person to a more serious crime. Maybe a kidnapping." The word kidnapping stuck in his throat halfway through saying it.

"Well have you found any evidence?" Louise asked. She knew she was just stalling for time. Her neighbour's milk bottles were in perfect line of sight to her machine.

"No. I found her hair clip on the floor by the milk bottles, but no sign of blood or anything."

She couldn't stand here and watch him suffer any more. The evidence did not look good. She said reluctantly, "Dave, I think I know where your Nan might be." She could see no merit in hiding the truth from him, mainly because she was a terrible liar.

"Where? Oh that's fantastic. So I have been overreacting all this time, right? She left you a note to pass to me and you forgot to do it, right? She's just gone for a day trip to the dairy farm, or something?"

*No point beating around the bush.* "I'm really sorry. I think I might have lost your Nan."

"What? Lost her? Where did you take her to lose her?"

"I think I might have sent her back in time."

The point didn't register. "At what time though? It can't have been that far back because she was with me this morning."

"I don't think you understand what I'm trying to say. I'm a scientist and I'm currently working on a project to transport matter."

"What did you just say?" Dave asked.

"I'm working on a project to transport matter," she repeated.

"Is this some sort of joke?" Dave did not look amused.

"What, like in that movie *The Fly*?" her neighbour's chubby friend put in.

"Not exactly like that," she replied. "And unfortunately, Dave, I'm not joking. I'm an award-winning physicist – we don't tend to come with a sense of humour."

Her neighbour's friend chuckled. "That's pretty funny. She's right though, she has won a lot of awards," he said, rudely picking up and examining one of her prized certificates.

"So what does this have to do with my Nan?" Dave asked.

"Well, the experiment I'm currently working on is throwing up some strange results. I can get certain types of matter to transport over very small distances, but unfortunately the process also causes me to make the subject disappear. My experiments almost certainly suggest they are being transported to either the distant future or the past. I could, of course, be sending them into an entirely different Universe, if you believe the many worlds theory brought about by Erwin Schrödinger's famous thought experiment."

"Transporting matter? That seems a bit far-fetched."

"Well it might, hence why my peers called me crazy and pulled the plug on my funding. It's not that ridiculous really, a few scientists have successfully transported photons across a lab. I guess they are scared because there's such a big gap between the results from other studies and the successes I have achieved through my experiments. I mean, an entire test subject is quite a quantum leap away from transporting photons, if you forgive my pun." She let out a terse laugh, but they remained stony faced – the joke obviously fell on a wasted audience.

Dave's friend still wore a knotted expression of confusion, but she could see Dave was far closer to the point. He asked, "Can you explain in English please? Are you saying that in this case the subject was my grandmother?"

Louise looked at the floor so that her long mousey-coloured hair covered her reddening face. “Yes. I'm really sorry. Unfortunately, during my efforts I have discovered that time and space are intrinsically linked. You can't move through one without moving through the other. The machine was set to transport the subject about twenty miles.”

Dave's friend put his hand in the air and asked, “So you've teleported her twenty miles away? That's amazing! Can you teleport me to Australia? I've been trying to save up for the flights for about three years.”

Dave looked on the verge of collapse. “What's your friend's name again?” Louise asked as she showed him to a chair.

“Simon.”

“Well Simon, I could teleport you to Australia, but if my theory, and the equations that I'm in the process of devising, prove correct, I would have to make you travel more than 50,000 years through time. Dave's grandmother is only just down the road, but 5,000 years ago. I teleported her into the past.”

“Bloody hell,” said Simon.

Louise glanced at Dave, who had turned deathly white. “I thought you needed to build a star ship to travel through time,” he managed to say. “I thought you needed to travel at the speed of light.”

“That's a common misconception; in fact travelling anywhere close to the speed of light would cause space, which is virtually a vacuum, to become incredibly dense. You would die instantly of radiation poisoning from the unthinkably vast amount of hydrogen.”

“Well aren't you just full of cheerful anecdotes?”

“I'm sorry, but I revert to science when I get nervous. It makes me feel in control.”

“So,” said Simon, “the way I understand it, this machine you've built is more like the one out of *The Time Machine* than it is the one out of *Star Trek: First Contact*. In other words, you don't drive in a ship but get teleported by a machine. But how does it work exactly?

Even the one in *The Time Machine* has these bars that move around with that scientist bloke in the middle, so it looks like all the world is changing around him."

"Well that's where the trick is, you see," replied Louise, "Arguably, space is only really ordered like it is because of the way it is being observed. Experiments on particles under really extreme conditions show they act more like waves than solid matter, called the wave-particle duality. In fact, it is only when the particle is viewed that the wave-function collapses and the matter appears to behave as we see it.

"I realised, after many failed attempts to transport inanimate matter, that I could only get the machine to work on living beings. I knew I couldn't build a machine powerful enough to change the space around the being – that's like changing the whole Universe. However, by doing it in reverse, I only had to alter the state of one tiny little brain."

"Sorry, love," Simon said, "you lost me with the wave particle duplicity thing. I didn't exactly pass my science GCSE with flying colours. Well, I didn't even turn up to the exam if I'm being honest."

Louise didn't have a movie to compare the situation to, so she gave up trying to explain further.

Dave, on the other hand, seemed to be much more intelligent than appearances would suggest, and she knew he had followed everything she'd said. He now wore an expression of muted astonishment, as if he had just been told his winning numbers had come up, but the ticket was thrown away with last week's rubbish.

"Either this is an elaborate hoax and there are hidden cameras filming me, to make me look stupid, or I live next door to the greatest scientist in history, who is also stupid enough to not put a safeguard on her machine. Which one is it?" he asked.

Louise knew it sounded ridiculous so tried to make as sincere a face as she could. "I'm afraid it's the latter. I really have built this machine. In my professional opinion she really probably is in the past."

"That's what I love about scientists," Dave retorted, "their absolute faith in guesswork."

Louise didn't know how to respond. There was a long silence as everyone contemplated the enormity of the situation. Simon picked at a scab on his elbow.

Eventually Dave asked the question everyone was thinking. "How are we going to get her back?"

"Can't we just cut the problem at the bud? We could just teleport back to when she first went missing," Simon suggested.

Louise frowned. "It's not that simple I'm afraid. I was in the room at the time, which throws up all kinds of complications. Stopping me from turning on the machine could create a paradox."

Dave's voice was desperate. "It's got to be worth a try though."

"It's not worth the risk. It could collapse the Universe. I'm really sorry Dave."

"What do we do then?"

Louise was at a loss. "I don't know," she admitted.

"It's obvious, isn't it? We need to go back in time and save her." Dave looked up at her with surprisingly intense eyes that reminded Louise of a small brown bear she had once seen at a zoo in Thailand – the poor thing an unfortunate target of the cruel locals, empty McDonald's wrappers and Coke being cruelly thrown at him in a forbidding cultural mélange of East meeting West.

She looked away, conscious of the eye contact lasting longer than she would have liked. "Possibly. I'm not really sure *when* she is though."

"How unsure are you?" Dave asked.

"I think I'd be able to tell you the precise date if I knew the exact place she was standing when the beam hit her. The hat I put on the mice records their position and feeds the information to the computer. My first concern would be the high degree of speculation brought about from so many variables, since we don't have all the data essential to the process. A few millimetres might make the difference of decades."

"What makes you so sure these mice you're testing the machine on – and I'm not particularly comfortable with the idea of animal experiments, by the way – are being sent into the past or the future?"

"When the mice came back they were covered with bacteria completely alien to our time, suggesting they had long since evolved, or that they were further along in the evolutionary process," Louise replied. "A combination of mapping the genomes of some of the bacteria and measuring the atmosphere allowed me to make fairly accurate calculations when dealing with the past. The future is much more difficult, and so I was prepared to send myself through time to gather more accurate data."

"You were going to use that thing on yourself?"

"I'm fully prepared to, yes."

Dave paused, and then decided, "Well that seems conclusive enough. I want you to use that machine on me."

"That's very brave of you, Dave, but I must warn you. The mice don't always make it back."

"Send me anyway," Dave stated boldly, although his voice was almost an octave higher than it had been.

"And me," said Simon. "I've always wanted to go back to the future."

Dave let out a groan like an angry tugboat. "You can't go back to the future because you haven't even been there in the first place. And we want to go back in time, not forward."

"I just thought it was an expression, that's all."

"Well it's not an expression; it's the name of a movie," he shouted, a little harshly Louise thought.

She decided to cut in before they filed for divorce. "I can't send you back after her. It would be unethical. I need to call the police, or even some agency higher up – the Government or MI5 maybe." She didn't really want to. She would rather risk her life in a human experiment than go to jail, ending years of hard work, or worse, having her ideas stolen by an opportunistic government scientist.

She prayed he would be determined and talk her into it.

"I don't care," Dave said. "You're going to send me back. I need to find her, I owe it to her."

"I'm not even one hundred percent certain that the being we temporally shifted was your grandmother; for all we know it could have been a passing cat. My machine isn't capable of recording the species of the subject."

"Believe me, Louise, she's not the type to disappear without word of where she was going, so the evidence is pointing towards her being the – subject. It's a risk I'm willing to take."

As noble as he was, she trusted him about as much as she did her mice. "OK, if you insist. I'm coming with you though. Simon, you'll have to stay here."

"What? I wanna come too," he whinged.

"You can't. I need someone to stay and make sure the power is kept on. We'd never make it back to our time if something happened to the machine this end."

"Well you stay then. If something went wrong I wouldn't know how to fix it anyway."

"I have to go with Dave because I'm the only one who can make the calculations for our journey back. My invention uses a bit more power than the national grid likes you to suck, so it's prone to tripping. The machine self-diagnoses and fixes itself anyway, so the only real danger is the power cutting. If we try and shift back to our own time whilst there isn't a machine to steer us back this end, God only knows where we'll end up. You know how to flick a tripped switch, right?"

"Not r..."

Simon started to speak but Dave cut in. "Simon, of course you do, you trained as an electrician for a year at college. I'm sorry, I know it sounds fun but I need you to do as she says."

"You just want her all alone 'cos you fancy her."

Dave went bright red. Louise stifled a laugh.

"Simon, please. My Nana's missing. This isn't a game."

"Well what about the dead deer decomposing in my trunk, or the fact your aunt will be here any minute? You're always askin' me to help you solve your problems, but you don't never help me with mine."

"Did he just say he has a dead deer in the boot of his car?" Louise asked.

Dave ignored her and looked his friend in the eyes. "OK, I will help you Simon, as soon as I come back – I promise. We'll teleport back here half an hour from now so you won't even notice us missing. I really need your help with this, mate."

Simon couldn't make eye contact with Dave; he appeared to deliberate for some time. Eventually he said slowly, "Oh all right. But I'm coming along next time. And make sure you bring me back a souvenir, something really old I can sell on *Antiques Road Show*."

## Louise

Half an hour later and with barely a clue as to what might happen to them, Louise and Dave prepared themselves for their journey into the past. They were wearing clothes Louise thought might be at least passable for prehistoric: Dave in one of Louise's mock fur coats and Louise in a ripped leather shirt and a hemp dress she had bought one year at a music festival. They looked ridiculous, but it was better than pyjama bottoms covered in machines that won't be built for a few millennia.

Louise measured the distance to Barbara's milk bottles, made a few calculations and entered the information into the hand-held remote. They said their goodbyes to Simon, put on the little nylon hats and steeled themselves in preparation.

To say she was nervous would be the understatement of the century. She was petrified. For some reason she didn't want to show this to Dave, and so with a forced grin Louise held Dave's sweaty hand and pressed the large red button that would send them on their way.

The last thing she heard was Simon saying, "Wowowowowow..." The word echoed and rebounded like a dance record stuck on a scratch. With her heart in her mouth as though she were reaching the edge of a huge precipice, Louise looked down and saw her atoms disengaging from her body, as she had seen happen to the lab mice countless times before. It felt quite tingly, almost euphoric. She tried to concentrate on the moment, but her thoughts were difficult to focus. She was thinking about everything and nothing at the same time. There was a bright light and she felt warm and tingly all over...

Twenty miles and five thousand years away a wolf that had been happily minding her own business, trying to hunt down a small mammal whilst avoiding the humans that would eventually wipe her species from the British Isles, found herself unexpectedly thrust into the future. Her prey was still a short way in front of her and, with its attacker's cover gone, suddenly made a dash for it. The wolf set off in pursuit, much to the amusement of a watching two-year-old boy, who made his presence known by shouting, "Doggy!"

The wolf, suddenly too incensed to question why she understood the human, stopped in her tracks with the intention of pointing out to her next meal that she was in fact a much more graceful and proud animal than her domicile cousins who had opted to live a life of servitude.

Before she had the chance to tuck in she was hit by a bus, knocked out cold and thrown into the bushes that lined the road. The little boy started to cry.

# CHAPTER 6

## The Uninvited Guests

## 16:27hrs, June 15th 2013 C.E. – Nether Wallop, England

### Jonathon Scabbers

Mr Scabbers liked to think he could hear foreigners coming a mile off. It was his neighbourly duty, of course, to keep an eye out. In particular he would make sure the parking spaces on the street were only taken up by the residents. He would tell no one in particular that he could recognise the sound of most of the cars belonging to the residents of Freecock Gardens, and he had decided this certainly wasn't one of them. (Of course he always had to check to confirm his assumptions, which he would conveniently forget if he got it wrong.)

He peered through his net curtains to see two very well dressed gentlemen park their car outside the house next to his. Mr Scabbers felt a pang of jealousy, followed by a strong feeling of resentment; if he didn't get any visitors why were they allowed any?

After a few seconds of trying to look round to see the front door of number 17, the two foreigners looked as if they were returning to their car, but instead walked right past it and to the door of the house opposite. His resentment was instantly replaced with glee – they were unsolicited salesmen. He should have known, what with those smart suits. He decided to watch and see what they were selling.

Despite walking right up to it, they didn't knock on the door of number 18 but instead had their mobile phones out, writing some sort of texting message no doubt. No sooner had they put their phones away when they turned on their heels and made towards his door. Mr Scabbers decided to become scarce. If there was something he hated above anything else in the world it was anything that controlled your mind, and three of his least favourite things fitted into that category: Jehovah's Witnesses, Unsolicited

Salesmen and Derren Brown. With a shudder, he disappeared into the back bedroom.

There was a knock at his door, which he ignored. He picked up a copy of the Daily Mail and started skimming through the pages (which we Web-spinners find ironic, since by definition the national newspapers were our greatest mind-controlling invention since politics).

A minute passed before there was another knock, louder this time. Persistent weren't they? They didn't spend so long at the other houses, so perhaps they'd seen his curtain moving when he was looking out of the window. He cursed his mistake, resolving to wait it out, make it clear he didn't want disturbing.

What seemed like an unnaturally precise minute later, there was a much louder knock at the door, so loud in fact that it shook the foundations of his bungalow.

"Go away. Don't you get the point, I don't want to buy anything," he shouted.

There followed a short silence; maybe they had finally got the message.

He had mistakenly allowed himself to relax when a deeply serious voice replied, "Mr Jonathon James Scabbers of 19 Freecock Gardens, we know you are there so please open the door. You have twenty seconds to comply or we will use necessary force."

Mr Scabbers used everything in his power to stop himself throwing up. He had only been in trouble once in his life, when a supermarket security guard caught him accidently driving the wrong way round the car park one-way system. He still had nightmares about it to this day.

He tried to console himself with the thought that he hadn't done anything wrong, so it must be a case of mistaken identity. It brought him little comfort as he hurriedly slid the door off the latch, unlocked the three separate catches, slid two deadlocks out of place and finally, with two seconds to spare, turned the main front door key.

As soon as the door was open he was pushed back inside by two very well dressed identical twins.

"Sit down Mr Scabbers," they both said at exactly the same time.

It was all he could do to stop his bladder emptying of its own accord. He fell on to his sofa, crossing his legs to help hold it in. "What do you want? I haven't done anything wrong," he pleaded.

"Mr Jonathon James Scabbers of 19 Freecock Gardens," said the man on the right, "we, the Time Police, have travelled here from your future. We have a number of questions we wish to ask you. We will know if you are lying so please do not waste time by falsifying your answers."

"First question," said the other man, before Mr Scabbers had time to comment or interject. "Did you operate a time travelling device, set to transport one person, at approximately 10:31hrs and 51.43 seconds, today June the 15th 2013 Common Era of the Gregorian date system?"

Both of the men took out their extremely expensive-looking mobile phones.

"Wha...?"

"Answer the question immediately please."

"N–no, I don't know what you're talking about."

"He's telling the truth," said the man on the left.

"I am receiving the same reading," said his colleague.

"Second question. Did you operate a time travelling device, set to transport two people, at approximately 16:19hrs and 18.217983 seconds recurring, today June the 15th 2013 Common Era of the Gregorian Date system?"

"No, that wasn't me," he replied.

"He is telling the truth again. Do you know of anyone within half a square mile of this house who owns a time travelling device?"

"No, I'm sorry but I don't."

"Final question. Do you know of anyone on this street who unexpectedly disappeared today?"

"No," he replied.

Mr Scabbers felt a lot more comfortable now he knew he was talking to a couple of crackpots. He suddenly felt very silly for being so nervous, but they had looked extremely intimidating walking in together, almost... alien. They were obviously off their rocker whoever they were, talking about time travel and the like. They must be scientologists, he decided. He vowed to call the *real* police as soon as they had left.

"Can I ask you a few things, if I'm not the one you are looking for?" he got the courage up to ask.

Both the men turned to each other. "His questions have less than a ten percent chance of yielding information beneficial to our search," said one.

"Agreed," said the other. "But there is still potential merit in letting him speak. We must limit his questioning." Turning to Mr Scabbers he said, "Proceed. You have one minute."

He didn't want to keep them there any longer than they needed to be, but their enquiry didn't make any sense, and he wanted to point as much out to them. "Answer me this: if you knew exactly when this time travel thingy-majigy was set off, and you say you've travelled here from the future, why didn't you just teleport straight to your suspect and catch them at it, before they even set it off?"

"Our instruments are not precise enough to tell us the exact origin of the ripple in space-time. However, from the periodic alternating fluctuations in the regional wave-function oscillational breakdown, we were able to ascertain roughly when the ripple was caused, and from the quadrangulation of the ripple origin based on the Spencer's Law depreciation, we were able to narrow the region to within the Freecock Gardens area by half a mile."

*Well that clears that up then.* Mr Scabbers, although completely baffled, wasn't finished yet. "Well why don't you just keep coming back then, until you catch them at it? That's got to be a better route than bothering us poor folk, the innocent bystanders, hasn't it?"

"Every instance we travel through time, the fabric of space loses a varying amount of energy. If it loses enough then the Universe will collapse. Our job is to stop the Universe collapsing."

Mr Scabbers was thoroughly dejected and felt as if he had lost an argument somehow. "Well I'm glad I asked," he said indignantly. Although he refused to admit it, he was a little unnerved by their answers.

"Your minute is up," said one of the men. "Your questions did not help us in our enquiry, save to eliminate you from the list of suspects. You will be pleased to hear we can now terminate your existence."

"Wha...?" he started to say, before a large glowing beam of light appeared from one of the mobile phones and hit him on the middle of his forehead. He felt a strong burning sensation and his life flashed before his eyes.

## Mrs Ellis

Mrs Ellis's knees were hurting from bending down behind the pampas grass bushes in the front garden of number 23. About twenty minutes ago she had made up an excuse (she didn't even like coffee) so she could leave her son and his best friend, safe in the knowledge they had exhausted their search of the street. The good thing about young people, thought Mrs Ellis, is their lack of commitment.

After keeping watch for about twenty minutes, her quarry finally made an appearance. Her son had just driven off in the Cadillac he was borrowing, when a black car rounded the corner and parked against the curb. The two men from her dream got out, checked the front door of two properties uncertainly and then approached a third. They entered through the front door of number 19 in a rather forceful manner. Mrs Ellis allowed herself a satisfied smile; she had been right to follow her gut. She thanked her lucky stars she had encouraged the boys to keep a wide berth of old Mr Scabbers and his blabbering mouth.

Despite the broad summer daylight, she saw an incredibly bright light shine from behind the blinds, followed by the briefest of screams. She was instantly regretful for thinking so badly of the poor man, because it was quite obvious what had just happened. Not long after that the two men left. They were soon going to approach the house where Dave and the young lady must still be, and she would have to distract them and make sure she kept them away. She was extremely scared because she had seen in her dream how dangerous these men could be, and she suspected she had just witnessed the extent of that danger. But she knew what she had to do, and if her life was taken in the process then that's a small price to pay for the salvation of all humanity.

# CHAPTER 7

## Pyre for a Goddess

## B.C.E. 3071 - Salisbury Plain, England

## Nana Barb

Barbara had accepted the idea of death many years ago. Not long after her husband Robert passed away, she had come to terms with her own mortality – not because she yearned to see his face again and expected she would in heaven; she wasn't religious. It was more that she had been forced to think about something humans spend a great deal of time trying to avoid thinking about. When thrust into the reality of a situation you have to face up to the truth: death happens to us all.

For her, death was nothing but dust, certainly nothing to fear because she had already been dead. What else could you call the period of time before your own existence?

She thought that if she were diagnosed with cancer or some terminal illness she would accept it with quiet acquiescence, but she hadn't quite considered that she might one day be tied to a post and set alight by a prehistoric tribe.

It was a shock when they grabbed her arms. She thought she had managed to talk them out of any barbarity. They had been laughing, building rapport. Where did it go wrong?

She could see the tribe members gathering kindling and logs, attaching them to a wooden post in that cursed temple of theirs. Her Stonehenge used to be something that filled her with awe. Now it filled her with nothing but dread.

She tried not to cry because she wanted to remain civilised, a quiet protest against barbaric ways. If she screamed out, lost control of her emotions, then what difference was there between them and her?

As her hands were tied behind her back to a large pole, any thought that she might have misunderstood their intentions left her. They were going to burn her. At the stake. This death would not be fast like an accident or peaceful during sleep, nor would it be lingering like a terminal illness such as cancer, with too much time to contemplate the loss your loved ones would feel in your absence. It was somewhere in between, where you had time to realise the end was coming but without any time to prepare for it. This way came with unprecedented fear of excruciating pain (hadn't she heard somewhere that burning was the most painful way to go?); this was protracted, lonely and undignified.

As they raised the pole she wanted to be brave, to be supportive to those she would leave behind. Instead she opened her throat and let out a pathetic scream.

The flames were lit and were getting close to her feet. The pole she was tied to was starting to feel ominously hot. She knew she was going to die now.

## Oc-ri Dér

Oc began the incantations as the boy fuelled the fire. The Goddess was screaming in agony; the sound was pure bliss, the sound of eternal gratefulness. Suddenly, completely unexpectedly, the Goddess turned into an animal they didn't recognise and the binding ropes fell to the ground. As the boy tried to catch the animal, everyone present began to pray for the miracle they were witnessing. The previously sceptical tribe members from the villages nearby dropped to their knees in disbelief, saying such things as, "It is the Goddess!" and "Oh blessed one, please forgive us for being weak of faith."

The timing was so perfect that Oc couldn't have requested it any better. There were tears in his eyes as the thought struck him that the Goddess had chosen him. He would rule alongside the Gods. As they tied down and set alight the frightened rodent, he made a vow to never miss his prayers again.

A small voice could be heard coming from the flames, "Let me go you idiots, it really hurts!"

"What was that?" one of the elders asked.

Who just said that? Was that the voice of the Goddess after she had changed form? Oh well, time for a cover up. Over the crackle of spitting animal fat he said, "Nothing your graciousness. I just stubbed my toe."

"Oh, I see."

# CHAPTER 8

## Oc-ri La

## B.C.E. 3090 – Salisbury Plain, England

### Dave

At the beginning of his temporal shift, Dave's attention focused on nothing in particular. Then his thoughts began to concentrate on his home planet, Earth, which appeared in his mind like an immeasurable entity, an organism of limitless life and energy. Then he found himself contemplating vast swathes of rich emerald woodland, punctuated with bright green patches; pastoral clearings in an ancient forest that appeared luminous in the setting sun.

Then he realised he was thinking about Louise, which was a pleasant feeling, and then slowly, along with the scenery, she began to appear in front of him, her delightful head materialising in amongst a large thicket of raspberry. It became apparent they were in the middle of a forest, but how deep in it was difficult to tell because the evening sun had set and foliage was blocking out what little light it still offered.

Dave's head was spinning. Louise had been telling the truth. There weren't any hidden cameras and this wasn't a dream – it certainly felt real enough anyway.

He hadn't fully committed his belief, right up until the point he could see his body start to break apart. First of all he had been gripped with a terrible fear, but then he'd started to travel through time and he found that particular emotion drifting away with his body. *How could you be scared of your human form ceasing to exist when you no longer inhabited it?* And now he found himself in the past, once again solid flesh and bones, and he noticed the fear hadn't returned with his body. He felt an inherent calm that a skilled proponent of yoga might display, or a samurai whilst training in his dojo. He felt clear of mind and spirit, renewed and reinvigorated.

And then he heard the wolves. They were howling and it sounded like they were hunting. The noises were terrifyingly close, and

Louise was stuck in the bush.

"Dave, you need to get me out of here. Quickly," she called to him urgently, with her voice as close to a whisper as she could keep it.

"All right, just don't panic," he shouted back far too loudly. He tripped his way towards her and frantically began cutting his hands on the raspberry bush with little effect.

"What are wolves doing in England?" he demanded as he tried pulling his shirt sleeves over his hands to protect them from the thorns.

"Dave, they are indigenous to this county. Our prehistoric ancestors obviously haven't managed to wipe them out yet."

"Didn't you think of warning me first? We should have brought a knife, or a gun even." Louise's shirt was too short on his arms, so he couldn't keep the sleeves over his hands which were now raw and bleeding.

"I think they're getting close, Dave, I can hear them near us."

"We'll be fine," he lied. He was now trying to pull at her leg, but it was stuck firm underneath a root. His hands were grasped around her bare thigh but they were slipping because of the blood and the sweat, of which there was a plethora because he was touching her bare thigh.

Then he stopped pulling, giving up because it was too late. The next few moments took mere seconds to play out, but seemed to last an eternity. Dave knew the wolves were upon him because he could see the bushes shaking as they crashed through them, and so he surrendered his masculinity and screamed like a little girl. He held his arm over his eyes to blind him from the terror that was about to befall him, and soon after felt the wolves begin to tear at his leather trouser legs. He tried to shake his leg to ward off their powerful jaws, but they came at him again and again. The hand that remained on Louise's thigh squeezed tight, and he felt her stiffen against the pain.

He wondered how his life might have been had he only been given the chance to live a few more years. He had so many regrets, so many things he had wanted to do. He had wanted to find a girlfriend, like Louise or Stacey Dawson, settle down and maybe have children one day. He wished he had stuck with his education, got a decent job and proved wrong all the people who doubted him. He had wanted to climb Everest, or at least do one of those guided tours to the base camp.

He wondered why it didn't hurt. Were they just toying with their food before they ate it? Then Louise began to laugh. Why would she be so cruel? Why wasn't she helping to fight them off?

He decided to face his killers bravely, to review the scene of devastation. Maybe get one last look at the beautiful face that was mocking him in his savage death.

He relaxed his grip on Louise's thigh and slowly lowered his other arm to review the devastation. Instead he was met with the sight of two wolf pups fighting over his trouser legs. One of them jumped right up into his arms and started licking his reddening face.

"Ha ha, very funny," he said as he held the panting puppy in front of him at arm's length. The wolf started peeing.

"Sorry Dave." Louise tried to control her laughter. "But seriously, we need to think about their mother. She can't be far away from us and I wouldn't want to test her maternal bond with her pups. Now, get me out of here, and try lifting the root this time, rather than pulling at my leg with your sweaty hands."

Silently, Dave left the puppies to play with the laces on his slippers as he reached down and put all of his weight into lifting the root, which sure enough gave Louise the room to pull her foot free. They were reluctant to leave the wolf pups, but equally reluctant to meet their parents. With one last belly rub they turned away from their cute little companions and ran into the dense, dark forest.

## Louise

Their primary aim was to move away from the sound of the howling wolves, although they had little idea which direction to head in, or how they might conduct their search. Louise had a vague idea that they would search for a settlement, in particular for columns of smoke that would give away the presence of humans. They could only hope that Nana Barb would have sought the relative safety of human contact, and that her extreme age, for this era at least, would have given her an air of innocuousness that might provide her some security. They walked into the dark trees, hoping to find some prehistoric people she could attempt to communicate with.

Louise was surprised that she had displayed more calm than her nervous neighbour, since she'd never had herself down as particularly courageous. Her leg was hurting where Dave had squeezed it so hard during his brief overreaction, but she refrained from telling him so. He was embarrassed enough as it was. He was very bashful, but she actually found it quite endearing. It was much more pleasant than the sleazy college professors she was used to handling, the type you would be forgiven for presuming had never seen a woman before.

Louise had found her temporal shift extremely educational, significantly more than she could have ever hoped. The very process was enlightening, as well as the outcome. She had felt as if all knowledge was available to her, if only she could focus her attention long enough to remember some of it. It was far too early to tell, but potentially temporal shifting could be utilised as something more than a simple transportation device; it could answer most of the more difficult questions about the Universe.

Before the events of today, she had already been close to using herself as a test subject for her experiments, but had wanted to gather some more statistical evidence first. When she experimented with her mice, they would fail to return to their own time in only a handful of cases, assuming their temporal shift didn't last any longer than eight hours. Any more than eight and only a handful returned.

Self-experimentation is an extreme measure one has to take if your peers refuse to accept your theory, but more often than not it will result in disaster. She would obviously like to see a positive outcome, such as Barry J. Marshall experienced when he famously proved his sceptics wrong by intentionally ingesting the H. Pylori virus, to demonstrate it was the cause of the majority of stomach ulcers. Conversely, she could be the first person to die from a technology that is ultimately dangerous, like the pioneering Marie Curie who passed away from leukaemia well before her time, after years of exposing herself to her discovery, the highly radioactive element radium.

Statistically, excluding any unknown factors, there was a 1.5% chancc of failing to make it back if she stayed less than eight hours. If they were gone longer than eight hours, she only had a 3% chance of making it home. She obviously had to consider the fact she was larger than the mice and perhaps more capable of moving herself away from dangerous situations. She also had to consider the possibility some of her mice might have succeeded in removing their data chips, which recorded their movements, vital signs and time spent away, and most importantly perpetuated their return journey at a time of Louise's choosing.

They also contained a GPS tracking chip so she could find them when they returned. Originally, the tracking chip was included so she could see how far her subjects had teleported, but when she realised they were actually time travelling instead, it was useless for the original task, but became useful for a different purpose entirely. For reasons unknown, she could never get the mice to return to her lab; instead she would have to capture them in traps around her garden and the local area.

Like a good girl, she had completed her risk assessment and concluded the danger was fairly minimal. Of course, she had always expected to shift herself to an era closer to hers, where law, society and rules would reduce the possibility of threat. Going to a time before recognisable civilisation, where dangerous predators still lurked, and where communication with the natives would be a near impossibility, was never part of the plan.

Now she knew the machine itself was comparatively safe, she could return to these experiments at a later date. For now she had a task, and that was to find Nana Barb.

After an hour of walking in near silence, both deeply engrossed in their own thoughts, they came to a clearing in the woods, which was atop a large hill. Away from the foliage of the trees, they could see from the light of a full moon. The full moon concerned Louise. The indigenous folk of this land allowed their religious practices to be governed by the moon's movements, and so the level of unpredictability had suddenly increased.

## Dave

Dave walked on with Louise at his side, struggling to find things to say to her. What topic would he have in common with a female scientist? He wanted to know if she had a day job, and how she had managed to find the funding for all her machinery. He wondered what type of music she liked, or what she did for fun. For some reason it didn't seem an appropriate time to ask any of these questions.

Instead he reflected on his feeling during the temporal shift, the feeling of complete lack of control, and yet the serenity that came with it. He wanted to share his experience with Louise but, put off by his attempted conversations with Stacey earlier that morning, he was worried it would come out in gargled English. He kept quiet instead.

When they reached a clearing in the woods they found themselves high enough to view their surroundings. Thankfully the moon was full so they had a better view. It's amazing how much of an effect light pollution has on your visibility at night-time, Dave thought. He could see hills and valleys a great distance away, which the light of cities would normally obscure in his own time.

And then he spotted what they were looking for: a faint slither of smoke and a bright glow when he traced it down.

"There," said Dave, and pointed towards his find, "I think we've found our settlement."

"Right then. Let's go," she replied. "But Dave, when we get there, let me do all the talking, OK?"

"Yeah, sure." She obviously thought he was completely inept. When the opportunity arose he'd show her though.

## Louise

Louise took the initiative and led the way through the trees. She prayed Dave would hold his tongue and not confuse her attempts to communicate with the locals. She had planned to use pictorial representations, which Neolithic people were known to communicate with. Before they had left their own time, she had used her limited artistic skills to draw a picture of a stooped woman, and to represent age she had drawn a sun and lines that represented its movement across the sky. She had decided to leave the colouring pencils at home, in case the locals found their strange inventions too bizarre to comprehend.

Louise could see a large fire burning in a clearing through the trees, which was casting flickering shadows across the path in front of her. She could hear the heavy tread of hundreds of feet dancing together and supposed a ritual must be taking place. As she walked closer to the edge of the forest she realised the large structures that she had assumed were huts were actually large stones. They weren't nearing a settlement, but walking into the building site of a large temple. And not just any temple, but a hugely impressive Neolithic stone circle that had a vague resemblance to Stonehenge.

Between the stones she could see the natives dancing in the moonlight. Some were banging drums to form a rhythmic beat, while children chased each other with delighted faces.

"Dave," she whispered. "Don't do anything brash or unexpected. We don't want to attract too much attention and end up changing the course of history."

"Of course," he replied, "I'm not stupid, you know."

Louise edged forwards to get a closer look.

The dancing stopped; they had been spotted. Louise swallowed hard and took a step towards the revellers. She lifted her hands to show she carried no weapon. She glanced at Dave, whose crossed arms betrayed his nerves, and glared at him until he followed her lead.

If the locals felt threatened then they didn't show it; indeed some were apparently quite amused. One or two were smiling widely as though they were meeting old friends. She took this as a cue to try communicating. She reached into her pocket to retrieve her drawings. One or two stepped backwards as if she might be about to produce a weapon, but were soon curious when they saw it was something too small to be dangerous. She triumphantly proffered the picture and made the first steps towards interaction.

"That's a nice painting," said a young boy, and Louise's heart almost stopped as she realised she could understand him. "Did you draw it?"

"Yes I did," she automatically replied in their language, much to her surprise. Her rational brain immediately sought a reason; the cognitive process involved in time travelling must somehow stimulate the Broca and Wernicke areas of the brain, thus allowing the subject an unexpected control over language. She suddenly felt very silly, holding out a badly-drawn picture when she could simply ask them what she wanted.

"It's very pretty," a small girl said, as she twisted her dirty hair in even dirtier fingers. "Is that a bear in your picture?" Dave started laughing, which in turn prompted some members of the indigenous people to laugh.

"Yes, it's a bear," Louise answered indignantly. She stared at Dave, daring him to tell them otherwise. "You can have it, if you like." She offered the picture to the girl, who took hold of it gratefully, with an amazed look on her face.

Suddenly there was a commotion stirring behind the crowd. A person too short for them to see was trying to make his way through, and was hitting anyone who got in his way with a large, gnarled stick. People were grunting in pain or annoyance as they let him pass.

"Move out of my way," a heavy-set sidekick shouted, "your priest is coming through, so clear a path." The crowd parted to reveal an angry-looking man, who must have been the priest.

The man looked ancient. He was short and his face was covered in warts, but his belly was round, portraying affluence superior to his subjects. He looked straight past Dave, staring in awe at Louise who suddenly felt very uncomfortable. The old priest licked his lips.

"I, Oc-ri La, one who sees the future, formerly known as Oc-ri Dér, one who sees far, greet you strangers. Have you come with messages from the Goddess?" He didn't take his eyes off Louise's legs as he made his grand introduction.

Louise thought it would be appropriate to mimic his way of greeting. She looked at his shoes and said, "I, Louise, err, one with long legs, greet you Oc-ri La. We are not here with a message from the Goddess. We are here to seek some knowledge."

"Then we shall help you with that." The priest walked towards Louise and grabbed her hand, pulling hard so she was forced to lean in towards him. "We shall indeed help you with that."

Louise tried not to break any customs, but nonetheless recoiled from the smell of stale fish emanating from the man's mouth.

"But first, we must continue the festivities. The Goddess is great, but can be cruel if you do not satisfy her wishes. We will tell stories, and then we can help you find the answers you are looking for." He turned, and led Louise by the hand to the centre of their circle.

His proposition sounded reasonable enough, but Louise prayed the stories would be short. They only had four hours left.

## Magda

Magda, despite having lived for fifteen summers, was still without a man. The people in the village found her wilful, her hips too narrow and she wasn't very good at cooking. She was still a virgin, which meant she only had a year to be allocated a husband, otherwise she would be sacrificed by the crazy old priest. The arrival of the two strangers brought her great interest.

To her, the newcomer was extremely exotic, and she had heard it was a good thing to breed with people from outside the village. He was so clean, and his tidy, floppy hair was mesmerising. She couldn't tell whether the woman was one of his wives, but didn't suppose that mattered too much anyway. She was much younger so would bear him many more children, if her narrow hips allowed.

They were dressed in really odd clothes, she thought. The woman was covered above the waist, despite the warm weather. And they must have made the clothes from some very strange animals. She spotted her opportunity to start a conversation. Being festival day, they should be dressed in the correct attire. She would fetch him a set of ceremonial bearskin cloak and cuffs, and the man's wife the traditional weaved skirt.

She ran quickly to the tent of dressing and searched through the clothes to find garments that would fit them. The man was really big, so she grabbed the largest cloak she could find. The lady's skirt would be quite short on her because she was so tall, but it was the largest they had so it would have to do. She ran back to the temple.

Quickly spotting the visitors, she approached them. She went straight up to the man and presented the bearskin cloak. "Hello," she said, eyeing the man flirtatiously, "my name is Magda."

The man's face went bright red. His wife, for she must have been so because she answered for him, replied, "And my name is Louise. His name is Dave, and we are very pleased to meet you."

She noticed the man, Dave, briefly looking at her bare breasts. His red face went even brighter, and then he looked at her no more. What was so interesting about her breasts that could make someone look like a hungry baby?

"I have brought you ceremonial clothes, so you can take part in the festivities," Magda said, trying to catch the man's eye again. Although she had never been with a man, she knew what she needed to do to get one. It's all in the eyes, her mother used to say. You can tell what a man really thinks by searching into his eyes.

"Thank you," said Dave's wife, "we will happily wear them." She nudged her husband.

"Yes, thank you," he mumbled.

He held out the clothes, looking confused. "They're a bit – scarce. Do you have something a bit less revealing?"

"Come on, lighten up," said his wife, "we need to consider the customs of the locals. If they have ceremonial dress then we will wear their ceremonial dress."

"Look around," she heard Dave whispering, "they are all topless. If you put that skirt on, are you going to walk around with your (she couldn't hear this word clearly, but it sounded like 'waps') out?"

"Oh, I hadn't considered that. Well if it is custom, then yes I will follow it. Our society might have come up with the idea that our naked bodies are something to be ashamed of, but I for one think that it is just flesh."

The nice man with the floppy hair – Dave, she reminded herself – went really white this time. She had never met a man who turned so many different colours. She wondered if all the men from his village changed colour as much as him.

"What about me?" said Dave. "It's bad enough that I'm surrounded by a bunch of natives with no clothes on, do you really have to get half naked too?"

"What's the difference? You don't really know me. We only met a few hours ago."

Magda was getting bored listening to their strange conversation, so walked straight up to Dave and started pulling at his shirt. "Come on, take this off," she said, trying to sound playful.

Dave folded his arms to stop her from lifting the shirt up.

"Come on Dave," said his wife, "let the girl change you."

"Why?" he insisted. "I don't have to."

"No," she replied, "but it's polite to let her."

"You'll laugh at me."

"No we won't," said Magda. "Please." She looked up at him with eyes she hoped were seductive. "I think you have a healthy body. It is large and everyone knows that means you are wealthy."

Dave's wife laughed behind her arm and Dave's arms softened. Magda pulled his top up and he conceded by lifting his arms. She pulled the cuffs over his wrists and wrapped the cloak over his shoulders and around his waist.

The old priest was sitting and watching the whole thing. He had obviously taken a fancy to Dave's wife, which was good news for Magda. She was still in the age of marrying, so was safe from Oc-ri La for now. Those already married were less fortunate, for the priest would always make use of his ethereal right to spread his heritage through any woman he wanted. Magda grabbed Dave by the hand and dragged him into the crowd, leaving his wife at the priest's mercy.

## Dave

Dave felt stupid in his new clothes, and he was annoyed that the little man was giving Louise so much attention. She wasn't rejecting it either, despite his face being covered in hairy warts and seeping boils. So he's now less attractive to Louise than the ugliest person in pre-history. Great, just bloody great.

He was grateful that she had left her top on, for now at least. He didn't think he would be able to handle seeing her breasts, and he also didn't want to see that smelly old man drooling over them. As he watched her from afar, she put the short skirt on over the top of her dress, which she had to hitch up because it was too long. Now she was showing even more leg, which seemed to excite the old man even more. Hopefully he would have a heart attack.

Both men and women had rings of bright paint circling their nipples, which tended to draw the eye towards them. They obviously weren't naked for sexual reasons, but that didn't make the situation any less uncomfortable. He supposed Louise was right, that perhaps their culture is the one that's screwed up. Didn't the Victorians used to cover up their ankles because they were seen as sex objects? Was he being as narrow-minded by feeling uncomfortable? Magda was clearly too young for him, but they used to marry younger because they didn't live as long, so she doesn't see that. It still didn't stop the situation feeling wrong.

Dave was really glad Simon wasn't there. Cultural understanding or tact weren't two of his strongest abilities. It wouldn't have mattered if the natives couldn't understand them, but for some reason they could.

He didn't know why they could speak their language, but he suspected the ability was related to their temporal shift. He wasn't a particularly religious man, but this smacked of something like divine intervention. It seemed a bit too convenient that they could communicate freely wherever they ended up.

The tribe had returned quickly to their festivities after the short interruption they had caused, and soon the entrancing drum beat returned. It was incredible that these humans enjoyed themselves in such a recognisable way millennia before the invention of nightclubs.

Dave sat down next to Magda on a reed mat, taking a moment to absorb his surroundings. They were at a building site of a temple of stones, much like Stonehenge, which he'd visited a few times before. These stones lay in a small semi-circle, with some resting on their side awaiting their turn to be placed into the ground. The circle wasn't as large as he remembered it being at Stonehenge, but was impressive nonetheless.

The people of the tribe didn't let him sit still for long; if the priest was transfixed on Louise, the children of the tribe were completely bewitched by Dave. One small girl, the very same who was now the proud owner of a drawing from the future, was approaching Dave tentatively with the encouragement of her friends. She was clearly emboldened by her recent successful interaction with these visitors and so ran forward to demand a dance. He looked at Magda, who stood up in response.

"Come on Dave, let's dance with her."

Dave was a terrible dancer. There are some certainties in life, one of which is that if you are male, white, middle-class and a little unfit, you cannot dance. The other certainty is that clumsy people should not attempt to dance in public. Dave realised these things, but was powerless in the face of these two young girls from the Stone Age. He allowed Magda to take his hand, but he glanced over towards Louise to check she wasn't being harassed by the priest. Louise looked over, caught his eye and smiled. He relaxed, and was soon allowing Magda to teach him the moves. The other children whooped with delight, and pretty soon there was a small entourage of small children running between their legs.

In return he showed Magda his robot dance. The group of children found this hilarious and were soon trying to copy him.

All the while, Dave attempted to keep one eye on Louise. He could see the priest getting closer to her now, and feverishly licking his lips as he continued to eye Louise's legs. He spotted the priest's hand as it darted towards her knee, where he made no attempt to move it once it had settled.

That was enough for Dave, so he shot a look of apology to Magda. "Sorry, I have to go and see Louise."

"She is your wife?" she questioned.

"Oh, no – goodness no!" he replied, "but we came here together, so I need to check she's OK."

Magda looked disappointed, but let him leave. He marched over to Louise. "Louise, one with long legs, would you like to dance?" is how he intended it to come out.

"You want long legs? What do you mean, Dave?" she asked him, genuinely confused.

Come on Dave, get yourself together. "I, err, I said would you like to dance?"

Louise looked at the priest, who now had an angry expression knotted across his brow. "I think it would be good to try and involve myself in their customs," she replied.

That was good enough for Dave. He grabbed her by the hand and dragged her to the centre of the stone circle. Louise was smiling – laughing even – and Dave didn't remember ever feeling so happy. His missing Nana momentarily forgotten, he took her into his arms and hugged her. She hugged back.

She hugged back!

Louise looked up at him and smiled, then returned to dancing the bouncy, repetitive routine of the tribe folk.

Suddenly inspired, he grabbed her by the hands and started to dance in a quasi-rock-and-roll style, swinging her from side to side and twisting her under his arm – much to the amusement of the watching locals. Pretty soon the natives had stopped dancing and were stood in a circle around them. Dave didn't care what they thought of his dancing, or whether he was breaking some sort of tradition; he was on a roll now and nothing could break his confidence. He twisted her round, leant her back in his arms and shook his hips. Then he grabbed her by the waist imagining he would sweep her up in the air, high up above his head.

His weak arms hadn't the strength to support her weight and so he dropped her on to the floor. Louise let out a small gasp of pain, and there was a sickening noise of snapping plastic as her small duffle bag broke her fall.

"Dave, what the hell have you done?"

*Great, just bloody great.*

## Oc-ri La

Oc was wary of these new visitors. The girl did not seem impressed by his title, which suggested she had not even heard of him. They were visitors from lands further than the reach of the Goddess's powers, and that would make it much more difficult to engage in carnal ecstasy with her, with her permission at least. Thirty summers had passed since the Goddess's visit, and much had been achieved in that time. He hoped the arrival of these new guests would not upset their progress. If they looked like upsetting his plans, well then he would have to dispose of them accordingly.

He had been watching that annoying man try to take the pretty girl's attention away from him. He would certainly have to get rid of him; the girl would have her uses, he thought with longing. He watched the man make a fool of himself as he dropped her, and took that as an indicator to begin the next stage of the festivities. There had been enough dancing, and so now he would tell his stories. Then he would discover their intentions.

"My subjects, be quiet and listen to the ethereal voice of your priest. It is now time for the stories of the Goddess."

He waited impatiently as the tribe formed a large circle around the fire, which stood in the middle of the first few temple stones that had already been set in place. Finally they were in position, and he could begin to tell the legend of his visit from the Goddess.

"Those of you gathered here today, listen in awe as your priest tells the story of his blessing by the Gods, and received his task;

his initiation that would allow his passage into the kingdom of the Gods.

"Many many summers ago I had been met by two brothers who looked exactly the same, which is an indicator they were to provide a sign or omen. They were prophets sent from another place, prophets who were sent to tell your blessed priest the Goddess's intentions. I was to meet the Lady of Wolf and Full Moon – the Goddess as she is commonly now known – and she would give me a task. Many summers later, still before most of you were born, the Goddess revealed herself to Oc. I was walking alone in the *Phaal*down Plains, awaiting the meeting that had been foretold to me. She appeared suddenly and greeted me warmly. She told me how to gain my passage into the kingdom of the Gods.

"This task was the most ambitious ever given by the Gods, the Goddess explained to me. She wanted me to build a temple in the name of all the Gods. I was asked to build the circle of stones.

"The Goddess first commanded me to perform a number of smaller tests, to prove I was worthy of the grand task I had been given. First, she demanded I travel to the village that lies in the valley below the *Phaal*down Plains, and fight the greatest warrior of their tribe. I walked for two whole days and immediately walked into their camp. Without resting first, I confronted their most feared warrior and demanded he meet with me in battle. After days of trading blows with spear and dagger, I eventually pierced his heart with my spear. I returned victorious, with his head for a trophy." A few of the younger members of the crowd who were hearing this story for the first time gasped. Everyone else cheered and rejoiced.

"Then, the Goddess came to me once more. This time I had to show I understood the enormity of the role bestowed upon me. My next test was to carry stones to the top of a hill. I had to lift all of the rocks and boulders strewn across a vast field. Your priest, without help from a single soul, had to move all of these rocks to the top of a hill. This hill was so high, even the highest hill in the Plains would seem like a small molehill in comparison. Once again, I exceeded her expectations. To save time I lifted the rocks high above my head, throwing them further than the greatest champion can throw." He lifted his hands above his head and squatted to demonstrate the action; the crowd cheered him on.

"Finally, I had to commit the bravest act of all. I had to burn the Goddess's human form on the stake, so that she could return to her true home."

The male visitor let out a yelp that sounded like a small puppy being kicked.

"As her human form was about to burn in the flames," he continued, "the Goddess disappeared in front of our very eyes. This sight confirmed to all who witnessed that I was beginning the journey of my apotheosis. Visitors from neighbouring tribes were also present to witness the miracle, and that is why we enjoy their support today."

He continued telling his story and continued to delight and inspire his subjects, demonstrating the same zeal that had so far convinced them to complete the gruelling, dangerous work involved in the construction of the temple. He embellished, invented and falsified to a degree never before seen in the history of his race. Fortunately, anyone who was young enough to remember the true version of events had previously perished in the great quarries of Wales, where the stones were still being laboriously cut.

Hours passed, and not a single person showed sign of losing concentration. He was proud of who he had become and once again thanked the Gods for being so kind to him. He finally brought his tale to an end, rushing through the parts about laying the first stones, where he couldn't make the story sound more epic than it actually was because most of the people involved were present.

He held out his hands towards the silent crowd, and took a deep breath.

"And now, to our guests," he said as he turned towards the beautiful female visitor. "Tell me who you are searching for."

## Dave

Dave's head was spinning and he felt sick. He had called this Goddess the Lady of Wolf and Full Moon. Nana Barb had been wearing her wolf jumper when she disappeared. They had just admitted to burning her alive.

The priest had said she disappeared while being set alight. Perhaps, maybe she had a temporal shift before any damage had been done. He wasn't losing hope yet.

Although the priest wasn't looking at him, Dave spoke:

"We are searching for answers about the Goddess. We are pilgrims from another part of the world."

He looked at Louise, who seemed happy to let him run with this idea. Her approval gave him confidence and so he pressed on.

"We wish to know more about the human form she adopted when she visited this place. We also have a request. We have a trophy, kind of, that we need to fix. We were wondering if we might be able to use some tools, or anything you might have around that can help us fix it."

The old priest turned to look at Dave for the first time, and seemed to consider his request.

"Then I am the man you need to speak with to fulfil both of your requests. You will both come and stay with me, and you will be extended the hospitality of the tribe."

This was a popular idea with the tribe, and Dave warmed to his hosts even further.

"I regret to say," the priest announced, "that the festivities are being brought to a close. We sacrificed a number of animals today, and the Goddess rewarded us with these inquisitive guests. I will fulfil the Goddess's wishes by giving them what they want. We will have another Goddess Cycle of prosperity because of these things." The crowd once again cheered.

Gradually, the crowd diffused and Oc led the way back to the village. While they walked, Dave took the opportunity to have a quiet word with Louise.

"How badly is it broken?" he asked.

"I don't think it's beyond repair. That was a pretty stupid move you pulled back there."

"I know. I'm sorry," was all he could think to say back.

They walked on with Dave feeling relieved. They might still be able to rescue the situation. He pushed any thoughts of his grandmother deep into the back of his mind.

The walk took around half an hour, by which time the full moon was starting to disappear over the horizon. The rest of the tribe dispersed to go and sleep in their own huts, while the priest walked them on into the centre of the settlement. His own lodging was much grander than everyone else's, being made from wood rather than the tipi-like animal hide tents that made up the majority of the tribe's accommodation.

The priest's sidekick followed them all the way, but stopped outside the main hut. Dave looked at him as he passed. Although he was a foot shorter than Dave, he was much stockier in comparison. And his spear looked sharp and painful, so he decided he wouldn't want to put his strength to the test anyway. With this man taking guard outside the hut, Dave wondered if they were being kept as prisoners.

Dave ducked under an animal hide canopy as he entered the priest's wooden hall. It stank of something dead or dying, and a poor infusion of burning incense that might have been trying to cover it up. Or perhaps the old man was working on his very own love potion to pull young women like Louise.

Inside there were low beams that Dave had to duck under to avoid banging his head, and resting atop each of these beams were rows and rows of clay pots and figurines. In the centre of the hut lay an enormous fire with a wooden spit resting across the middle. A half-cooked boar carcass was hanging off the spit, and Dave suspected this might be the source of the smell.

Louise took the initiative: "Please, your greatness, we need a tool to fix an object of ours. Do you have a knife made of the sharpest flint and your finest twine that can tie small items together?"

The old man pondered this request with a deeply furrowed brow. "Yes, I have these things you ask me for. But they are very valuable items and I would expect something in return."

Louise looked towards Dave, who responded by shrugging his shoulders. He had a pretty good idea where this was going.

"We're not sure we have anything of value to you," Louise said.

"Oh, come now," said the priest as he licked his dry, cracked lips. "You have much to offer me."

Dave's blood boiled, but he kept quiet. "We only want to borrow the knife," he said, "the twine we will need to take with us, but I wouldn't have thought twine would be that valuable."

The old man ignored his comments. "But today is a celebration, in name of the Goddess and my pretty guest. You may fix your object while I prepare you the customary feast of welcome." The priest walked towards a stone cabinet and removed a number of items, which he took over and handed to Louise. He moved towards the front doorway and called for the man outside. Once he had joined the priest inside, they walked to the corner of the hut and began talking in hushed tones.

Louise took out the remote and started getting to work. She prised the casing open, causing springs, wiring and circuitry to pop out like a jack-in-the-box.

Louise said, "Excellent, the main circuit board is intact. I just need to fix the casing and reattach the broken wires. You're a lucky man, Dave."

He stayed silent and watched her work. Her hands moved deftly around the small items. Someone with such precision and skill would never be attracted to a clumsy oaf like me, Dave thought woefully.

"Dave, there's something I didn't tell you before we left."

"What?" he asked, worried as usual.

"Well, the experiments I performed with my mice always showed the same results. If I ever sent them away for longer than eight hours at a time, they would virtually never make it home."

"Oh." He let her announcement sink in. "How long have we been away now?"

"Seven hours and forty-eight minutes."

"Great. Just bloody great. What the hell are we gonna do? Can you fix that thing in time?"

"I can try," she replied. She continued to toil before exclaiming, "Oh shit."

"What happened?" *Oh no, this is it, we're screwed.*

"I really need a file."

"What, to smooth down a circuit board or something?"

"No, I just broke a nail. The remote's fine – I told you I just need to tie the casing back together."

"Jeez Louise, don't do that to me!"

Louise laughed. "Jeez Louise? I didn't realise you were a 1960s American."

Dave turned his face away knowing it was filling with blood.

There were sounds of rattling and clinking as the priest was moving around in the back of the hut. He walked over to them, for the first time making eye contact with Dave instead of Louise.

"Now," he said, "we will complete the traditional welcome civilities."

Dave wondered what the priest had in store for them. The look in his eyes suggested he had an ulterior motive. "Just tell us what you would like us to do."

"First we need to greet those who are here, and I do that by passing you each a bowl of nectar." He passed them each a steaming bowl of thick amber liquid. "The Goddess and the Gods who sit beside you, we thank you for providing us with this sweet nectar."

Dave watched the priest put the bowl to his lips and so deemed it safe to drink. As the beverage neared his nostrils he smelt a sickly and slightly alcoholic smell. He took a tentative sip, which was surprisingly pleasing. He soon gulped down the rest with delight. Louise had put the remote down and was drinking readily too.

"And now Louise, one with long legs, you do not participate in this part. We will now complete the traditional test of a warrior," the little man said.

*Did he just say warrior?* "I think you misunderstand me, I'm not claiming to be a warrior," Dave said.

"But it's a sacred rite, and all men, whether priest, hunter or warrior, must take part."

Dave gulped. Louise shot him a stern look.

"Now you must eat of the flesh of a bear. If you can hold the raw meat in your stomach then you are truly a man and I will consider you friend. If you fail to hold it down then we shall make you a slave, as is our custom."

"What happens if I have an allergy to bear meat? I've been told by the doctor to steer well clear, in case I have an anaphylactic fit."

"Oh Dave, man up and eat the bloody meat will you," Louise said as she continued to work at fixing the remote.

The priest held it out in front of him. "You must take the test. It is the tradition."

Dave very much doubted it was traditional. He wanted to get rid of the competition. The reality of the situation hit. He improvised, pushing the bear meat back to the man as he said, "In my village it is sacrilegious to eat the meat of a bear. We see them as sacred."

"You are visiting my village, so you adhere to my rules," the annoying old man persisted.

He pushed the plate of raw meat towards Dave. The smell was rancid, and immediately he realised this was the source of the awful smell that had hit him as he entered the hall. He gagged just from the fumes. He'd never hold it down if he ate it. "Louise, how are you getting on? I think I might be happy eating this meat if we had our talisman fixed."

"It's getting there," she called back to him. "Just eat the meat and it should give me enough time to sort it out."

The priest stared at Dave. "I will ask you one more time. If you do not accept my hospitality, I will invite Uthal to give you a welcome of his own."

Dave could see Louise frantically trying to tie the plastic casing that contained the circuitry of the hand-held device that would lead them to safety.

"Uthal, please can you come in. Our visitor has proven to act uncooperatively." The heavy-set man walked back into the hut with an insatiable grin on his face.

"Yes boss. Do you want me to kill him quickly or painfully?"

"Oh, get rid of him quickly. He's already wasted enough of my time." He licked his lips, eyeing Louise longingly.

*What the hell do I do now?*

# CHAPTER 9

## Nostalgia Trip

## Evening, September 5th 1941 A.D. – Salisbury Plain, England

### Nana Barb

Barbara felt relief such as never before when she realised she was about to embark on her second trip through time. Initially she recoiled from the tingly feeling in her feet, thinking it was the heat from the fire getting closer, until she remembered that she'd felt a similar sensation only a few hours previously. Even though she currently had no lungs, she imagined her breathing calm and tried to think clearly again. She was being teleported away from the sacrificial burning; she was, hopefully, now safe. It didn't matter where she ended up, anywhere had to be better than where she had just left – although she longed for it to be forward in time, when people will be more civilised. Obviously she wanted to go back home. The way her day had been going she held little hope of that.

She tried to focus on the experience, which was moderately easier when you knew what was coming, but still so difficult since you didn't appear to be in control of your thoughts. All around her she could see what appeared to be a network of shimmering anthill-like tunnels, although seeing probably isn't the right word. Her eyes weren't working in the traditional sense. It's almost as if she felt they were there and so accepted they existed.

She found herself thinking of Robert, her husband who died ten years ago. Her memory of him had started to fade like the colour on an old photograph, but while she was travelling through time it was fully refreshed, as if she was once again experiencing the feeling of meeting him for the first time. She was at once apprehensive, excited, curious and confused. His face, touch and smell were overwhelming to what felt like her senses, and she longed to be near him and talk to him, to have an opportunity to tell him she loved him.

She was cherishing the feeling until it abruptly came to an end and she found herself standing in a rubbish skip. Before she even had time to consider the stench, an almighty siren sounded. It was a sound she hadn't heard in years. She was in the middle of an air raid.

She panicked. Not knowing where she had ended up was disorientating enough, but to someone who had lived through the war, not knowing the location of the shelter during a raid was absolutely terrifying.

She fell out of the skip and on to a pile of cardboard boxes, surveying her surroundings as she brushed off some decaying potato skins. She was behind a concrete building with doors and windows that were inexplicably familiar. As she poked her head around the corner of the building, the sense of recognition began to grow exceptionally strong. She let out a gasp of surprise: this was where she had met Robert almost seventy years earlier.

She contemplated the building in front of her, which had considerably more roof than she remembered, when the unmistakable sound of a squadron of Messerschmitts buzzed into life like a swarm of angry wasps. She instinctively ran, despite not having done so for at least ten years. She now knew exactly where the shelter was; she'd remembered every detail of a cocky young American soldier showing her around this camp upon his successful return from Operation Overlord. How could she ever forget?

She ran away from the sound of machine gun fire, towards a low building with a corrugated iron roof where a fresh-faced young man with the letters ARW emblazoned on his arm was ushering people inside.

"Quickly please, no need to panic. All non-combative personnel this way please," he shouted in a stern but excitable voice. "What are you doing here?" he asked, taken aback at the sight of the aged Barbara. "Civilians aren't meant to be on the site after sundown."

"I'm sorry, I got lost on a walk," she replied, feeling guilty for lying but deciding it sounded less crazy than *"I am from the future."*

"Well, never mind that now," said the man, eying her sceptically, "hurry along, and get yourself to safety."

Nana Barb stooped down and entered the shelter, finding herself inside a dank-smelling room with a low ceiling and a few nervous-looking inhabitants. They were mostly dressed in indistinct military attire; doubtless they were the lorry drivers, mechanics and cooks who helped to keep the base operating twenty-four hours a day.

Robert had explained to her a lifetime ago that Middle Wallop airfield was in a very important strategic position in relation to London. This daring dusk-time raid was probably not a direct attack; likely they were leftover bombs being jettisoned upon their return from an attack on the capital. However, the fact that the bombs weren't planned for them didn't make them any less deadly.

Everyone instinctively ducked. A bomb must have hit a building fairly close by, because there was an incredibly loud bang and the air in the shelter was immediately thick with concrete dust. She realised it was the roof being taken off the storage shed next to the shelter. She wondered: if she had made the twenty mile journey to this base sixty years ago, would she have stumbled across her future self cowering away from German bombs? It was mindboggling to even think about.

Then, almost as soon as it had begun, the sound of machine gun fire died out. The shrill voice of the young warden barked at them to stay where they were until the siren had stopped. The whirring sound continued for a few moments and then faded away as if losing all self-belief.

Nana Barb realised she'd been holding her breath, and as she exhaled it was as if the entire camp had been doing the same. The world outside their refuge became a hive of activity as order was restored to the camp. The shelter quickly emptied, except for the air raid warden who stayed behind, clearly wanting to talk to Nana Barb.

She would have liked to have made herself scarce as quickly as possible, what with her unusual attire and sudden appearance, but it looked as though she would have to stay and talk to the young man. She hadn't been particularly fond of the air raid wardens the first time around, after they had fined her parents for allowing a slit of light to show after the blackout boards had slipped.

This time travelling business was a tricky one, Nana Barb concluded. There were so many things to take into consideration, and even though her brain activity felt somewhat youthful, these were clearly adventures more suited to someone with many fewer years than herself. She felt herself clutching on to her mobile phone, desperately hoping they wouldn't search her under suspicion of being a spy.

"You had a lucky escape there," said the warden, "that machine gun fire was quite devastating, and thankfully not to the back of your legs."

"Yes I suppose it was quite lucky," replied Barbara, "although the way my day's been going today I'm surprised it didn't turn out worse."

The young man smiled and proffered his hand. "Clifford Ellis, but you can call me Cliff. I'm very pleased to meet you."

Barbara took his hand, returning his smile. "Barbara Wilson. What a nice young man you are, so polite – something of a rarity nowadays." Barbara had momentarily forgotten where she was; being able to talk to someone in English came as something of a relief, as if making it back to reality was once again a possibility.

"Ellis, I recognise that name," she suddenly thought out loud.

"Well it's not that uncommon in this area," Cliff replied. "Anyway, now is not the time for discussions about my family tree. I have work to do, and unfortunately I must bid you good day."

"Oh, aren't I in trouble though, for being on the base after hours? I might be a spy you know."

Cliff clearly found the idea amusing. "I wouldn't have thought the Germans were employing their grandmothers for undercover operations," he said with a chuckle. "Just make sure you keep your walks to the afternoon next time."

As the young man left the shelter, Nana Barb suddenly felt very alone. Deep down she had probably wanted to be searched, so that she might be forced to explain what was happening to someone in a position of authority. Now she had nowhere to go and she was starting to feel quite tired. She sat down on a bench and tried to decide what to do next.

It was difficult to comprehend, being so close to the home where she grew up. She had lived in the small village of Imber only twenty miles away, before it was forcibly evacuated by the Ministry of Defence to train the troops that would help to liberate France. A tantalising thought came to her: her parents would be alive. Would it be safe to visit them? Might she cause the Universe to explode if she accidently met her past self? That's what they always claimed in movies, to make the plotlines more interesting.

She mulled it over for a number of minutes, trying to think of any danger that might arise from seeing them, from a distance of course. The thought of being able to set eyes on her parents again made the idea of the Universe exploding seem insubstantial. Getting to Imber wouldn't be that difficult. Perhaps she could go and speak to one of those lorry drivers. She didn't have long until the evening light faded completely, and she wouldn't be allowed to wander around at night.

Decision made, she dashed off to see if anyone was going her way.

An hour later and she was thanking a nice young man called Frank for dropping her by the church in the village. Frank helped her down from the high step and she waved him away as he drove off to his destination. Her head felt light and a feeling of nostalgia was putting her on the verge of tears she thought had long ago dried out. Imber was a beautiful village and ever since the army had closed off the surrounding area she had been incapable of visiting her childhood home. She asked to be dropped in the village centre so she could absorb the memory, which she welcomed like a long-lost friend.

Crossing the village square and past the plaque commemorating the soldiers who died in the Great War, she walked past the Bell Inn and down American Street. The country lane was very dark; no light escaped from the blacked-out windows of the farm houses. At one stage she saw a familiar kindly face peering at her from behind the open front door of Seagram Farm. Sheila Dean; when Barbara was a youngster she seemed ancient, but she was probably a good twenty years older than her now. Sheila called out to see if she was lost, being out so late and all. Barbara replied, saying she was perfectly fine and would be turning in soon anyway.

And then, there it was. She stopped and stared, transfixed at the building she thought she would never see again, a building that had long since collapsed from years of shelling practice. Barbara had always considered buildings as nothing but bricks and mortar from which you make your home, and couldn't understand how people could grow sentimental attachments to objects or material things. Today she was prepared to contradict herself. She had always hated the expression 'having a lump in your throat' because it was a load of old nonsense really, more often than not just a spot of dry mouth. But now she couldn't swallow, overtaken by a strong emotion she hadn't even felt when Robert died, and she realised what people really meant when they said it.

One thing Barbara hadn't taken into consideration was how she could possibly see her parents when their windows were covered over with boards covered in thick black paper, to stop the light giving away their position to passing German planes. There was no chance of peeking a look through the windows so she could remain unseen, just in case.

The only course of action she could decide upon was to wait by the woodhouse out back and hope her father would come and collect some logs for the stove. If the situation arose and she was stuck for the night, she would simply sleep above the pigs in the top of the barn. It was a warm evening so she wouldn't freeze.

She brushed the woodchips off the chopping log and sat, experiencing various feelings of anticipation, dread and curiosity. After a while, her heartbeat started to slow and her breathing was close to relaxed. Most people would find it tedious waiting outside for someone who might not come, but Barbara was so lost in her own thoughts she didn't notice the time pass.

After waiting for a couple of hours with no sign of activity, she reluctantly began to contemplate a night with the pigs. She checked her watch, which displayed a time that now only belonged to her, when the back door of the house opened quite unexpectedly and a sliver of light illuminated a section of the back garden. She was overcome by a strong sense of déjà vu, which was borne from more than just familiarity with the surroundings. The memory returned to her as soon as she saw her mother walk towards the woodhouse. She remembered a night during the war when her mother claimed to have met a strange old dear in her garden, but had all but forgotten it soon after. Suddenly everything became clear and she knew what was meant to happen next.

She made herself aware of her mother – a strange name to call someone so much younger than you – by stepping into the light. "Sorry dear, I didn't mean to startle you," she said, knowing that she must have looked quite a sight hiding amongst the bushes.

"Who are you?" her mother demanded, "and what are you doing in our garden?"

"Please don't panic, I'm just a trifle lost. It's so dark and difficult to see with the blackout and I was trying to find the Seagram place." Barbara was concerned with the ease with which she found herself making up lies. She blamed her recent discovery of poker for the deftness of her deceits.

"Well it's over that way. It won't take you very long to walk there, but you really shouldn't be out this late on your own."

Nana Barb smiled as she was reminded of the caring nature her mother always displayed to strangers. "Mary," she said, for she couldn't very well call her Mummy, "I have to tell you something. It's very important that you listen, even if it sounds particularly strange."

"How do you know my name? I don't believe I've ever met you before."

"Yes, you're quite right. I'm just a nosey old busy-body that's all. I like to keep track of the goings on of young folk. Now, that young man your daughter met in Salisbury at the dance. I know you are concerned about him, but I should like to give you some parental advice about their relationship, advice that has, should I say, been passed down through my family."

"How did you...?"

"Never mind that, I've got to be going soon, so you can listen to my advice or we can spend the short time we have discussing the sources of my information." She watched her mother recoil, despite not speaking out. She knew her mother had an old-fashioned respect for the elderly that was so sadly lacking in her own present.

"Please, go on."

"I know she is young, but your Barbara has a very sensible head on her shoulders. It's quite possible that her support helps that young man get through the war alive, and the last thing she needs is to become estranged from a mother who does not understand what she is going through." Nana Barb had watery eyes and had to wipe them with her handkerchief.

Her mother looked lost for words. They both were clearly experiencing something supernatural, and she could see her mother had felt it too. "Thank you," was all she could say. Her father's voice called from inside the house, querying his wife's absence. "I've got to go now," she said, "I've left the light on and I wouldn't want to be fined by the wardens." With that she turned around and walked back into the house.

Nana Barb felt like she was walking a tightrope as her long dead father's head peered into the garden to see the cause of his wife's distraction. "Evening," was all she could manage to utter, anxious of betraying her true identity somehow by saying any more. She felt her legs buckling and she feared she wouldn't be able to carry herself any further. As she stumbled into the darkness, the now familiar tingling returned and she knew that she would soon be leaving. She willed her legs to carry her out of sight, and once she disappeared into the shadows she disappeared into time.

# CHAPTER 10

## Righting Wrongs

## The Hyper-real Universe, Dimension Alpha $2^{-32}$

There may be a few of you who are beginning to question the implications of time travel. I hope you are. The answer isn't simple, because, as with most sciences, there is always a degree of complexity even if the surface appears calm and ordered. Some of your questions will be answered as the story progresses, but I'll give you a brief idea to help you understand some of the things that have been going on.

The means by which our protagonists are travelling through time is extremely difficult to elucidate, even to an open-minded proponent of the sciences, but I shall still attempt to explain the basics. Our minds are typically accepted as vessels of consciousness, but in truth they are the exact opposite. The human brain acts as a focusing device that channels thoughts from the web of consciousness. The matter that makes up the physical world is, in a sense, an illusion.

If you prefer to view it this way, you think yourself into existence.

The only way to time travel is to build a device that encourages your consciousness to disengage from its corporeal restrictions. This consciousness will then travel through time and space until it settles upon another consciousness, however weak it might be, that it can trade places with, thus thrusting the unexpected proponent of this exchange back to the past or forward into the future. By way of comparison, the only non-sentient matter that is capable of performing this feat does so when completely *unobserved*: car keys and remote controls.

Suffice it to say that our very existence as the Fates, as you would have us called, means that there is some degree of control over the time travelling that has happened so far in this story. But we don't have complete control over the Universe – far from it in fact. The only thing we do control is consciousness, which if you like to view it as such is one large organism that simply uses the Universe as its home. Humans should know this more than anybody, that no matter how much you have control over your thoughts and actions, you never have control over your environment. These things exist separately. So whilst we are setting in motion the events that take place in this story, there is always an element of guesswork.

The importance of this is two-fold: the idea of fate actually existing is probably a surprising idea, and difficult to comprehend as it is. Then the realisation that this 'Fate' doesn't even really know what's going to happen is doubly hard to accept. It might even make you scared to be alive.

Well it shouldn't. You're lucky to even be given the chance to live and breathe, and all life is a precious thing. So now that you know you're not in control, and neither is the entity that controls you, all that's left is to hang on and enjoy the ride, like riding a rollercoaster as it is being built backwards.

## B.C.E. 3090 - Salisbury Plain, England

### Dave

Dave faced the sharp end of a spear, and in a desperate last attempt, tried to reason with their captors. The old priest was pulling Louise by her arms and was now sniffing her hair.

"Please, I will eat the meat. Pass it back to me now."

"It is too late for that. You had your chance, but you instead decided to mock me and my beliefs."

"What can I do to change your mind?" Louise put in.

"Well," the old man replied, "there is much I can think of. We can wait until your friend is dead, then we can discuss these things. Uthal, kill him."

"Wait!" Dave shouted. "We are friends of the Goddess. You will forever be condemned if you kill us, and you will lose your right of passage to the kingdom of the Gods."

Uthal paused, unsure whether to believe Dave's desperate claims. "How can you prove this?" he asked.

The old man cut in, "I'm the priest, so I ask the questions."

"Sorry, oh revered one."

"How can you prove this?" he asked, looking at Dave.

"I can tell you she wore a blue jumper, with a picture of a wolf and a full moon."

"Everyone knows the legend. Your futile attempts will not sway my decision."

The spear was pressed close to his throat.

"OK, so she goes by another name: Barbara; her favourite TV programme is *Bargain Hunt* and she is always trying to get me to go on the show with her; her favourite drink is tea, and before the doctor told her she had high blood pressure she used to have one sugar after dinner as a desert tea, and no sugars before dinner because then it was savoury."

"What did you just say?" asked the priest.

"I said she had no sugars before..."

"You said the name of the magic tincture. This *Tee*, I have been attempting to make it for years. You know its recipe?"

Dave was taken aback. "Yes, and I know exactly how to make it," he replied, sensing a shift in power. "But I'll only tell you if you let me know what happened to the Goddess when you set her alight. Did she burn at all?"

"Do not be so foolish. Of course she didn't burn, she is a God. Like any respectable God, when we initiated the fire, the opening of the passageway into the otherlife, she transformed into a small animal. We then set light to the small animal, just to make sure."

"So you saw her disappear, without a burn on her?"

"Yes, she broke into thousands of tiny little pieces without a mark on her. That's more than can be said for the small animal, which was broken down slowly by the fire, as is normally the case."

Dave felt bad for the poor animal but was about ten stone lighter with that news. Wherever she had gone, she was safe. She had temporally shifted away from the fire.

With the distraction of the conversation, the priest must have let slip his grip on Louise. Suddenly Dave heard a whelp of pain as she aimed a well-directed kick between the old man's thighs. He saw Louise dive for the remote as Uthal stabbed his spear, aiming directly at Dave's throat. He started to scream and he felt the sharp edge of the spear touch his Adam's apple. All of a sudden, time slowed. Dave saw his body start to break apart, seemingly floating into the air around the plunging spear. Louise had fixed the remote. The joy of seeing Uthal's confused expression gave way to the now familiar feeling of elated indifference.

After the usual out-of-body experience had passed, Dave materialised in some bushes on the side of the main road. He could see Louise halfway up a tree on the corner of Freecock Gardens. They began their argument over distance as they extricated themselves from their awkward locations.

"You have to be careful," Louise whined, "you could have a) got us killed, or b) changed history and singlehandedly brought about the destruction of the Universe."

"Impossible," Dave shouted back. He didn't elaborate because he knew that would annoy her more.

"What do you mean, 'Impossible'? Where is your scientific proof to back that up? You can't just form an opinion and decide that it's fact!" Louise dropped down from the tree.

"Isn't that how you scientists go about creating your theories?" They started walking back to the house, keeping a few metres apart. "And I'm not deciding it is fact. It's just my opinion, which happens to be right by the way." Again he refrained from explaining why he was so sure of himself. Their shouting had disturbed the neighbours' dogs, who were now barking aggressively in their direction.

Louise lowered her voice: "Actually the accepted approach is to come up with a theory and spend the rest of our lives attempting to disprove it before someone else does."

"And what part of this self-proclaimed moral code covers the loss of elderly relatives?" Dave pointed towards Nana Barb's house. "The lights are off. If she's back in our time then she's still not found her way home."

"Actually Dave, I'm afraid it's highly unlikely she'll be back in the present. Without the machine acting as a focusing device on a certain part of her brain, she could be anywhere in time."

"Assuming she's still alive."

"She will be alive, Dave. You've got to keep faith. We'll just have to search harder. And we'll have to agree to disagree on the nature of time travel."

"It's not as simple as agreeing to disagree! If you didn't believe in your stupid paradox idea I could simply teleport back to stop you turning on the machine."

"You're willing to risk the stability of the Universe on a whim?"

"And you're willing to sacrifice my grandmother?"

"We are not having this argument. Yes your grandmother is important, but the Universe more so. We will carry on trying to find her by sending a rescue party and that decision is final. Next time can you please be a bit more tolerant of the cultural differences of our ancestors and not lead us headfirst into an early grave?"

Louise unlocked her side door and walked into the house. Dave followed, trying to look indignant.

"It was raw mouldy bear meat! What did you expect me to do? Eat up and beg for seconds? It could have killed me. We've evolved out our ability to eat festering, uncooked food a long time ago, since it probably kills about half the people who eat it."

"It was their custom. They clearly don't use it for sustenance, but for ritualistic purposes. Our sudden appearance obviously led to them deciding we were Demigods, an interesting prospect for social anthropologists and further proof of our dualistic tendencies."

While Louise was blabbering on, Dave realised they were alone in the room. He interrupted: "What time did you teleport us to?" He looked out of the window.

"Half an hour after we left, about half past four."

"I'm going to kill Simon. The car's not in Nana Barb's driveway. He's gone somewhere."

"He left a note," Louise said, picking up some of her post that had been scribbled on.

Dave looked over her shoulder at the envelope:

> *Got hungry so gone for crisps.*
> *Loiuse your food supply's are rubbish.*
> *Dont worry about fuses. Ill be back in a mo so will cheque there ok.*
>
> *Si*

"That explains it then," said Louise.

"I don't believe that man, he's always doing things like this. Next time we'll have to find someone else to keep an eye on the equipment. We can't trust him to do it."

"So you want to go again, after we came close to dying two or three times?"

He thought about this. It was an exhilarating experience but he had no intention of dying so young. He weighed up the value of wasting his so far short life in an effort to save a much older one. If time travelling was this dangerous what hope did his Nan have anyway? And where would they even begin to start looking for her? Their only lead had burned (forgive the pun) and so they needed to stab wildly in the dark. He had half hoped she would be standing outside the door of her house, that the machine returned her to her own time after a certain amount of, well, time. However, the front door of Nana Barb's house remained firmly shut, without so much of a suggestion she had made it back home safely already.

The familiar feeling of guilt returned, and the thought of trying to explain to his much more narrow-minded aunt that Nana Barb was lost in time. Death by tribal spear sounded a lot quicker and less painful. And if he was being totally honest, once he'd accepted Louise wasn't off her extremely gorgeous rocker, he started to consider the enterprising opportunities the ability to time travel might offer. All the budding business ideas and high-flying city jobs he had dreamed about during his unemployment bore little relevance if he could travel to the future and have a sneaky peek at the lottery numbers.

"Yes," he eventually replied, "I'm absolutely ecstatic about going again, if it means I can rescue my Nan."

"Well that's very brave of you," Louise said. "I, however, value my life too much. You'll have to go on your own next time, or with Simon."

She was abandoning him. "What? How dare you? You lost her in the first place. You're not ducking out of this that easily."

"I'm not ducking out of anything. I have simply realised I should never have gone with you in the first place. It isn't safe to leave the machine in the hands of someone ill trained to use or fix it. I thought I might be more useful on the other side, but I didn't foresee this ability you seem to gain from a temporal shift – this ability to speak the local language of your destination. It changes the rules in our favour. Now we just need to research the culture of our intended destination next time, so you fit in better. We have all the time in the world this side, so there's no reason to rush."

"But Louise, you can't leave me with Simon. Hasn't he already demonstrated how useless he is?"

"You said it yourself, we can't rely on Simon to make sure the equipment stays safe. This way I can guard the machine from this end and I'll teach you how to use the remote that will get you home safely."

Dave couldn't believe she would quit on him after one tiny little scrape with death. He was furious. "What are you, a chicken?" was all he could think to say.

"Dave, I'm not Marty McFly. You won't persuade me with topical movie quotes."

Dave blushed then forgot how to speak, as he often did when he suddenly remembered he was talking to a girl he liked. He had hoped he was going to go on some amazing adventures with Louise, where he might have the chance to impress her with his bravery – assuming he was actually capable of being brave. Until the wolf pup episode, he hadn't ever been in a situation that required him to be particularly courageous (except for the time he had turned down the offer of a cigarette as a teenager, and all the risk of exclusion from the popular group that came with it). Failing that, at least he would have spent a bit of time with her and she'd be able to get to know him on a more personal level. He felt that the real Dave was a much more pleasant bloke than the bashful and awkward man she was currently getting to know.

A car pulling up in the drive broke the silence, and Dave used the opportunity to vent his disappointment at Simon. "We'll talk about this later," he mumbled, then went outside.

## Simon

Simon pulled back into the driveway, angry and annoyed. He could see shadows moving in the window, which meant they were back already. He was late, and Dave was going to shout at him. It wasn't his fault some old bloke had slammed on the brakes pulling out of the petrol station forecourt. The bloody idiot was wearing glasses about twenty inches thick, and was clearly due a new subscription. Sue was going to kill him, literally kill him. His only hope was the time machine. He had to go back and stop the accident from happening.

He saw the front door open and Dave came storming out. Simon momentarily forgot his concerns and burst out laughing.

"What the hell are you wearing, mate? You look ridiculous!"

Dave stopped in his tracks and looked down at the new clothes given to him by the prehistoric teenager. That seemed to knock the wind out of his sails, so he carried on down that route.

"I can see your hairy chest – better not turn around so I can see your hairy back too!"

Making Dave embarrassed, actually quite an easy task, was a sure-fire way of getting him off your case.

"Yeah, well, you're fat," was all his mate could offer in return. A bit pathetic really; he expected better.

"Mate, that was a low blow." This could actually work, Simon thought, trying to look annoyed. He could feel the tide turning in his favour.

"Forget it, I didn't mean it. Hmph." Dave walked off, trying to pull the bearskin over his back hair.

Simon waited a bit before following him back into the house, feeling triumphant and relieved at having got away with it so lightly. Back inside the house he saw Louise, who was grinning as if enjoying a private joke. "Boyfriend trouble?" she asked.

"Nothing I couldn't handle."

"Simon, as funny as you might find Dave's new clothes, you shouldn't have left us. It was a pretty irresponsible stunt to pull. If you were hungry I had some crisps in my bedroom, you only needed to ask."

"Well I didn't realise I was hungry until you'd gone. I was too excited to see you disappear. How'd it go anyway?"

Louise frowned. "Not great. We nearly died."

"What happened?"

"I wouldn't worry about it. We're here now aren't we?"

"Did you find Dave's Nan?"

"We found out where she had been, but we're no closer to tracking her down. It seemed as though she spontaneously shifted a second time, which means she could be anywhere. We need to decide whether we try to intervene at a known location, or try to work out a way of tracing her movements through time. The good news is that you've got your wish, because you get to go with Dave the next time."

"Oh, how come?" He tried not to show his relief.

"I think it's safer for me to be here, that's all."

Simon contemplated. This was his perfect chance; now all he needed was to find out how to operate the machine, then he would change the destination to ten minutes before the accident. Once he was back in the future, or past, or whenever it was he would be, he'd find that stupid blind man and stop him from slamming his brakes on for absolutely no reason.

## The same time, a couple of hundred metres away

## Mrs Ellis

Mrs Ellis was laid flat on the floor. The two men from her dream were standing over her, one of them operating a device that looked like a gadget from Star Trek. She had lied to them and they somehow knew. They shot her with some kind of beam and now she was frozen to the ground.

She had succeeded in drawing them away from the street to a small copse of trees out of sight, and they had followed her without aggression while she talked to them. That part was easy. Lying to them apparently wasn't.

One of the men spoke: "You have proven you wish to act uncooperatively and so we must use force. As you now know, we can tell when you are lying to us. We have the ability to make your pain receptors believe your body is being skinned alive and if you fail to respond truthfully again we will use this power. Now, answer without lying, do you know of anyone on this street who unexpectedly disappeared today?"

Mrs Ellis was prepared to take the pain, but how could she protect someone off the back of a vision in a dream? She hadn't seen why it was so important to keep her from these men, she just had a feeling that it was the right thing to do.

## A few minutes later, Louise's house

## Dave

Dave had calmed down enough to be in the same room as Simon. Louise was teaching them how to use the hand-held device that controlled both distance and time, but he was struggling to take in what she was saying. He was furious with Simon for putting their lives in danger, and now he had made him look even more foolish in front of Louise. He didn't even know why he liked her so much. Stacey Dawson had stayed the night at his, even if he couldn't remember most of it. He was going to go on a date with Stacey and he was going to be popular. He was better than this, letting himself get upset over someone he had absolutely nothing in common with.

Louise's instructions were quite complicated and Dave couldn't follow. Simon, whose concentration was normally as focused as a two-year-old at a birthday party, seemed to be engrossed in what she was saying. Perhaps he was being unkind to his best friend; perhaps he should trust him a bit more.

At this point he would normally become suspicious of Simon's dedication, but that train of thought quickly dispersed. Louise had such a beautiful voice, it was almost hypnotic. She had taken off her hemp dress and was now wearing a bright pink lab coat, which Dave found something of a turn-on. Most of the girls in his village were just that – girls. Here, talking to him as an equal, was a real life, professional woman. Maybe he was falling in love.

"Did you get that, Dave?" asked the voice of an angel.

"Yes, loud and clear," Dave lied. He felt his face get hot with blood, but the other two seemed not to notice. Simon was pressing buttons and Dave suddenly feared for his life.

"So I can input whatever I like and nothing will happen until I press the action button then enter the safety code?" Simon enquired.

*Safety code?* What was that? Had she told them what it was?

"Yes Simon. It's there to stop you pressing all the buttons when you sit down on it or something." They both laughed. Dave forced himself to laugh too, even though he didn't see why it was funny.

"So, that's all you need to know to control your temporal shift," said Louise.

"Just an idea," said Simon. "Why don't we give it a little test run by shifting somewhere local? It can't do no harm going back about an hour or so, just to make sure we know what we're doin'."

"I like your thinking," replied Louise, "but there are inherent dangers with time travelling to a familiar location, theoretically speaking of course. You could meet your past self and change the course of that history."

"But surely we would have met ourselves already if we'd bumped into each other when I sent us back in time."

"Well that depends on which theory of time travel you believe. Besides, maybe I succeeded in stopping you from going back because my argument was so strong."

Was Dave hearing this right? Was his imbecilic friend having a debate about time travel with a Quantum Physicist? And amazingly, he agreed with Simon over Louise. He also agreed with his friend that a test run was a safer option than their last approach. At least Simon would have the chance to prove if he'd been listening.

Simon carried on confidently: "It depends where we end up and how long we go back for. If we make it so we come back to this house at the exact moment I left to get the crisps then we couldn't possibly meet our past selves."

"That's true, but you would have to be precise with your calculations into the machine. You couldn't accidently stay longer than you intended and run the risk of meeting your past self. So whilst this test run is safe in some respects, because we'll know exactly where you're going to end up, it also has to be incredibly precise in timing and positioning, assuming I am correct and we have the ability to influence our past of course." She glanced at Dave when she said this, which annoyed him even more.

"Fine, it sounds like we've got it all worked out then," said Dave.

"How excitin' is this?" said Simon. "Does it hurt, going back in time?"

"Not at all," replied Dave, "it actually feels quite nice." The only thing that's going to be hurt from the test run, Dave wrongly assumed, would be his pride.

Simon really was full of surprises. With some trepidation Dave allowed him to operate the hand-held remote for the time machine. After all, how dangerous could time travelling back an hour or so possibly be?

## Simon

Simon adjusted the settings on the hand-held device, exactly as Louise had showed him. He couldn't believe his luck. Not only did Louise buy into his idea, but his normally suspicious friend was so busy ogling that he hadn't paid a blind bit of notice to her instructions. It was all he could do to stop himself pointing this out.

Louise looked at them reassuringly; Dave looked nervous. Simon pressed the button.

Dave was right, it felt quite nice. It started at the tips of his fingers, a tingly warm sensation, then moved all the way up to the top of his head. The tingly feeling penetrated his brain and he could see his body separating into tiny little pieces. Eventually the world around him also appeared to break apart until all that was left was light. The colours looked like a mixture of tie-dye and Windows Media Player visuals. He was as close to being enlightened as he ever would be.

He found himself thinking about the garden next door to Louise's house, and the dogs they could always hear barking from Nana Barb's back garden. He found himself thinking about their kennel. The world was coming together like a pixelated television channel finding a better signal and he found himself looking at Dave's body forming next to his, inside the dog kennel.

Once they were fully formed, Dave looked over at him nervously. "Do you think they're still in here?" he whispered. Simon didn't wait to find out. He unlocked the door of the kennel and started running. Dave shouted after him as he ran through the stranger's side gate, cutting through the trees that would take him to the path around the back of the petrol station forecourt. He had set the device to transport them to just before five o'clock, about five minutes after Dave and Louise made their first shift. He had ten minutes to get to the petrol station, which was much closer on foot than it was by car. All the more annoying that he had taken the bloody thing in the first place.

He could hear Dave's footsteps behind him which spurred him on to run faster. He hadn't exercised in years and so the running soon became a slow jog. About one hundred metres from the petrol station Dave caught him. "What the hell are you doing?" he demanded.

"You," breath, "wouldn't," breath, "understand," cough, followed by a succession of quick breaths.

"Try me," offered Dave.

"No, I know," breath, "what you're like. You'll," breath, "side with her and stop me."

"Now you definitely need to try me. I don't tend to agree with her that much, even if she is the so-called expert. What did you really bring us back for? What mess did you manage to get yourself into in that brief moment I left you unattended?"

"Nothin' I can't fix. But I've got to be quick." Deep breath. "Or else I'll miss my window of chance."

"Are you sure you know what you are doing? I feel as if telling me might help."

"I'm running out of time. Sorry Dave, but I'll tell you when I get back."

"OK Simon, but you won't change anything."

"We'll see."

With that he ran off towards the petrol station. As he rounded the corner he saw the old man's Fiesta pulling out of the forecourt. He tried to pick up his speed and the old man turned to look at him. Not concentrating on what his legs were doing, Simon tripped over his own foot and came crashing down on to the tarmac like a stampeding elephant that lost its footing. He heard the old man slam his brakes on and the screech of metal. He looked up in time to see the number plate that said GR8 SCOT smash into the rear bumper of the Fiesta. The windscreen remained just out of sight.

Dave came running round the corner. "Simon? Are you all right?" He was winded so couldn't answer. "Simon, quick, we need to get out of the way. Your past self is in that car and I'm in no mood to test Louise's theories against mine. We need to leave. Now!"

"I can't, I think I might be dying!"

"No you're not, get up."

"Seriously," Simon managed to say through the sobs, "I hit my head. Really hard."

"Simon, I'm not going to ask you again. Press the button!"

"Owww." He managed to get the remote out with one hand – the other was holding the side of his grazed head – just as he heard the Cadillac door open. He tapped in their return destination and once again he felt tingly. They were returning to their present.

# CHAPTER 11

## A Change of Luck

## The Hyper-real Universe, Dimension Alpha $2^{-32}$

And so now the mantle of storyteller will be adopted by our final Web-spinner, Ogg. The androgynous Ogg has different characteristics than either me or the fearful Craag, characteristics that the observant reader might well glean as the next few paragraphs progress. This break isn't due to a natural reason such as a toilet break; instead it is an intentional switch to a more suitable narrator. The reason behind this will be made apparent later on in our tale.

I am not a cruel Web-spinner, but then I'm not completely kind either. The Universe needs balance and so whilst Ogg and Craag are polar opposites, I sit somewhere in the middle. We have a little joke here in dimension Alpha $2^{-32}$. When someone claims to be having a bad day we interrupt with, "That's what Craag said!" The joke doesn't really translate into any language, but the people of Germany still find it hilarious.

## 17:48hrs, June 15th 2013 C.E. - Nether Wallop, England

### Mrs Ellis

The two men, who called themselves the Time Police, once again asked Mrs Ellis if she had heard of someone suddenly disappearing from the Freecock Gardens area. She genuinely didn't know anyone who had built a time machine, so had answered their first questions truthfully. However, she did know that Nana Barb had gone missing, so that was creating a bit of friction between her and her newfound friends. One of them had made his gadget produce a beam of light that caused her so much pain she felt the skin of her hand peeling away, despite her eyes telling her the hand was still intact. They asked her again. She tried diversionary tactics this time by saying yes, she did know of someone who had gone missing. As she hoped, the Time Police registered her response as the truth. "Do you know the name of the person who is presumed missing?" asked one of the suited men.

"Yes," she replied, buying herself a few more seconds. Now the men were talking about time travel she wasn't quite sure why she was stalling for time. If they could transport themselves to whenever they wished, what difference would a few extra minutes make?

"What is the name of the person who has gone missing?" they persisted.

She had decided to take a gamble. "Jonathon Scabbers," she replied.

"Her answer is correct," said one of the men.

"His disappearance is not directly related," replied the other.

What? Are they stupid or something? Of course they know it's not directly related – hadn't they made him disappear? That was her gamble, that the bright light she'd seen from his window signalled the end of Mr Scabbers' life.

*And wasn't she next?*

But why did their logic seem so unnatural, so un-human?

"Do you know of a second person who has gone missing?" asked suit number 1.

She couldn't bear the agony again. She had almost cracked last time. She wrestled with her logic that told her she didn't want to feel pain protecting someone she barely knew against a bizarre voice in the back of her head that told her to hang on just a minute or two longer. "No," she lied.

"That answer is incorrect," stated suit number 2. She tensed in anticipation; this time it came like a tsunami of torture, starting in the tips of her toes and sweeping up the length of her body. It increased in intensity until it felt like her tissue, sinews and bones were simultaneously being torn apart, nerve ending by excruciating nerve ending.

She was going to crack. She would rather die than this. Dying she could do, but this level of pain she couldn't bear any more.

Then, as quickly as it had come, the earth made a small tremble and straight away she felt normal again. The pain was almost immediately forgotten. Mrs Ellis opened her eyes to a couple of dogs barking aggressively. She looked up to see the arm of the suited man being attacked by an angry-looking Alsatian. The device was knocked into a bush and she was able to move once again. The second man went to get his own gadget out, but a second, equally vicious-looking dog jumped up towards his face, biting hard. It knocked him to the ground and began tearing at the man's skin. Despite having his flesh torn away, the man didn't bleed. The first man was frantically looking for his device while the dog tore at the backs of his legs. The other man had managed to pull out his own gadget, pressed a button and they both disappeared.

"Good doggies," Mrs Ellis called. The two Alsatians turned to her, tails wagging with apparent delight. "Aren't you good boys!" They both went over to her and rolled on their backs. Mrs Ellis happily responded by rubbing their bellies. When they thanked her, she didn't find it the slightest bit strange that she could understand them.

She was, however, a little taken aback when the dog she was stroking suddenly turned into her son. "Oh, hello love," she said. "How did you get here?"

"Mum! What the hell are you doin'? Gerroff me."

"Sorry love, but I can't help it if the dog I'm stroking turns into my son."

"Mum, you don't half say some crazy things sometimes."

"This is coming from the boy who just materialised in my lap."

"Well... All right, you've got me there."

"What kind of dog was it?" Dave asked her.

"Well Dave, it was an Alsatian," she replied.

"We materialised in the neighbour's kennel, and he keeps Alsatians. That can't be a coincidence."

"There's not much in this life that is coincidence, dear. You'll learn that as you get older. Now, we've got those suits off our backs for a bit, so let's go find this young scientist friend of yours, Dave."

"What 'suits'? And how did...?"

"There's a lot you don't know about me, Dave, or at least refused to listen to. I have told you many times before, I'm psychic."

"Before today I would have found that strange, but that really doesn't surprise me anymore."

Mrs Ellis followed her son and his best friend back to the house of that young scientist. She felt relieved, but then everything had gone to plan. Whose plan it was she couldn't say, but she certainly felt reassured at the turn of events, so it must have been done in the name of good.

They arrived at the house and the boys let themselves in. The first words she heard when she walked through the door were spoken in a heavy American accent.

"Well howdy son, so we meet again. I was beginning to worry about you."

"Oh bollocks," she heard her son reply.

## 1862 A.B. – London Township of Sarum and Winchestershire, Western Earth

### Nana Barb

Barbara forced herself to open her eyes, which were wet with the tears of grief. She hadn't expected she would ever cry in her life again – oh, she would well up from time to time if she was watching a particularly heart-warming moment on *Deal or no Deal*, but crying until no tears remained? What funny things the past can do to you.

Fortunately the next jump through time had sent her somewhere away from bombings or homicidal tribes, to civilised society from the look of things. It seemed safe enough that she could remain where she was for a short time while she 'got her head together', as her grandson would say. She had found herself inside a building that could only be described as an enormous warehouse, larger than any building she had ever seen before. It made the new Heathrow Airport terminal look like a doll's house.

She couldn't begin to imagine what purpose the warehouse might serve, because she was hidden behind some large machinery. It was comfortable enough; there were large pallets containing sacks that were filled with a cotton wool-like material, which she had used to fashion herself a crude bed.

She stayed there reminiscing for hours, although she didn't know for certain how long since she had stopped herself from looking at her watch. Doing so would only lead you into a false sense of normality.

Eventually she must have fallen asleep, for the next thing she remembered she was awakening from a restless sleep that involved dreams of a recurring explosion. She had been shaken from her slumber by the sound of machines, the ones which had previously been lying indiscriminately on the floor around her, beginning to buzz and whirr into life. This technology wasn't the kind from her time, but larger, sleeker and more advanced-looking. Rather than propelling things along on a conveyer belt or using a robotic arm to attach a car door or some such, these machines were *walking* around the place. Some were like giant spiders, with great metallic legs that chinked on the metallic floor; some were pulling themselves along with tiny feet, like long centipedes; others were strolling along like massive versions of the toy robots she used to buy her son. In the middle of the warehouse, previously hidden behind a large machine that had since wandered off, was an almighty structure. It was huge – bigger than Salisbury Cathedral, and it was clearly a spaceship.

The noise in the warehouse was now becoming immensely loud,

and Nana Barb was amazed to see some of these contraptions fly gracefully into the air, like seagulls catching thermals. They all looked highly advanced, all seemingly operating autonomously. Each machine was clearly working towards a common goal, which looked to revolve around the principal aim of latching on to the side of the unfinished spaceship. One of the floor-based machines, a forklift with no driver, rolled towards her, the two forks sticking at angles reminiscent of angry eyebrows. Like a road-raged driver, it beeped at her to get out of the way, so she jumped aside and watched it pass her to collect one of the pallets of material.

She desperately looked around for a person, hoping that she wasn't in some sort of nightmarish future where only machines remained. She had watched part of the second *Matrix* movie that depicted such a world, and whilst she hadn't understood either the story or what anyone saw in that Keanu fellow, she had understood enough to know she wouldn't want to ever visit the place.

Fortunately, she soon spotted a bright yellow hard hat, underneath which was a perfectly normal-looking human being. He was standing on a raised platform as if overseeing all the machines in operation. She was relieved to see another person, but at the same time her limited experience had taught her to be wary. She was in the future, of that she had no doubt, and it was quite likely that customs had changed from her time. And who's to say she can even speak their language? Her first time travelling experience was fine until she'd lost her ability to communicate. She'd understood at first, but as time progressed she had lost the skill of speaking their language, as if the magic fairy dust was wearing off; Cinderella turned back into a pumpkin. And she'd slept a number of hours now, so if they had a different language would she have already lost the ability to speak it?

Erring on the side of caution, she decided to look for an exit rather than approach the man. The walls of the warehouse were made of a smooth gleaming metal reminiscent of the stainless steel casing of her kettle, which stretched as far as the eye could see. As much as she could make out, the metal stretched from wall to wall and from ceiling to floor, entombing the contents of the warehouse completely. There must be a way in, otherwise how would that workman come and go?

She started to walk towards the wall closest to her and as soon as she walked on the path the floor illuminated to her footstep. She hadn't wanted to draw attention to herself, but the lights flashed up like a tacky Spanish holiday resort. The man in the hard hat spotted her immediately. From an unseen speaker a voice issued instructions in a language close to English, but not quite.

*"Cease, tufar agoing nomass."* Thankfully her mind translated for her: "Stop, don't go any further." Part of the wall near her became a television screen, which displayed the man's face.

"Oh dear, what mess am I in now?" Nana Barb muttered to herself. Amazingly, she got a reply. Even more amazingly it was in English.

"You must be from Mars," said the man on the screen. He spoke very slowly and clearly, almost as if he was talking to a deaf person who might be lip-reading. "You are lost. You have taken a wrong turn from the spaceport. Do not worry, it happens from time to time."

Nana Barb was quite taken aback. Why did this man think she was from Mars? It seemed like she wasn't in trouble, which was something to be profoundly grateful for. "Where do I go now then?" she asked the man on the screen. She said it in English, even though she knew she could have said it in his language if she had wished.

"Follow the lights. They will take you back to the exit," the screen replied. "Go through the main doors at the back of the concourse and you will easily find immigration." All of a sudden the floor under her feet illuminated with arrows. Amazed with what she was seeing, her eyes followed the lights until they came to rest on one side of the warehouse. A small rectangular section of the warehouse wall changed colour and then receded to leave the gap of a doorway.

Barbara took this as a cue, and so walked down the lit-up path and through the newly formed exit.

She was greeted by another world.

She looked around in wonder, feeling more like she had stumbled into the Eden Project than she had into an airport, or spaceport, as she guessed it must be. Instead of the metal she had left behind in the warehouse, the main building was made entirely of natural materials. As green as you can get, she thought. Large redwoods replaced what she supposed would have been concrete supports, holding up the structure in the centre. Extremely tall hedges divided the rooms instead of walls, and underneath her feet was grass – not just that plastic grass they put on football pitches nowadays, but perfectly trimmed lawns that would humble the groundsmen and groundswomen of the Lawn Tennis Association.

The people didn't look all that different really. Oh, the clothes looked far more bizarre than any science-fiction writer had been able to predict, and the men seemed to like wearing dresses. But they looked like they were made from the same flesh and bones as her. They were very multicultural, not something she was that used to seeing around her home town, but at least they were all human. She wasn't sure she could have handled a future crowded with alien species.

The only thing that seemed particularly odd about these people was their age. There were hundreds walking along the concourse, and yet she couldn't see a single person over thirty. They seemed to notice her too, and a few were staring at her as if they had never seen anything quite like it. If there wasn't such a dramatic difference between her age and theirs, Barbara would have put it down to her strange clothes, which admittedly would have looked positively archaic.

She tried acting nonchalant and looked around for anything that might give her guidance. She quickly spotted a sign written in a number of languages she didn't recognise. Apparently you could automatically speak any language, but not read it. That didn't matter though, because amazingly further down the board the word 'immigration' was written in English. She walked on in that direction, starting to worry that she had neither luggage nor a passport.

She decided to keep herself as near to other people as she could, hoping that the throng would hide her somehow. She walked close behind a young man in a green miniskirt with a haircut that looked like a Christmas tree, and who was being devotedly followed by his luggage – a small suitcase-shaped machine that had a tail and floppy ears. When she got too close to it the suitcase yapped at her.

After a short distance, the concourse tapered and the crowd were channelled into a narrow passageway. There was a large mirror on her left from which a buzzing sound was emanating. It seemed odd that a mirror should buzz, but then that was perhaps one of the least strange things to happen to her so far today. Then, from out of nowhere, there was a beeping noise, flashing red lights in the grass under her feet and a woman's voice shouting, "STOP."

She paused; she had a habit of feeling guilty when an alarm was raised, even if she was going *into* a shop when the shoplifting warning sounded. But for the first time in her life, she was the culprit and she had actually set it off.

"I'm sorry madam, but Puritans need to go to the queue signposted Martians, which you can find over there," a short-of-breath thirty-year-old woman poked her head around the side of the mirror and pointed to a sign on the other side of the concourse. "This machine is a bio-chip scanner only, so it cannot read your DNA," she said, as if Nana Barb would know perfectly well what she meant. She could have been talking gobbledygook as far as she was concerned, but she did notice that the woman automatically spoke to her in English. The words were a bit strangely pronounced, as if she was trying hard not to miss any vowels.

She thanked the uniformed lady and proceeded across the

concourse, where she bumped into a young woman who was clutching a small cactus. "Oh excuse me," said Nana Barb.

The young girl wore an expression of surprise, and looked at Nana Barb as if she was a fantastic novelty that she might never see again in her lifetime. The hand that wasn't holding the cactus pressed a button on a device that was wrapped around her arm. The device then spoke for the young lady. "It is fine. No harm was done. Are you from Mars?"

"No, I'm from Nether Wallop," Nana Barb replied.

"I do not know of Nether Wallop," said the robotic voice of her arm gadget. "My name is Lil, or Lillian in your language. I work in advertising."

"Pleased to meet you, Lil. My name is Barbara, or Barb in your language. I'm retired."

"Pleased to meet you, Barb," the device stated. The young girl put her hand out in a fist, which Nana Barb clutched and then shook. The young girl looked amused by this, but if Barbara had broken some sort of custom the young girl didn't mention it.

"Well I'd better go, I need to have some sort of scan," she said to the girl, who waved goodbye in response. Nana Barb started walking in the direction given to her by the airport employee, spotting a sign with something resembling shorthand, and underneath it, written in English, the word Martians.

Why did everyone think she was a Martian? Wasn't Mars a cold, barren desert, with no means of supporting life? And how was she going to get through their immigration checks if she didn't have ID or DNA or anything of the sort? They also all spoke to her in English, even though she could understand perfectly everything they were saying in their own language.

Before she had the chance to consider these thoughts further, she heard a boy's voice asking her to stop by the machine that she guessed was the scanner. She looked around to find the source of this voice, but couldn't see who might have issued the orders. Just as she was about to dismiss the incident as some sort of futuristic voice throwing technology, she felt a tug on her skirt, and she looked down to see a really small robot that she could only describe as, well, cute.

The robot, a little metal boy with a white angular head, stood at about 2'6" and walked on two legs like he'd been born with them. Someone had painted a little tuxedo on to his body, which made him look comical to say the least. Nana Barb had to stop herself from laughing at the sight of him.

"Hello," she felt herself saying in a tone usually reserved for foreigners or small children, "and what is your name?"

"Lady, I may be small but I'm no kid," the small robot said in an Italian-American accent. "You don't gotta use that cutesy-wutesey voice for me."

"I'm sorry, I didn't mean to offend you," Nana Barb replied, a bit taken aback from his cocky attitude.

"Hey, don't worry about it."

"Um, how do you do?" Nana Barb asked, not quite sure of the etiquette involved in talking to robots.

"I'm doing great, thanks for asking. Now, where do you wanna go?"

Was this some sort of trick? "I want to go through immigration," she replied.

"You've already passed through immigration, otherwise you wouldn't have me. Now, where do you wanna go? We can't hang around at the airport all day, unless you're into that kinda thing."

"Well, can I ask you a few questions first? I'm a bit new to the area."

"Yeah, of course, whatever you want. You the boss."

"Quite. Now, you said I *have* you. Can you explain what you meant by that? Are you saying you've been assigned to me? Am I in some sort of trouble for failing an immigration check?" she asked.

The little robot strode around her in a circle. "Jeez, you puritans are really backwards, ain't you? You guessed right first time, I am assigned to you. But you ain't in no trouble lady. You passed the immigration check, but we didn't have your DNA on record. You obviously ain't from around here, which means you got me, Guidebot 973."

"Oh I see, so you are a guide of some sort," she said as the little machine paced around in front of her.

"Yeah, I'm a guide and a robot. They ingeniously combined the two words to come up with my name, and ain't that just the cleverest thing you ever heard?"

"Why are you talking to me in that accent? Are you all programmed to speak that way?"

"No, I scanned your neural pathways to see which food is your favourite. And it turns out to be Italian."

His little voice, which had the slightest robotic tinge to it, suddenly became more animated. "Come on down to *Luigi's* on the corner of Spire and 52nd, it'll take you back to a time where Italian was the dish of the day."

"What just happened?"

"What do you mean?"

"You just said something funny."

"Oh that. Well I just advertised a restaurant to you. I guess they ain't got adverts where you come from, so you better get used to those. So, you got more questions, or are we gonna head off somewhere good? I can take you to see the Geldof Temple, or the Bioengineering Zoo. They're the most popular tourist hotspots."

"Oh, well the Zoo sounds nice. Maybe we could go there? Before that, could we find any food? I'd quite like to go to that Italian restaurant you just mentioned. It feels like I haven't eaten for a few thousand years." She chuckled to herself.

"Sure, you the boss," he said, striding off happily towards the airport exit.

"Keep up lady. I got short legs, but I know how to use 'em!"

Nana Barb trudged uncertainly after him, nervous about her lack of money. But if they could afford to give a robot to a stranger, then maybe they could afford to give her some food.

If the airport was strange, outside was even more peculiar. It was eerily quiet and Nana Barb noticed there wasn't a single car driving past, despite there being a network of roads capable of supporting many of them.

All around her were buildings that stretched to the sky, but rather than being made of bricks, steel or concrete, they looked natural, as if they were living organisms that had been encouraged to grow into the shapes of skyscrapers.

Guidebot 973 must have noticed her surprise because he said, "I know, ain't they quite some sight? That one," he pointed a little white finger to the largest of them all, "was built by Tyson Marmaduke, the foremost bioarchitect of our age."

"Bioarchitect?"

"Yeah, an architect that builds with biological material. You puritans really have been left behind, ain't you? I can tell this is gonna be hard work."

They walked past a shelter of some sort that might have been a futuristic bus stop. All of a sudden there was a deafening whoosh, and a huge vehicle fell from the sky. It landed directly adjacent to the bus stop. It almost gave Nana Barb a heart attack. As her pulse slowed to normal she surveyed the beast that gracefully fell from above. Running through the top of the vehicle was a suspension wire, which was presumably the vehicle's source of propulsion. It was as if a cable car carriage had just fallen off its runner and landed on the street.

The little robot tugged at her skirt. "We don't need the Skyway lady. It's just a couple'a blocks. It's a nice day, so we might as well walk."

With that the vehicle dragged itself back into the sky. As soon as it reached a certain height, it disappeared. Nana Barb stood with her mouth agape.

"Wow," she exclaimed.

"It's not that impressive," Guidebot said dismissively, "it's just a trick of light. If you could see the Skyway it'd ruin the view."

Wonders never cease. Nana Barb thought her head was going to explode. Bioarchitecture, Skyways. What else would she come across in the future? She had trouble keeping up with technology in her own time, but this was just too much. She wished she were young enough to find it even just a little bit exciting. In reality she just wanted to go home. She wanted to play with her grandkids in her garden, maybe play a card game. She always loved playing *Newmarket*. Whenever the younger girls won the pile of pennies they would shriek with delight. That sound was always music to her ears.

She looked down at the little pacing robot. He didn't seem capable of standing still. She thought he probably wasn't programmed to feel emotions, but at this moment he was doing an excellent job of acting impatient. She started walking towards the small robot when a man, who had previously been leaning against the bus shelter advertising boards, suddenly walked towards her and put out a fist. Once again she instinctively went to shake it, but this time her hand went straight through his.

"Hi," said a voice that sounded slightly electronic. "Nice to meet you *unknown name*. I'd like to introduce you to WallCo's patented Automatic Knitting Needles – they knit those sweaters for your grandkids quicker than you can say apple pie."

Nana Barb took a step back from the man. *He must be some sort of hologram.*

"That advert earned you 5ACs," the holographic man continued. "Come by again to earn the highest AC ratio in the market!"

"What just happened?"

"You just earned yourself some ACs to go towards dinner. Come on, let's go. We're not that far from *Luigi's*."

As she walked down the street, thinking she had never been so confused, she was met with an unexpectedly familiar sight. At the end of the street a car, driving on all four wheels rather than flying in the air along the Skyway, rounded the corner. It was a bright pink Cadillac with the number plate GR8 SCOT.

# CHAPTER 12
## A Boy Named Sue

## 18:05hrs, June 15th 2013 C.E. – Nether Wallop, England

### Simon

Simon was bricking it. Here he was, face-to-face with a man twice his size, whose car he had stolen, crashed and stuffed with a boot full of dead animal. He tried to go back and change things, but *he* had been the cause of the accident. The old man kept on saying to him *it was you, you made me crash.* He had got the wrong end of the wrong stick. He had literally made the old man crash, by distracting him when his future self tripped over his own stupid foot.

So far, he hadn't been hit in the face. That was a good sign. He made the first move.

"Hello Mr Sue sir. How are you? I was just about to call you."

"Were you now? That's funny, 'cause I didn't even leave you my number."

"I meant call for you, as in drive the car round to yours."

Sue suddenly raised his voice. "You'd shut your trap, boy, if you knew what's good for you. I didn't tell you where I live either. Now bend over so I can teach you a lesson." He started taking off his shoe.

Simon felt tears well up, but held them back. "Please sir, I didn't mean to. I'll pay for any damage, I promise."

"Damage? As well as stealing it, you also damaged my pride and joy? Oh son, what have you done?"

*Why don't I keep my stupid trap shut?* He bent down all the same. His mother, rather than supporting him, started to laugh.

"Mum! What the hell do you think you're doing? Please Mr Sue. Don't be violent with me. Is there any way we can reach a complement?"

Sue laughed heartily. "Son, you are quite the find. Don't you mean compromise? And you can stand up now; I'm just playing with you."

Simon turned round, not quite sure he had heard him right.

"Stand up," Sue repeated. "The car will be fine. Play time is over and I ain't got time for dilly-dallying. Believe it or not, there are more important things than the state of my pride and joy."

"I promise I'll pay you back sir." He was still bent over, afraid moving might make him change his mind.

"Honestly there's no need. And please call me Sue. The important thing is that you're all safe. For now."

*Safe? What does he mean? Why wouldn't we be safe?*

"Err, Mr Sue? What the hell are you talking about?" It irked him that Dave was suppressing a grin, but he was still shitting a brick so didn't shout at him.

His Mum suddenly joined the conversation. "Simon, I think I just met the people he's talking about. There was two of them, and I got their thingy."

"Mum! Leave it out, you're being weird again."

"The weird are often just misunderstood," said Sue. "You'll do well to listen to them from time to time."

"So," Simon asked. "Is your name Sue because you travelled back to our time and heard the Johnny Cash song? Did you think the guy in the song sounded hard as nails and thought it would be a good name?"

"What? Where did you come up with that one?"

"Don't mind him," said Simon's Mum. "I used to read him *Hitchhiker's Guide to the Galaxy* when he was a boy. In it one of the main characters has a little cultural misunderstanding and calls himself Ford Prefect after a make of car."

"Oh, I see. No, my full name is Suegard, and I'm aware of how effeminate the shortened version might sound to you, but being feminine is actually quite popular in my time. The gender lines are less rigid. I hate it of course, but loved my dear mom. I'd never change it or she'd turn in her grave."

"Fair enough," Simon said.

Sue turned to Louise. "Thank you for your patience, Louise. I said

I would explain everything when your friends got back. Now is the time to, as you say, 'spill my guts'."

Now he addressed the room. "There have been two incidents of time travelling in the past True Hour – a True Hour being an approximation of the normal human perception of an hour passing on the traditional time-line of existence. These occurrences have alerted my attention, as they will have done the Time Police." He turned to Simon's Mum.

"These two people you met, I assume they were twins?"

"Yes, big cruel men they were. They had these devices that could make you feel pain such as you never thought possible. I got one of them." She raised the hand-held remote she took from one of the Time Police.

"You did incredibly well to get that." Sue smiled at her approvingly. "It's no mean feat getting one up on the Time Police. We need to be careful though, they have a tracer on that thing."

"So there is a police force dedicated to time travel?" Louise asked.

"It's kinda complicated, sweet cheeks, but that's about the gist of it. They always come in twos, and after you meet them you will never feel comfortable around twins again."

"So they're twins?" Dave asked.

"I've only said it twice. Whatever they are, they look like twins at least," Sue replied. "They are infinite in number, technologically advanced, capable of regenerating and scariest of all, relentless in completing their task."

"Sounds like Arnie in *Terminator*," Simon said, "he was hard as nails."

"They're worse than Arnie, son," his Mum said, "they come in twos."

"That's a bit of a coincidence," Dave said. "The dirty old priest from the past mentioned something about prophets who were identical twins. Could it have been them?"

Sue scratched his chin. "Could be. They are programmed for one function only, which is to track down time travellers. For reasons I'll explain later, they still have to limit the number of trips they make. We all do for that matter, so no more little unnecessary trips through time." He looked sternly at Dave and Simon when he said this.

"How do they know when someone travels through time?" Louise asked.

"I will explain the full details to you later, but in a nutshell you are changing the shape of the Universe every time you travel through time. You are effectively ripping apart the fabric of space-time and stitching it back together again."

"That sounds dangerous," suggested Simon.

"Actually, it's a necessary part of the evolution of the Universe and it helps to sustain its stability."

"Ha, I knew it!" Dave exclaimed. "Did you hear that? 'Time travel is necessary', which means I was right and you were wrong, Louise."

Simon didn't know much about women, but he guessed his best mate had just blown any chance he might have had with her. Louise did not look happy.

"Explain how you came to that conclusion, David," she said, crossing her arms in a huff.

"Gladly. If it's necessary to maintain the stability of the Universe, then we were meant to time travel all along. It was fate, if you will, that deigned we would meet. Time is a patchwork quilt, stitched together piece by piece rather than being spun in a linear fashion. We would never have blown apart the Universe by meeting our past selves because we never would have met our past selves. Fate would have intervened to stop it happening, or we would have remembered it happening had it happened."

Sue smirked from the side of his mouth. "Other than too many happenings, that was eloquently put, boy. It's a nice theory, but it's wrong. If you had actually met your past self, this version of existence would have collapsed. That's why the Time Police were formed in the first place, because time travel is a dangerous game that could possibly end in the destruction of a Universe."

Dave's face dropped like an innocent man in the dock being told he's going down for ten years. Louise smiled and Dave looked down sheepishly, suddenly interested in his trainers. Simon was just pleased the attention was off him for a bit. Stupidly, he allowed himself to relax.

"So about six months ago," Sue continued, "I met a lady by the name of Barbara Wilson. She was lost in time."

Simon looked across to his mate. His face was scrunched up like he was looking for a trick.

"Does that mean we can go and rescue her?" Dave asked, more hopeful than certain.

"That's what we're going to try and do. It's not as simple as it sounds I'm afraid. She's stuck on a continuous shift and I don't know how to stop it."

Dave was clearly disappointed. Louise looked guilty.

"That's – not the news I was hoping for." Dave looked like the wind had been taken out of him.

"Oh deary, don't you worry. We'll find her. And on that little bombshell," said Mrs Ellis, "I could murder a cuppa. Louise, I don't suppose you'd mind, dear?"

"Oh, no. Of course not."

"Ta dear, milk and one sugar."

"Great idea," said Sue. "Take a bit of time to digest everything I've just said. In a minute I will explain what we need to do to sort out the situation. Simon, I hope you don't mind but I have something I need to chat to your mother about."

"Huh? What could you have to talk to her about?"

"That's my business, son."

"Son? By 'chat' you don't mean you're trying to chat her up are you?"

Sue just chuckled. Simon didn't see what was so funny.

"Come on Simon," Louise said, leading him into the kitchen. "You can help with the teas."

Dave followed them out of the room as Simon wondered what the hell a time traveller could be talking to his old dear about.

## Sue

About ten minutes later, everyone was assembled to hear Sue's immediate plan. Sue looked over the young group in front of him, revelling in the moment. These are the people from the history books. Oh, not the ones they taught from at school. The Master's followers had seen to it that the inconvenient truths were well hidden. However, if you searched hard enough you would find the true history, the turn of events the Master would never want you to read about.

"So, bit of a coincidence that you bumped into me last night, what with you bein' a time traveller n' all," Simon said.

"There's no such thing as coincidence, boy. Do you seriously think the first time traveller you met would just happen to turn up just before you took the first temporal shift of your own?"

"Temporal shift?" Louise put in. "That's what I call it too."

"I know dear, you invented the term."

The young scientist blushed, managing to look both surprised and smug at the same time.

"Hang on," Simon said, "are you sayin' you meant to meet me in that pub last night?"

"That's precisely what I'm saying. You were my entry ticket into the first ever time travelling party."

"So this whole thing was a set-up. You meant to meet me in that pub, you had it planned all along that I would keep your car and use it to bring you to Dave. I bet you even knew I would crash it into the back of that old bloke's Fiesta."

"No, actually you stole my car, and you crashed it all on your own.

I never gave you permission to drive it, and if you ever touch my car again, boy, you better be kissing my boots with your grovelling."

"In that case, you might not want to look in your trunk."

"What?"

Before Simon had the chance to reply, the earth shook. The Time Police. They were here, and he needed to get these kids to safety.

"Right, all of you in the car, now. I was hoping I'd get the chance to explain what the hell's going on, but it appears we have a change of plan. We need to get out of here, now!"

Mrs Ellis looked terrified. "It's them back, isn't it? The Time Police have come back to collect their thingy-majigy."

"I'm not gonna lie to you. You were lucky to escape them first time round. They won't be so easy to fool this time. You need to listen to me and do what I say and we might just make it out of here alive. Oh, and we're going on a little trip through time."

All of them, except Mrs Ellis, emitted an audible groan.

Sue led them out of the back door where they all crouched down below Louise's fence. He saw a black car pull up, a car that had moulded itself to look like a three series BMW.

The two robotic forms walked towards the front door of Louise's house and didn't waste any time knocking it straight in. They both hit the area around the lock with the sides of their fists, and the door caved in like a prisoner in the Master's torture chambers. He took that as his cue to lead his charges into the safety of the Cadillac.

"Run," he called at the top of his whispering voice.

They broke their cover of the fence and ran towards the Cadillac.

"Shotgun," Simon inexplicably called as he ran towards the front passenger seat.

His shouting alerted the attention of the Time Police. The first suited TP swung around and fired a beam from his device. Sue looked across and saw that all the others had made it to the car, except for Mrs Ellis. The beam went straight through the middle of Sue's hat. Mrs Ellis reacted by pulling out the device she had acquired and pressed buttons randomly. A beam of light generated from her device and struck the policeman square between the eyes.

"Mum! Where did that come from? That was a great shot!"

The TP's face disintegrated like melting metal and the pigment of his skin disintegrated to a shiny silver.

"Robots," Mrs Ellis exclaimed, before suddenly disappearing.

"That's our cue to go, girls and boys," said Sue as he jumped into his seat.

"Go?" Simon said. "What are you talking about? What in Tupac's name just happened to my Mum?"

"It's fine. I know where she is, and all you need to know is that she's safe. Let's go; I've already got a hole in my favourite hat, I don't wanna get one in my favourite head too."

He suddenly caught a waft of decaying animal. "What the hell is that smell?"

Simon went bright red.

"Oh for goodness sake. What the hell else did you manage to get up to in that short space of time?"

"Sorry Mr Sue sir."

"Well," Sue said with resignation, "not much we can do about it now."

He started the engine and accelerated the Caddy away from one danger and into the next. "On the road again then ladies and gen'lemen. Yeeha!"

# CHAPTER 13

## Sucker for Adverts

## The Hyper-real Universe, Dimension Alpha $2^{-32}$

And once again I take over the storytelling from my colleague, Ogg. You may have noticed he has a romantic view of coincidence and chance. If you are winning a game of poker, you can be sure Ogg is writing your narrative. If you find your long-lost car keys down a drain after the twenty pound note you dropped down there is helpfully retrieved by the handsome young plumber, who then invites you for a drink, and then one thing leads to another and you get married, have five kids and live happily ever after, then you know Ogg most certainly set that particular little scenario up for you. However, when you get divorced after he unexpectedly grows fat and loses interest in the bedroom, that's when Craag took over the storytelling.

So now you have experienced the varying natures of the three fates, and therefore I hope I shan't have to explain them all again. I'm indifferent at the best of times, and repeating myself is one of my least favourite pastimes. It's a bloody book, so if you missed it you can go back and read it again. Capiche?

You may not understand the relevance of three narrators with three different outlooks on luck and chance, but there is a good reason why our story needs it. Matters of life or death are resolved depending on who is leading the narrative, so our choice of narrator is extremely important. You will see the relevance of it later as characters will undoubtedly die, and others will survive almost impossibly deadly situations.

Now that we've got that sorted, we can get back to your story.

## 1862 A.B. - London Township of Sarum and Winchestershire, Western Earth

### Nana Barb

Barbara saw the bright pink Cadillac drive past her. The driver was a young man touching thirty (*of course he was – they all are here*) with long brown hair and wearing a cowboy hat. He looked strangely old-fashioned here amongst all the futuristic buildings. He tipped his hat as he passed.

"He looked like he came from my time," Barbara said.

"What do you mean 'your time'? He's just a lover of classic American style, as I assumed you were with your love of Italian food."

"Now that's a confusing statement for geographical reasons. Yes I suppose the classic American style must give me some sort of comfort from its familiarity," Barbara reasoned. She had gone to Vegas with Robert the year before he had died and had instantly fallen in love with the place. The only food she could eat there was Italian though – everything else was burgers and steaks, which was far too rich for her stomach.

"So," her robot guide said, "*Luigi's* is just round this street, one block away. After we've grabbed some grub I'll take you wherever you wanna go in the Greater London area."

"So this is London?" Nana Barb meant to ask rhetorically.

"Nope, this is the London Borough," – which he pronounced as borrow – "of Sarum and Aylesbury. I can take you to any London Borough on the SuperTrans Express."

"Well, that's a strange thing. What is this super thingy XS? It must be very fast."

"Oh it is. It can go over four hundred miles an hour, and gets into Queen Brittney station in under twenty minutes."

"Very impressive."

Nana Barb wasn't surprised that technology had moved on so far.

But how far ahead in time was she? She didn't want to ask the robot, because she had let slip a few things already. If robots were capable of suspicions, then she didn't want to arouse his.

She walked past a nice young couple holding hands. They smiled at her and so she wished them a good day. They stopped and thanked her for saying so.

The young man (or more accurately the device on his wrist) asked, "Where are you from? You look as if you are Martian, but then I heard they have a colony of Oldies in the Northern AT States of Canada."

"I'm from here and there," Nana Barb replied, slightly put out that this seemingly nice young man just called her an 'Oldie'.

"We are both from Even Newer Castle in the north east. We're here on a day trip. We are having a break from our job in advertising."

"Oh that's nice for you. Are you going to visit the zoo?"

"Yes, we have heard it is nice there. We do not have a zoo in Even Newer Castle."

"Well I'm off to *Luigi's* for some lunch. Good day to you both."

"Good day," both their wrist gadgets replied in unison. They walked off smiling.

Five minutes later and Barbara was sat in an American diner-style restaurant having the menu read to her by her table. She watched in amazement as the solid-looking surface became translucent and showed her examples of the dishes. "Traditional spaghetti Bolognese, served with out of this world rocket salad and Parmesan Cheeseish." A picture of a juicy plate of spaghetti appeared on the table, making Barbara's mouth water. "Perhaps you would like to try a pizza pie, done in the old American-Italian style with Pepperphony and fresh green tomatoes? They're a 'pizza' history lady!" That didn't sound as nice as the Bolognese, so Nana Barb hit a button on the table that said 'back', and then clicked 'order'.

"That's a great choice," said Guidebot. "I've heard the elderberry 'shake is also particularly divine. I ain't got it on nothin' but authority, of course, bein' that a single sip would fry all my circuits."

"Quite. I'm not a big fan of milkshakes. Can I get a cup of tea?"

"Sure, they got the Lapsang Souchong, the Black Delight, Glorious Green, Chai Latte."

"What about normal tea? I just want a tea with milk and half a sugar. I used to have two, but then the doctor warned me about my blood sugar, so I had to cut out that luxury. I have half of one if I've had a tough day, and they don't get any tougher than this."

"So you want a..." he paused for a minute and his eyes – for want of a better word – rolled back, "Breakfast Tea. Sure, they got that. They might have to programme it into the remoleculator, but it'll taste pretty much the same."

Nana Barb was infinitely more cheerful. "Oh good. Can I ask you a question?" She shifted nervously in her seat.

"Sure, fire away."

"You said I earned myself enough for dinner. Does that mean I haven't to pay for this meal? I don't want to be stuck with the washing up. Not that I'm work-shy, mind. More than happy to help if I need to, but I'd like to know where I stand."

"It's fine to ask. I know you got the free market on Mars, so it's probably confusin' for you down here. You have to pay for this food using ACs. Because you've been on the planet less than an hour your account is pretty low, so you gotta expose yourself to more advertising. This place was perfect for you, because they advertise in situ, so you can earn some more credits while you're sitting down to your meal."

The little robot pointed towards a couple of extremely muscular men, brazenly wearing just shorts and vest tops, despite the room being cold from the air conditioning. "See them? They respond to high impact visualisations, so get ready for the show. This will be spectacular."

Suddenly a snowy mountain appeared on the wall next to them. A man could be seen in the distance skiing down the mountainside. As he got closer, Nana Barb could see that he was equally as muscular as the two watching men, and despite the obvious cold, he was also wearing virtually no clothes. He approached a ramp that was built into the face of the mountain with great speed, causing him to lift off into the air like those brave people who she once watched on the BBC. They were doing something called a 'big air' according to that nice young man who commentated on the Winter Olympics programme.

The skiing man from the video on the wall did a double back-flip, flying over the heads of the two real men watching. He skidded to a stop, lifted his goggles and said a load of words in that close-to-English language. She couldn't hear very clearly, but she could pick out a few words. The words 'extra value' and 'special offer' assumedly meant the same thing now as they did in her time.

"What is he saying?" she asked her guide. "My hearing isn't so great."

"That's OK, I got enhanced hearing. He's telling them about Glorytex's new transparent Thermogear. It maintains body temperature whatever the conditions, whilst appearing completely transparent. Useful if you've been working hard getting that perfect gym body into shape."

"How can the clothes appear transparent?"

"They are made from materials that are smaller than the wavelength of light, which can then be used to control that light. The really high tech stuff is used by the military to make soldiers invisible."

"The invisible man, coming true. It's enough to give you the heebie jeebies. How do I earn these apps then?"

"ACs. It's an A and a C, which is short for Advertising Credit. Just watch the wall and it'll come to you."

The woman on the table next to Nana Barb turned and made a fist in her direction. The space behind the woman wobbled and solidified into a real wall. Come to think of it, this woman was the first person over thirty that she had seen. She realised she had been sitting next to a projected image all along.

"What do I do now?" She glanced nervously at the little robot.

"Just relax. It'll scan your neural pathways, find out what makes you tick, then advertise according to your profile."

She looked back at the woman.

"Now my dear, if you want anti-aging treatment then you just need to pop into Reducto's of Station Road." The woman gradually appeared to reduce in age before Nana Barb's eyes. "You too can look as young as me. Then you can give the grandkids the energy and vitality their playtime deserves."

The hologram disappeared, and she was now sat next to a solid brick wall. Nana Barb suddenly felt very far from home. The mention of her grandkids made her think of her family, and made her realise how homesick she felt. She wondered if poor Dave was looking for her back in her own time.

Guidebot pulled at her skirt and spoke, saying, "Hey, your food's here. You've earned enough ACs to pay for it."

She sat down at her table and started to eat. She pushed the food around her plate, no longer hungry all of a sudden. She hadn't eaten in a long time now and knew she would have to sustain herself somehow. She tentatively tested the food and was surprised to find it devoid of meat. It was tasty enough, but something wasn't quite right about it. She felt like asking if she had accidently ordered a vegetarian meal. But what if there was no longer any meat? Maybe they had stopped eating it in this future. Maybe she would be a barbarian in their eyes, just like she considered the people from that prehistoric tribe barbaric.

A few minutes later she was finishing her meal, when an unexpectedly familiar face appeared behind the glass doors. For a minute she struggled to remember where she had seen him, until she realised it was the cowboy from the Cadillac. The doors fell apart to let him through and he walked in, surveying the room with interest. When he spotted Barbara, he walked in her direction smiling.

"Howdy," he said in English, offering his hand.

She shook it, realising it was the first hand she'd shaken since arriving in this time.

"Howdy to you too," she replied.

"My name's Sue."

"Let me guess, Susan in my language and you work in advertising?"

"No, actually my full name is Suegard, and I have just quit my job with the Government. I now work in advertising insurance."

"Oh I see. And what is advertising insurance, exactly?"

"It's a policy that covers companies in the event of an unsuccessful advertising campaign."

"Oh, of course. Well, what can I do for you Sue?"

"Well my dear, it's more what I can do for you."

Nana Barb was a bit taken aback. "What on Earth could you possibly mean?"

"Barbara, I think I might be able to help you."

*How did he know my name? I didn't tell him what it was.*

"Oh, and why, pray tell, do you think I'm in need of any help?"

"Because you're lost in time, my dear."

"Oh, yes. That. Please, go on." Nana Barb, dumbfounded, sat back and waited for the man to explain what the bloody hell was happening to her.

# CHAPTER 14

## Back to the Future

## 18:26hrs, June 15th 2013 C.E. - Nether Wallop, England

### Louise

If Louise was scared in the psychotic tribal priest's hut, then she was terrified in the back of the Cadillac. For a start it stank of a dead animal, and she couldn't open the window to let in some fresh air.

"I wouldn't do that, darlin'," Sue warned.

Louise stopped trying to reattach the window lever and looked at Sue's reflection in the rear-view mirror. "Why not? It stinks in here," she replied.

"In a few minutes we're gonna shift through time. It's a whole different ball game doing it in a vehicle."

Simon interrupted before she could ask him to elaborate. "What the hell is happening when we travel through time anyway?"

"You are not travelling through time, but through different dimensions. This car is a vessel that allows us to break free from the confines of space-time so we end up in a dimension of space that surrounds us, a dimension of space that can't be seen but is nonetheless proven to exist. You end up in a different time and place as a by-product."

Louise was amazed. "I had posited the exact same theory," she said. "It was impossible to incorporate the apparent results of my experiments into the existing framework of the perceivable Universe."

Dave surprised Louise by asking, "How do you mean?"

"Well David, the Universe we know, and think we understand, is made up of three spatial dimensions: effectively height, length and depth. We are also fairly used to one further dimension: time. These are the four dimensions of the perceivable Universe in which we live, a space-time Universe. In return for the relatively stable living environment that provides us with, we must adhere to the relevant rules. We can no more change the forward nature of time than we can spontaneously relocate ourselves to the other side of the planet, or so physicists once thought."

"Why did they used to think that?" Simon asked.

"It's difficult to explain without teaching you the maths, but from a philosophical standpoint it's easier. My teacher, Professor Armitage, used to say that if you could go back in time you could create a paradox, which is basically an impossible series of events that would stop the world from making sense."

"The Grandfather Paradox," Dave said. "If you went back in time and killed your grandfather, you would effectively stop yourself being born; therefore you could never have gone back in time to kill your grandfather, because you don't actually exist."

He was confirming her suspicions all along; he wasn't as stupid as he looked. Louise flashed him a smile, which she quickly toned down in case it looked patronising.

"Don't look that surprised," he said, "I only picked it up from sci-fi movies."

"Don't be so hard on yourself," Louise said. "A lot of real science gets used in science-fiction story lines. It still takes someone with brains to relate that to this current context."

She twisted her hair in her fingers while maintaining eye contact with Dave. He looked away, uncomfortable.

"So," Louise continued, "couple Dave's eloquent description with a bit of Einstein's theory of relativity, and there you have a convincing argument for the impossibility of time travel."

"Fair enough," Simon said. "But if that's the case then how the hell have *we* managed to do it?"

"As far as I had surmised, my machine makes a conscious mind aware of a fifth, and possibly sixth dimension of space. Once your mind is retuned – for want of a better word – to become aware of these extra dimensions it can travel around in much the same way as we can move through normal space. There is an entire alternative reality surrounding us, and most people don't even realise."

"A bit like that Speccy Wizard, when he ran through the wall at King's Cross St. Pancreas," Simon suggested.

Everyone went silent. Louise stifled a laugh.

Before Dave could cut in and nitpick about his friend's confusion between organs of the human body and mainline railway stations, Louise continued. "Now the obvious contradiction is the fact this conscious mind can't leave its body behind, which apparently isn't a problem. It seems as though the matter our bodies is made of relies on our consciousness to maintain its stable position in space. Apparently it is perfectly capable of breaking apart to travel with our minds, as surprising as that sounds. I can only assume the quantum world suddenly takes charge over the atomic. The energy is never lost, just moved, kind of spooky action at a distance on a massive scale. It could also go some way to explaining why particles in their smallest state appear to act like waves until they are viewed, and then they start acting solid like they should.

"Just think for a second what that really means. Nothing, even your body, is made up of solid, unmoving matter. It is all a series of oscillating waves, which only 'collapse' into a solid state when looked upon by an observer. If that doesn't impress you then you haven't fully understood. Waves are normally sound waves, magnetic fields or electricity. Your body might as well be made of the same stuff as a digital TV signal.

"This idea got me thinking about the strange results my attempts to transport matter threw up. If I could manipulate that trigger switch that causes the collapse, you might just be able to encourage the matter to adopt its wave-like properties. This was a pivotal point of my experiments: the moment I realised the conscious mind was the proponent of these effects. After years of perfecting, I worked out how to manipulate the wavelength of the newly formed waves, making them oscillate at just the right frequency to travel certain distances and therefore lengths of time. Then my machine makes the conscious mind return after a certain number of oscillations. When the matter is observed again – i.e. when the conscious mind is brought back to the space-time dimension – the waves that had been moving through space once again collapse and matter is apparently reformed."

"I've spotted a problem with that theory," Simon said.

Louise didn't want to see him make a fool of himself, but allowed him to talk anyway. "Go on."

"You said you make the wave oscipate to just the right frequency so you can control how far you travel through time. Well how come we don't just land in outer space every time we time travel?"

"I don't understand," Louise said. *He couldn't possibly have worked it out, could he?*

"Do you have a pen and paper?" Simon asked Sue.

"Sure, it's in the dash," he replied.

Simon searched around in the glove compartment until he found a pen. "Is there anything to write on?"

"Take that thing that looks like an etch-a-sketch. It's a writing tablet."

"Cool, thanks."

Simon started drawing something on the writing tablet, and then leaned over his shoulder to show Louise and Dave what he'd drawn.

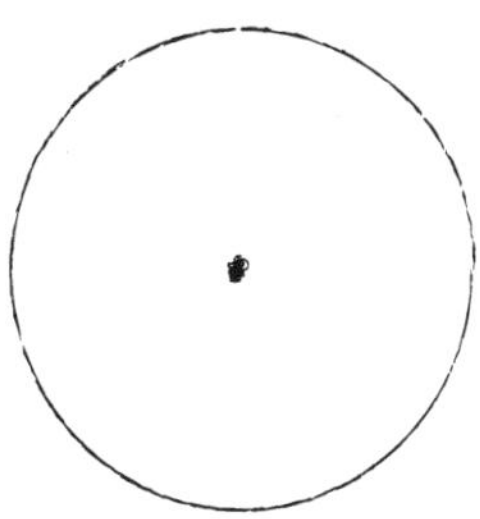

"This," he pointed at a circle he had drawn, "is the Earth. This little splodge is our car. When we travel through time we move, say, one mile." He drew the little car again in the empty space right of his original drawing, a little higher up this time.

"Now, if time has moved on by a couple of centuries, and the Earth resolves around the Sun..."

"Revolves," put in Dave.

"I'm getting there," replied Simon. "And if the Earth resolves around the sun at a gazillion miles an hour, how do you know that it hasn't moved over here?" He drew another planet Earth a few inches right of the little car.

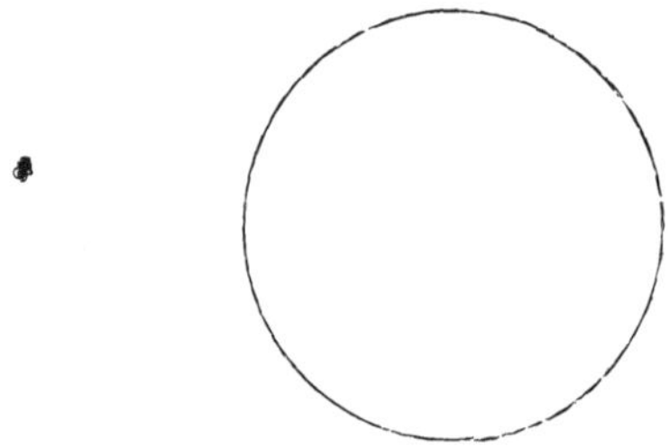

He pointed to the black dot. "That's us, in space."

Louise looked at the picture for a minute, realisation dawning on her. She was stuck for something to say. How had he worked out a problem in minutes that had taken her months to realise? The singular part of her theory that she had never been able to solve had just been recognised almost instantly by a complete halfwit.

Sue burst out laughing. "I think he's got you trumped there, sweet cheeks."

"I... how did you work that out?"

Dave clapped Simon on the back. "Nice one, mate! Where did that come from?"

"I don't know, mate, it just sort of came to me."

"What – that took me months to work out. The numbers didn't add up, which made me question how you define a precise spatial position. Is it a fixed point in space, or is it a position that's relative to objects such as stars or other celestial bodies? If you move through time, what's to say the solid object you were standing on hasn't moved? That's a pretty difficult concept surely? Fair enough, the idea is taught in college physics, but still..."

"I wouldn't worry your pretty little head about it," said Sue, "I'm sure your head was simply stuck in all the maths."

Louise eyed Sue thoughtfully. "Presumably things have moved on from my time, a deeper understanding of the laws of nature and all that. How far in the future are you actually from, Sue?"

"About two thousand years."

Louise realised she could jump forward two millennia of acquired knowledge, if she played her cards right. "So why do we so conveniently end up back here on Earth, even though it never stays in the same place?"

"As y'all know, time travel is most definitely possible otherwise none of us would be here today. D'you remember talkin' about that alternative dimension, the thing you said permeates all of space? It is closely associated to the matter we can see around us, and the thing that links it is gravity. It's difficult to explain and I ain't no physicist, but the very gravity of matter ties everything together. Whatever region of space exists in this alternative dimension also moves through space and orbits our Sun as Earth does. As Louise said, you can't make something outta nothing, so in a sense there needs to be matter on both sides of the coin to make it work. If you happen to be on a ship in outer space, now that's a different story. You shouldn't expect there to be a ship there again when you come out the other side, that's for sure. No one knows what happens in this situation because no one has ever tried. The theory is that you keep travelling through time until a passing asteroid ends up in just the right place."

Louise thought about it, and realised Sue's response had still given her the key. Gravity. What was the one problem with the current understanding of physics? Gravity.

This could lead to a unifying theory of the forces, which in turn could help her convince the naysayers – Professor Armitage *et al.* She made a mental note to write these thoughts down later. The Nobel Prize commissioners were notoriously difficult to sway, and a unifying theory was said to be a guaranteed route to the coveted prize, and therefore scientific immortality.

She recovered her resolve, or revolve, she supposed she could call it. "Initially I wanted to call this alternative dimension the Ether, but thought there would be a danger of confusing it with the Victorian sense of the word."

"Isn't Ether that drug he takes on *Fear and Loathing in Las Vegas*? They get off their trolley breathing it in off a rag. Are they travelling through dimensions when they take it then?"

She knew this one, which meant she could once again regain control through her knowledge of science. "You are confusing it with an unrelated chemical compound, also called Ether; the one he takes in that movie is Diethyl Ether, making the example in that movie a case of solvent abuse."

Simon turned around in his chair.

"Whoa, tone it down please, brainiac," he said, "you forget who you're talking to here."

"Drugs, Simon. The guy was taking drugs," Louise said. Was this the same guy who had just recognised an extremely difficult concept that scientists had only discovered comparatively recently?

"Don't interrupt her," Dave said, "I was finding it interesting."

"Thank you Dave." Dave went up a notch or two in her esteem.

"In fact," she continued with renewed vigour, "our Ether is shortened from its full name: the Luminiferous Aether, which translates from the Greek for 'light-bearing' and 'Aether', the region of space in which the ancient Greeks believed the Gods made their home. The Luminiferous Aether was thought to be a region of space that permeated the entire Universe. Newton, and others, suggested its existence to explain the unusual properties of light, which they believed must travel through a medium in waves, like sound or electricity. See where I'm going with the name now?

"The Victorians had closely studied the properties of sound waves, which they realised relied on the presence of a substance – water, an atmosphere, even rocks and walls – to travel through. In the absence of a substance, the waves dissipate so that no sound can be heard. To speak in a language you understand, Simon, in space no one can hear you scream."

"*Alien:* great movie," Simon said.

"The Victorians," Louise continued, "attributed similar properties to light, and therefore assumed the existence of the Ether, to allow light-waves to travel the way they do.

"Scientific practice relies on the process of hypothesising and then proving your assumptions correct through observational experiments. They attempted to prove the existence of the Ether by completing a vast number of experiments, but to no avail. It seems it never existed. Its absence tells us a lot about the nature of the Universe, although some scientists still claim its existence to this day."

Dave looked thoughtful. "So, what's to say this substance we are travelling through isn't the Ether?"

"Well it doesn't bear any relation to the nature of light. The Ether was a region of space that existed to make sense of a natural phenomenon. The natural phenomenon we experience is different."

Simon started singing, "*Something like a phenomenon, something like a phenomenon.*"

Everyone looked at him. Sue shook his head like he was disappointed.

"LL Cool J. The guy was a legend."

"Was?" said Dave. "He's still alive you know, Simon."

"May he rest in peace," replied Simon as he tapped a rhythm on the dashboard of the Cadillac.

Suddenly the car spluttered. White smoke appeared around the edges of the bonnet. "What the hell was that?" Sue demanded.

Simon sunk down into his seat. "Erm, I think the crash might have done some damage to your car. Sorry Mr Sue sir. I think it's the radiator."

Louise heard a screeching sound in the distance. She looked behind her and realised she could see the shape of a familiar black car skidding into view. The way things were going so far today, she was starting to feel these episodes were more than coincidence. All the same, she wished that fate, luck, whatever you want to call it, would let them relax for a few hours.

"Oh crap. Guys, I don't mean to worry you but the Time Police are following us. Are we going to travel through time any, uh time, soon?"

"Bob darn it. That means they have logged our position. They only hunt in twos, so when Simon's Mum melted one of them back there I thought we'd sent them off our trail. Now they have quadrangulated our position in space-time, this era is no longer safe."

"What do you mean no longer safe? Surely an entire era can't be unsafe?" Louise asked.

"It can, and it is. They will keep coming back at us until they have wiped us from the face of this Earth. Worst case, they could implode this Universe to nip the problem in the bud.

"They can implode an entire Universe?" Dave exclaimed, disbelieving more out of hope than conviction.

"They certainly can, this particular brane anyway. They just need to pop the bubble of its space-time by creating a paradox, which is thankfully harder than it sounds, but possible all the same. The only way to make sure that doesn't happen is to beat them to the punch – destroy the Time Police."

They all went silent. How difficult was this task? How realistic their chance of beating an advanced robot race? This situation was unnerving. All this talk about the Universe being destroyed was unnerving. The fact she was about to travel through time to an unknown future was unnerving. And now she was told she might not be able to come home? She was unnerved, to say the least.

"Next thing you're gonna tell me we need get this car up to 88 miles per hour for it to work. Am I right?" Simon asked, far too excitedly under the circumstances, Louise thought.

"What? Where would you get that idea from?" Sue replied.

"Don't mind him," Louise said, "he thinks he's in a movie."

"Oh, I see. Well don't worry about it. We don't need to travel at any speed really. I'm just driving to a particular location so I can control the destination of our re-entry. We need to end up in my garage, so I need to drive exactly twenty two point four one miles from where I live in my own time."

"Yes, that makes sense."

"Buckle up then boys and girls. This is our stop."

Louise turned round to watch the black car quickly closing in on the Cadillac. *Wow they are quick.*

"Guys, the Time Police. They've caught up with us."

Dave was frantically searching around, presumably for a bag so he wouldn't cause any further mess in Sue's car when he threw up in it.

Sue reached across to the car stereo and pressed a button. The fascia popped off to reveal a series of complex digital images. A big red button sat in the middle of the display (*why is it always big and red*?).

"I've been trying to work out something, Sue," Louise said. "When my mice come back they never end up in the same place. How the hell do you know we won't end up fifty feet in the air, or on a motorway with hundreds of cars heading in our direction?"

"Now's not the best time, honey. Don't you worry your pretty little head – I've made you each a little Daemon, who is only too happy to swap places with you in your so-called Aether. Now I know that won't mean much to you yet, but I'll show you when we get there."

Louise hated not knowing the answer to something, and this car journey had yielded a high quantity of unknowns. She felt sick.

She turned round to see the black car bearing down on them. In the front two seats were another set of identical twins – female this time. She turned round and slumped down in her seat, shivering as she shut her eyes.

## Dave

The robots were bearing down on them, their horrible black car gaining ground at incredible speed. Dave felt sick to the stomach. Sue had just told them they could not return to their time until they had defeated the Time Police. What did that really entail? How difficult would they be to defeat? Did they have anyone else to help them, or was it the inhabitants of the car versus a mighty army of robots?

## Sue

Everything so far was going as he had planned it. He hadn't quite expected the Time Police to catch up with them so quickly, but they had a habit of surprising you. He now just needed to get these kids to safety and then phase two of the plan could begin. Assuming they made it to the Shift Location before those darned TPs caught up with them.

His DAEmap buzzed, informing him they had reached the spot. He lifted his hand in preparation of slamming it down on the red button. Just one second more.

## Simon

*Something like a phenomenon, something like a phenomenon, ohh. Something like a phenomenon, something like a...*

*Jesus wept, we're off again...*

## Dave

Dave felt the car vibrate underneath him. He no longer felt sick. The feeling was in fact wonderful – like last time but with a greater feeling of empathy, in particular for the others in the car. More than anyone he felt a connection with Louise, could feel her elation, excitement and intrigue. It was as if he was capable of searching deep into her soul. He hoped she was looking back at him. Without his social concerns he hoped she could also feel what he was feeling. If she knew how he felt – but then how *did* he feel exactly?

They reformed. It was dark, so dark that he initially thought the Time Police must have caught up with them. He tried blinking hard, but still nothing. Maybe the temporal shift had made him go blind. Were there any side effects? Surely it only took a small misalignment of some retina cells to completely mess up his sight. Were there any other possible long-term issues? Heart disease? Cancer?

Lights flickered on, each flick revealing more information about the room he was in. He wasn't in the car any more, instead he was behind bars. He was in another animal cage. Why *did* that keep happening?

The next flick showed the others, all lined up in cages alongside his. For a fleeting moment he panicked, thinking he had been locked up. But then, with a final flick, the lights stayed on. This time Dave could see the Cadillac, which looked as shiny as if it had come straight off the production line. The huge dent that Simon had caused by crashing it had disappeared, and the pierced radiator grill was once again whole.

Sue was out of his cage quicker than you could blink. He went to the other cages one by one, releasing the catches that set the inhabitants free. He reached Simon's cage and set him free.

"Sue, your car. It's fixed," Simon said.

"I told you not to worry about it. It has a habit of mending itself," Sue continued. "Follow me upstairs and we can have a little chat about fixing a few other things."

The car was fixed, but would the dead deer still be in the trunk? *Or even the boot.* He realised his friend's fondness for Americanisms was inevitable when discussing something that epitomised

America.

He called Sue to ask him. "So it appears your car has the capacity to regenerate or fix itself. What about any objects that might have been left in the car before it regenerates? Where would they go?"

Sue stopped walking up the steps and scratched his beard. "You're referring to the dead animal that was previously in the trunk. You want to know what happened to it."

It wasn't said as a question. Dave watched Simon try to slink down behind Louise, as if it would do any good.

"Well Dave, I'm hoping you and your irresponsible friend here stick around long enough to find that one out."

Dave thought it was a bit unfair that he was being lumped into the irresponsible category with Simon, but kept quiet all the same. He looked to his left and saw that there were many more cages lining the other wall. At first sight they all appeared to be empty. Suddenly, out of his peripheral vision, he saw movement. His first thought was that he saw something that looked like a small animal, with large eyes peering through the cage bars. As he turned his head towards the spot where he thought he'd seen the creature, the bars shook slightly and he was once again looking at an empty cage.

"Sue," he said as they walked towards the flight of stairs, "exactly what do you keep in these cages?"

"Nothing, Dave," he replied.

"I just saw something."

"I didn't say animals don't occasionally appear in the cages. But it would be cruel to lock them up, wouldn't it?"

Dave looked at Louise, who turned away from his gaze.

"Daemons?" Simon suggested.

"Very good, you were listening before. Aetherial Daemons aren't from our dimension. As their name suggests, they live in the Aether. Although, not the Luminiferous Aether of the Victorians, but a place more similar to the ancient Greek definition. We biologically generated them to solve an apparent problem with time travel."

"Who's we?" Louise asked.

"The small number of us who defy the rules of the Master: the Timeseekers."

"The Timeseekers, the Master?" Simon said. "This all sounds like it's been written by a bloody writer from *Doctor Who*. Who is the Master, when he's at home?"

"The Master is another biologically engineered organism. He was designed to do something humans could never do: rule fairly. Look, I know there are a lot of questions, but everything will be revealed as I explain our plan. If I try to tell you too much at once, it will blow your minds. We'll go upstairs and have a bite to eat, during which I will fill you in on the essentials. Just the essentials, mind; we have a lot to do and little time to do it in."

"I thought we'd put the Time Police off our scent by coming here. Why the rush? Is it not days, if not weeks that we have at our disposal?" Dave asked.

"There are other things that require our attention, and a particular time in which they must be completed. We also can't run the risk of alerting the TP again. This time we need to do it chronologically, and for the most part I know what we need to do."

A cage next to the stairs suddenly shook slightly, and a small reptilian creature appeared. Bizarrely it looked halfway between a monkey and a small dinosaur, with eyes that were large and inquisitive and a tuft of hair in the middle of its forehead.

"Ah," said Louise, putting on a silly voice. "Isn't he cute? Can I touch him?"

"Sure," Sue replied, "but that's a girl. You can tell from the stripe on her tail."

She put her hand through the cage and the Daemon nuzzled up to her hand. The little Daemon suddenly looked over her shoulder then disappeared. The shaking cage was the only evidence anything had been there at all.

"Enough of that, you'll get more of a chance to play with them later," said Sue. "Let's go. We've got work to do."

They walked up the stairs and sat down on some stools in what was presumably the kitchen. There didn't seem to be any cooking apparatus, except for one large serving hatch in the middle of the room. Sue went over to this hatch and started typing something into a small control panel on the side.

"You guys must be starving," Sue said. "What can I get you to eat?"

Dave's stomach rumbled and he realised the last thing he had been offered was mouldy bear meat. "What have you got?" he asked.

"Anything you want, as long as I've got the recipe for it. This is a remoleculator."

"Don't you mean a replicator?" Simon asked.

"No, I mean a remoleculator. It doesn't copy anything, it reorders the states of certain types of matter until it appears as a tasty, nutritious meal. You can't replicate something outta nothing."

Simon looked impressed nonetheless. "It's still pretty cool though. I'm a crap cook, but a great eater. This would come in handy."

## Sue

A few minutes later and Sue was putting three steaming plates of stew in front of the time travellers. He hoped they would like the meals from his own time. He hadn't been in the past long enough to spot their eating protocols. As his guests began to, thankfully, devour their meals, Sue started talking.

"So I have explained a bit about the time travelling, and touched on the political situation here. All of this information is relevant to our situation. Everything I tell you now is based mostly on experience, but a large part on presumption. I am no genius, so you don't have to trust my judgment if you don't wish to. I can only guide you, not command you.

"Starting from the beginning, you are the first time travellers in history. Louise, as you might have inferred, you invented the first ever time travelling device, chronologically speaking of course. In this era, time travel isn't exactly a common thing, but the science is well known. Think of it like nuclear power; only a handful of people know how to make it work, and the secret is kept in check to restrict the damage it can do.

"The reason I knew where to find you is twofold: firstly, it was written in the history books. Not the ones that are taught in schools, but the ones well known in certain underground circles. Secondly, I have a device that tells me every occasion the timeline changes.

"This brings me on to a question of how the Universe allows for time travel." Sue paused to build the drama.

Dave coughed into his food, and eyed Louise as if expecting a reaction. She remained stony-faced.

Sue waited to see if he would be interrupted. They carried on eating, so he continued: "When someone changes the course of history by travelling through time they actually create a new region of space called a dimensional brane. When you go back in time and change something you don't necessarily create a paradox. Nor is time a patchwork dictated by Fate. Modern philosophers suggest Fate is partly at play, but even if this is the case, they all agree Fate has no control over Nature – natural disasters and the like. If this idea has any truth in it, that means there are two conflicting systems fighting against each other. I'm digressing a bit here, but this will all prove to be important.

"So what does that leave us with? We have the two ends of the spectrum of twentieth century opinion on time travel: the Patchwork Time Theory and the Classical Paradoxical Theory. So which one is right? Well actually, neither is correct. There is a third option, first suggested in the year 23 After Bob. You create a new timeline, which exists as a completely separate entity from the original. Once it is created, the consciousness that inhabits these worlds is split into two. The old brane feeds the new one with experiences and memories, although it feels fresh and new, just like you're living it for the first time. The predominant consciousness therefore experiences a reality formed of a combination of these existences. The dimensional brane I mentioned earlier is the perceivable reality the predominant consciousness inhabits."

Dave looked up from his food. "The only way I can understand difficult concepts is through a visual aid. Can you explain it a bit better for those of us who don't have a bloody clue what you are talking about?"

"Sure, sorry it's quite a difficult thing to explain. Think of it as cloning, but on a gargantuan scale. On first appearance this new Universe will be almost identical, but there will be a few anomalies depending on which genes you play about with. Instinctive behaviour is carried through genes, so in a way that is similar to our own reproduction. In fact, it was this comparison that drew scientists into creating the idea that the Universe itself is a replicator, and time travel is the way it reproduces."

Louise stopped eating. "Can I ask something?" she requested.

"Be my guest."

"What if you travelled back in time and did something as momentous as shooting your own grandfather to death? How would your dimensional brane concept deal with that?"

"It's a good question, well asked. And to answer you, you will quite simply cause the new dimensional brane you've created to collapse. A sure-fire way to destroy a dimensional brane is to create an Irretrievable Paradox. They actually aren't that easy to make, because the Universe will fight against you, but if you do succeed you wipe out that dimensional brane. The chances are that you die with it, since you are nothing but a memory in the old brane. But then there's another factor we can throw into the mix. Are you familiar with Schrodinger's cat?"

"Yes of course, it was a thought experiment used to explain quantum superposition," Louise answered.

"Come again," Simon said.

"Sorry, I forget who I'm talking to sometimes. No offence intended," Louise added.

"None taken," he replied.

"I'll explain it, if you don't mind Sue?"

"Go ahead," he said.

Louise mopped up the last bit of gravy with a slice of bread. She put her knife and fork together and pushed her plate away.

"So, you remember I told you how physicists discovered that individual particles can act more like waves than solid particles until they are looked at by someone? Schrodinger's cat is a concept that came from this discovery. It was a way of explaining how the subatomic world might have real-world consequences.

"I'm sure we can all agree, at any one time a particle can be said to be fixed in only one position in space. If not, our environment would be blurry and impossible to navigate. Because you can't look at subatomic particles with the naked eye, or even with normal microscopes, physicists use particle detectors to 'see' them. Photons, a fancy way of saying light, are the particles that allow us to see the world around us, and photons interact with other subatomic particles to effectively help them fix a position in space. In a very true sense, simply by observing a subatomic particle we are manipulating the outcome of its position. The difficulty of measuring an unobserved particle is trying not to manipulate its position by observing. A good analogy is measuring the tyre pressure of a car; by putting the gauge into the tyre you have to release some pressure, so therefore you will never get a wholly accurate reading. Certain particle detectors don't require photons to track the position of particles; therefore we can use them to measure their possible position in space.

"So we know that matter in certain states acts like waves because of results of experiments conducted with particle detectors. The problem is, when the particles are acting like waves, we don't actually know where they exist in space. Sometimes they even appear in two places at once. Quantum superposition explains the multiple possible places a particle might exist in space depending on all the given possibilities of the interacting fields.

"So how is it possible that the quantum world can act so differently to the atomic world? And does it matter? Perhaps the two systems just exist aside each other and don't really affect each other. Schrodinger spotted a way that the result of a quantum effect could have direct implications in our world. The story goes that he watched a cat playing around his lab one day and wondered if he could use the difference between life and death to answer the question. There are no grey areas with death.

"If he put the cat in a sealed box with a lump of radioactive material, that material may release energy in the form of small subatomic particles known as electrons; but with equal probability, the material may not decay at all. A small vial of poison is also placed in the box, and is linked up to a particle detector so that if the electron is released and detected the vial is smashed and the cat is poisoned. As the decay of a radioactive material follows the laws of quantum mechanics, a situation is created where a quantum effect can make a difference to an animal's existence. One would say that the cat would either die *or* not depending on whether the electron is released from the radioactive material. However, due to the nature of radioactive decay, the material has equal probability of either decaying or not and so the electron is said to be in a state of quantum superposition; without observation the electron has both been released *and* not released at the same time. So the cat can be said to be both alive *and* dead at the same time. It is only when the box is opened that the state of the electron is observed, its wave-function collapses, and the cat's fate swings towards life or death.

"If this sounds too supernatural to be real, that the results must somehow be incorrect – how can a particle possibly exist in two places at once? – understand that quantum effects have led to many of today's technologies. Your computer wouldn't work without it."

Simon seemed to consider. "So did his cat die or not? Seems a bit of an evil way to prove your point."

Sue knew he was going to say that.

"He didn't actually kill his cat, Simon," said Louise. "That's why it's called a thought experiment. It's a hypothetical explanation used to explain a complicated idea. He probably didn't even own a cat."

"Cool. I get it, I think."

"His ideas led to the suggestion of a Multiverse. The possibility of either outcome being true means perhaps the cat dies in one Universe and lives in another. Basically, the possibility of two outcomes perhaps means both happen. Maybe infinite Universes exist to accommodate the infinite possibilities of every event."

"Well explained," Sue said, "and if you apply that to my example then you are faced with a possibility of either killing your grandfather or not. In one Universe you will and in the other you won't. You couldn't exist in the one where you killed him and so you couldn't possibly remember pulling the trigger of the gun. But at this stage you are faced with a quantum possibility. Perhaps you are stood there pulling the trigger. As the gun misfires you have no idea that an entire Universe is collapsing somewhere due to your actions. This is extremely abstract thought here, so I apologise if it's difficult to follow, but the idea of a Multiverse doesn't exactly fit with our dimensional brane theory. If it did it would mean there are infinite possibilities within each brane and what would be the point in having multiple, infinite Universes? From a philosophical standpoint, it don't make sense. There must be a way of unifying these theories, which we must do because I believe the answer will have real consequences as to how we can resolve the situation we've got ourselves into.

"Imagine you have just two systems; for the purposes of familiarity let's call them Fate and Nature. Fate suggests all our actions are preordained, Nature suggests they are wild, uncontrolled and infinite in possibility. If there was a master puppeteer such as God, or any kind of omnipotent being who controlled our actions, then there is no need for a Multiverse. To use Schrodinger's cat again, God decides if the cat is alive or dead and the fact that someone is just about to open the box to sneak a look forces Him to make a decision over the cat's mortality. I use God as an example – I'm not religious or anything. In this instance, the dimensional brane idea sits better because technically the theory just becomes a tool with which Fate can work its will. It allows Fate to make complicated decisions over long periods of time within the framework of physical possibility.

"Now we've got the Nature argument. If you ain't got no one at the helm, the possibilities are endless. Sound familiar? That's because it directly equates to the lack of a supreme being, and therefore opens up the possibility of a Multiverse. For every possible action there are an infinite number of outcomes, and so time travel is perfectly plausible because it is one of a number of possibilities. In some ways time travel is inevitable. If something can happen it will, which includes scenarios that involve travelling back to change the past.

"Now if we want to unify our theories, why not just stitch the two concepts together? What if Fate *and* Nature coexist? What if they are two separate entities who are playing dice over the outcome of all existence? In this case there aren't infinite possible outcomes because Fate is controlling the number of possibilities. On the other hand, Nature is battling to break free of Fate's restraining hand, trying to force different possible outcomes. If you apply this concept then both theories can live together in harmony. Although harmony probably isn't the right word for it, because in truth this probably explains why it's so darn hard just to exist. Philosophers now agree that there is a battle – hypothetically speaking of course, Simon – between Fate and free will, Nature and ethereal nurture. The truth of the matter is, you can probably make choices that result in whether you live or die, but you gotta make sure those choices are the right ones. If not, it don't matter if there's another you living happily out there in another dimension, because you won't have a clue about it if you're already dead. Personally, I believe that your memories make you who you are, and if your conscious mind has stored the memories of just one chain of events then it has already chosen the path of least resistance. If you follow that path to find you're in a dead end, I don't believe there's any going back."

Louise seemed to consider for a moment. "What if time travelling creates a huge legacy that affects historical events?" she said. "Say for example you went back and killed Hitler. Surely you would still remember the Second World War happening, even though in that dimensional brane it would never have happened."

"You catch on fast. In fact, you wouldn't remember it happening at all. If someone killed Hitler by travelling back in time, then that dimensional brane would be a much happier place to live. Equally, if you cause a war that suddenly gets written down in the history books, you would remember it as though it had always happened. Although the confusing fact is that you will retain some memory of the events, although on a subconscious level."

This was met with completely blank faces (from Dave and Louise; Simon had virtually given up trying to follow the conversation and was now playing with the remoleculator), so Sue elaborated, "OK, let me try to explain it better. If you concentrate really hard and think about it logically, you have no choice but to experience the resulting changes of time travel two times. When you first go back to make the changes, you will later have no recollection of the events because they effectively took place in a different dimension. In the new dimension you have created by perpetuating a DAE, a Dimension Altering Event, you are only experiencing these new events for the first time, even though you created them. You would have no idea you created that war you read about in your history classes, right up until the moment you travel back and start it. Then when that moment happens, realisation will set in. Your stomach would drop as you realised you were the person who destroyed so many lives.

"Think of it in terms of an optical illusion. Consider these two dimensions to be like 3D glasses, which use our brain's reasoning powers to merge two images together. The two images that are displayed on a screen are displayed at different angles to give the illusion of one perspective-rich image. Your brain fills in the gaps because it couldn't possibly remember experiencing these events yet, although in a different dimension it already has."

Simon sat down with another steaming plate of food, stacked so high it looked as if he had put one meal on top of another.

"That's impressive, mate," he said, "but what does that all mean in real terms? You are very articulated, so it's not your fault I'm slow with science. I just haven't got a bloody clue what this all means to us. And if we're in such a hurry, why do we need to know?"

"I'll get on to the reason why this is so important. To answer your other question of what this means in real terms, Dave's grandmother went back in time and caused a DAE. She went back to Neolithic times and paid a little visit to a tribe, the tribe who were probably responsible for building Stonehenge. She obviously did something that resulted in the tribe deciding they would build the monument. I know that because when you woke up this morning, Stonehenge didn't even exist."

"How could you possibly know that?" Dave asked.

"Wait just a minute."

Sue took the hand-held device out of his utility belt. His DAEmap looked very much like the ones the Time Police owned, except this one didn't have all the nasty lie-detecting software or high-intensity photon beams. He placed it on the table in front of his guests, which responded by lighting up. A box now framed his device and the small display screen was replicated as a three-dimensional image in the middle of the table. The image displayed was of Simon's Mum, the moment of her holding out the Time Police's DAEmap frozen in time.

"That's bloody incredible," Simon said as he spat some of his mouthful of food through his mother's head.

Sue tapped a few buttons and the image changed. Nana Barb's image suddenly displayed, an image of them sat in the restaurant together. That was ten years ago now, but it seemed so much sooner. How time flies.

Sue keyed some more buttons on the table and her image disappeared. In its place was something that looked like a webpage, with the familiar word Wikipedia in the top right-hand corner. The word was familiar, but the logo was different. The page was also three-dimensional.

"This is a Gridpage," Sue said. "The Grid is the successor to the internet, and the software is capable of projecting three-dimensional images, rather than the flat, two-dimensional screens you would be accustomed to. This isn't a Gridpage from our dimensional brane, but from the so called 'Master Brane'. This is the original timeline before any DAEs took place – before Louise invented the time machine. That's the DAEmap's greatest ability, to retain information from the various timelines."

His three guests were reading as he was talking. Louise realised first.

"Oh my goodness," she said, "these are a list of Neolithic Monuments in Great Britain. And there is no mention of Stonehenge."

"So you're telling me my Nan went back into pre-history and convinced that tribe we met to build Stonehenge. Bloody hell." Dave seemed to think for a bit. Sue didn't like the way this conversation was going, but he knew they needed to know the truth if they were going to be any help at all. It was inevitable.

"What happens if we make changes?" Dave continued. "If I go back and change the past, stop my Nan from causing the building of Stonehenge, then I could wipe the slate clean. Is that what you're saying, that I might need to go back in time and stop the changes that have been made? If I do it right, then I stop my Nan from creating a DAE and we all live happily ever after. I was right all along. We just need to teleport back to when Louise accidently switched on the machine," said Dave.

"Actually, that's not what I'm suggesting. In fact, you probably wouldn't want to do that."

"Why not? It seems the most logical way of stopping the Time Police. No changes to history, no DAEs and therefore no need for the Time Police."

"Well for a start, if we stopped the Time Police ever forming then we would never have remembered them visiting you. They would be but a fading dream, existing only in the part of your consciousness your brain refuses to accept because it doesn't make sense. If you succeeded in destroying the Time Police before their formation, you would have created a new dimensional brane, but we aren't on that brane otherwise we wouldn't remember any Time Police."

"But we can change history, we know that. We just need to make the changes. Then this existence will be the one that was simply a dream. We'll create a new brane, one in which the Time Police were never made."

"But Dave, there are other things that have resulted from your grandmother's time travelling."

"Then we'll go back and fix that too."

"Dave. I'm sorry to say this, but if you did you would destroy yourself."

"How could you possibly know that?"

"I just do."

"That's no answer. How do you know? You're hiding something."

Sue tilted his head down in a feeble attempt to avoid the fact Dave should be told.

"You're sure you wanna know this?" he eventually asked. "It might be hard to hear."

"Tell me. I can take it."

Sue wondered if he could. The whole concept of alternative dimensions is a confusing thing to get your head around. It will more than add to his confusion to reveal his secret too.

*But then he had a right to know, didn't he?*

"Sue," he persisted. "Please tell me. I want to know."

After some deliberation, he decided he would want to know the truth as well. It's the worst thing about being human, not knowing the whole truth. It was only fair that Dave was given answers.

"Son, you might want to sit down."

# CHAPTER 15

## A Chain of Coincidences

## The Hyper-real Universe, Dimension Alpha $2^{-32}$

It might cross your mind in a few years that the future historical events portrayed in this book never actually come into fruition. If it does, then it is further evidence humans are extremely narrow-minded. Even though this story has introduced you to the concept of dimensional branes, most of you will still be selfish enough to believe that your narrative is the only one running, your timeline the one solid and unchanging timeline in existence. Welcome to your reality check.

Think about it logically: if these alternative dimensions are posited and the characters within them are created to talk, feel and think much the same as you, then who are you to deprive them of an existence? If they at some stage departed from your dimensional brane, it doesn't mean that their reality wasn't very close to yours, like two bubbles that spring from the same blow of a bubble-making wand. It's even possible they left you something as wonderful as Stonehenge as their legacy.

Stories are like windows that peer into alternative dimensions. We create our Universes through stories, but not just by sitting down with a pen and an infinitely large notepad. Stories become part of the cultural, even global psyche, and in the process become truer from the telling. Stories define your own existence, but they also create others. If enough people read a story and find it so compelling as to wish for it to be true, does it not make it so? One can almost hear the scribble of J. M. Barrie's pen as it inscribes 'I do believe in fairies, I do believe in fairies'.

## 1853 A.B. - London Township of Sarum and Winchestershire, Western Earth

### Mrs Ellis

Mrs Ellis was having an interesting day. So far she had avoided death at the hands of killer robots, twice, travelled through time, saved the Universe (hopefully) and bought herself a hat from the future. It was pink and fluffy, unless she wanted it to be a different colour or material, at which stage it would metamorphose into a different hat. The girls at the social club would be jealous, no end.

She was under no illusion; there was still a lot more work to do. But so far everything had gone according to the script. Now all she needed to do was find Sue, tell him the plan, then get herself back to her own time, which meant she had to remember the instructions Sue had given her for using the DAEmap. When Sue took her aside in the scientist's house, he explained to her that the device had a homing beacon that would alert the Time Police as to its arrival in their time. This would filter back to a main computer that tracked the location of all DAEmaps. She had to get to the younger Sue as fast as she could to tell him what was going on, which he had told her definitely happened because that was why he was there in her future.

What he didn't say, because he told her he didn't know, was what happened to her after she left him.

She probably shouldn't have bought herself the hat, because she might have drawn unnecessary attention to herself. She had had half an hour to kill before Sue would be at home, and the salesperson had told her that the only currency she needed to buy the hat was Advertising Credits, which she earned by watching an advert for a male strip club show downtown. This advert involved a load of half-naked men dancing around her.

She could get used to the future.

Now the time had arrived for her to meet Sue, so she was stood in a doorway waiting for him to walk back to his flat. The familiar sight of a leather Stetson hat rounded the corner, and Sue, looking exactly the same as he does/did in about ten year's time – should she say centuries ago – was wearing it.

She watched him walk up to the front door of his ivy-clad apartment, scan his eyes in an eye scanner thingy, and enter his apartment. She waited a minute then walked to his front door and rang what she hoped was a doorbell. Sue's face quickly appeared in three dimensions, in a square box next to the ringer.

"Yellow," he said a familiar Southern US drawl.

"Oh, hi Sue. You don't know me, but I am called Mrs Ellis. I am a friend of yours, although you don't know it yet."

"Err, sorry lady but I've become a bit disillusioned with religion of late. No chance of converting me, I'm afraid."

"Oh, no, that's not what I'm here for. You told me to tell you I have news the Timeseekers might find useful."

"Lady, keep your voice down."

There was a long pause, then, "You better come in."

The sound of a lock sliding out of place came from within the big metal door. It swung inwards. Mrs Ellis pushed it ajar and walked in. The house of the future was a sparse place on the inside, which was exaggerated by the contrast of the leafy and natural exterior. The walls were shiny and industrial, almost purely aluminium. Perhaps that was down to the apparent lack of female companionship in Sue's life.

"Through here," Sue's voice called from the end of the hall. She followed the sound of his voice until she found herself in what was presumably a kitchen. It had a large table in the middle, which was again made purely of metal. Sue was sitting down, a couple of cowboy boots elevated on to the metal table in front of him.

"Hi Sue," she said with familiarity. He didn't look as surprised to see her as she thought he would be.

"Are you the messenger, as was foretold by Lord Armitage?"

"Haven't got a bloody clue. I am a messenger, but I was sent by you, from your own future."

"Well that probably makes you the messenger then. I can't see myself sending someone with a message, without making 'em stipulate they ain't the messenger. So the next decision I need to make is whether I trust you."

"You said you would say that. You told me I just need to tell you something no else could possibly know, a secret that only you are privy to."

Sue eyed her suspiciously. "Go on then, tell me this secret."

"Well when you were still a nipper..."

"Sorry, a 'nipper'?" Sue interrupted.

"Yeah, a little one. Wee slip of a lad, youngster. Now when you were a nipper, you were a very religious person. You dreamed of travelling back in time to see a prophet, someone I know from my time: Bob Geldof. See in my time he's just a singer, well he's not even one of those really. I guess he's a humanitarian who really likes swearing."

"That doesn't tell me anything, other than the fact you've done your research."

"Hold your horses, I'm not done yet." Mrs Ellis took a seat at the table. "When you grew up, you started working for the Department of Bio thingy-majigy."

"Biotechnology."

"Yes, that's the one. When you were there you were working on a project that would make time travel safer. You broke all sorts of laws to go back to the time of Mr Geldof, just to get a sneaky peek at the man you so revered."

Sue had turned white but didn't say anything, just looked at her through intense eyes.

"Despite me knowing this, right now you still don't trust me. Fair enough. I could be a Government agent trying to make you slip up.

So here is the part that definitely no one knows, other than the other you, and of course me. You went back and found your prophet, and you didn't like what you saw. The real Bob was nothing like the scriptures suggested. He was a disappointment compared to the legend. Oh, of course he was a lovely bloke – still is for me, because he's not dead yet in my time. And he did some wonderful things. But he was manipulated into something he wasn't by your Master, so he could be used as a tool for controlling the population. You couldn't stand the truth, could you?"

Sue's face softened. "They knew he was mortal." He paused as if thinking what to say. "Just human, like you and me. Our rulers have travelled to every era past and future, so have unprecedented access to the true course of humanity's history. Our naive civilization believed everything written in the history books, because why would our rulers lie? I became disillusioned with everything I had lived for my whole life." Sue paused, thinking. "You're right. No one in the world knows that except me."

"So now do you believe I am who I say I am?" asked Mrs Ellis.

"I will believe when you tell me who the chosen one is."

"Oh, I will do more than that. I will tell you where you're going to meet her."

"So it's a her?" asked Sue.

"She is indeed. A lovely old lady by the name of Nana Barb."

Mrs Ellis got Sue up to speed with everything she knew, aware that she needed to get going before the Time Police noticed her DAEmap's signal. She told him about her dreams, about the robots who tortured her, and about being rescued by the Alsatians. She also told him every detail she could remember about her conversation with the older Sue. She explained about *Luigi's* and that he would meet Nana Barb there. Sue listened intently. He even recorded the conversation so he didn't miss anything.

When she was done, Sue asked her if she wanted to stay for something to eat.

"Oh no thanks," Mrs Ellis replied. "I've got to get going, otherwise the Time Police will find me."

"Why would they be able to find you?"

"Because I've got their DAEmap thingy."

Sue very suddenly looked extremely mad, and the atmosphere changed completely. Mrs Ellis immediately knew the situation had turned bad. "What? Why in Bob's blasphemous name would I ever let you bring a DAEmap into my house?"

She was suddenly very worried. "You didn't mention it."

"Did I happen to mention what happened when you left me?"

"No, you didn't say what I was meant to do next." Mrs Ellis really didn't like the look on Sue's face.

"In that case, you're not gonna be very happy with this."

Sue quickly reached over and pressed a button in the middle of the table. Mrs Ellis felt her body being pinned to her seat, a sensation very similar to the time she had been restrained by the Time Police.

"What the hell are you doing?" she demanded. "I thought we were on the same side."

"Sorry ma'am, but you can't go bringing a DAEmap into my house. Because of my position they will wipe my memory. You will spend the rest of your life in prison, but I simply cannot afford to miss my date with this Nana Barb. There are bigger things at work here."

"But you must have known this in the future. Surely you could have told me in a different way."

"I can't answer that I'm afraid. Perhaps I will tell you next decade."

Mrs Ellis's heart dropped.

"What is going to happen to me? Will they kill me? I've already experienced the pain they can put someone under. I don't want to go through that again."

"Don't worry, that won't happen to you – that much I can promise."

"Why not?" Mrs Ellis replied, puzzled.

"Because I've just wiped your memory," came the blunt, uncaring reply.

What could she do? She had to warn her son and his friends, but without any memory of the events, how could she do this? It seemed as though she had failed in her quest. At least they would be safer with her not knowing about what they were up to. That gave her some small solace at least.

No less than ten minutes later, Sue was letting two androgynous identical twins in through his front door. The twins walked into the kitchen. She tried to wriggle free, but could barely move her arms an inch.

A chillingly familiar, emotionless voice issued a command. "You are under arrest, in the name of the Master. Come quietly or come dead."

Mrs Ellis, never having felt so let down in all her life, kept her mouth shut and as she felt her memories leave her head like a hard drive being wiped clean, she let them take her away.

## 1862 A.B. - London Township of Sarum and Winchestershire, Western Earth

### Nana Barb

Barbara sat back in her seat and awaited the story the cowboy promised to tell. She felt incredibly nervous, but at the same time hugely relieved that someone knew what was happening to her. Hopefully he might be able to get her out of this mess.

"I wouldn't get too comfortable because we're going outside," Sue said. "It's not the best place to talk in here."

"Oh, well in that case I'd better finish my tea."

Nana Barb finished her tea then followed the cowboy outside, her intrigue rising all the time.

They walked a few hundred metres down the road and turned into an empty street. Before the cowboy spoke to her he turned to the robot and issued some commands that her mind translated.

"Guidebot please enter reprogramming mode, authorisation 2, 7, 9, Lima, Echo, 6."

Guidebot peered up at the cowboy. "Confirm your name please," he said in an alien monotone. Nana Barb much preferred the Italian voice.

"The Colonel," the cowboy replied.

"Please submit password."

"Gloria," he replied instantly.

"Finally, please submit your iris for verification."

The cowboy pulled something out of his belt and waved it in front of the little robot's face. He appeared to shut down.

Sue continued, "Now please disable your Grid connection and reroute any messages directed to the Master to internal storage pod G16."

Nana Barb had no idea what was happening, but let the man make changes to her robot. He seemed to know what he was doing.

"Now, create a secure connection to the Grid with a new untraceable GPID. I am placing a new chip into your main circuitry; recognise it and accept the reprogramming. Now reanimate and return to your task of serving this lady."

Guidebot's eyes lit up once again and he winked at Nana Barb. "Back with you ma'am. At your service."

"Oh, jolly good," said Nana Barb, "I was rather enjoying your company."

"Ahh, ain't you the sweetest?"

"What did you do to him?" Nana Barb asked, turning to Sue.

"All Guidebots are programmed to feed information back to the Master, so he can keep track of non-civilians. You don't have an ID chip, which makes you a non-civilian. Time travel is illegal, so if you had slipped up by revealing you came from the past, you might have been sent to the interrogation chamber."

Barbara felt the blood drain from her face. *Interrogation chamber?* That didn't sound like a cheerful place.

Sue laughed, inappropriately she felt. "Don't worry," he said, "they haven't resorted to torturing old ladies just yet. They have a way of telling if you are lying, so you only need to tell the truth with them. Fortunately for you there was no intent, so they wouldn't have harmed a hair on your head."

"Thank goodness. At least the people of this time have retained some civility then."

Guidebot chuckled, if a robot was capable of such things. "I wouldn't exactly call the Master a person, lady. You's is quite backwards, ain't you? Who are you lady? You must be important if The Colonel feels the need to reprogram me."

"Well actually Guidebot, I'm sorry to say that you've been duped. I ain't The Colonel, just an anarchic member of the Timeseekers. This lovely lady is a Time Traveller, but an unwilling one I must tell ya. Ain't that right, deary?"

"Yes, but I want to know how you could possibly know that."

"A Time Traveller and a Timeseeker." Guidebot made a whistling noise as if he was trying to mimic taking a sharp intake of breath. "Good job you disabled my reporting program. You would have turned me into a dirty, nasty snitch otherwise. And here we are, getting on so well."

"To answer your question," said Sue, cutting across Guidebot, "I had a chance meeting with someone. Do you know a certain Mrs Ellis?"

"Why yes, of course. She's the mother of David's best friend. How on Earth do you know of her?"

"Because I met her about a week ago, according to today's date. She travelled to my time, and came to find me. In fact she did more than simply find me – she knocked on my darn door and shook my hand as if I were a long-lost friend."

"Well I never, how very bizarre."

"I was shocked to say the least." He paused and cocked his ear as if he was listening for something. His voice lowered into a whisper.

"We can't talk much longer here. A screen has just been turned on in our area, which means a servant of the Master might overhear us. Follow me up the road."

Nana Barb followed the cowboy's lead. As they walked he carried on explaining in a whisper.

"Listen, the short version is this: She met my future self in the past, which is your present of course."

"Golly, this is confusing to say the least," Barbara tried to whisper back but her voice was too croaky.

"Yes I appreciate that, but try to bear with me. So my future self told Mrs Ellis that she would travel into her future and meet a ten years younger version of myself, and once she met me she would need to pass on a very important message to someone. That someone was you. I had to tell you what was happening to you, and how you can stop it from happening.

"Barbara, do you trust me?"

"Well we've just met, but what choice do I have?"

"Fair enough. Walk with me in silence for a bit, and when we get to my house I will give you the tools you need to get you back to your time. It's not safe for us to carry on talking like this in public."

"OK, then let's go. Does he come with me?" Nana Barb gestured towards the little robot.

"Of course, he's your property ain't he?"

"I guess he is."

"You didn't wanna leave me, did you lady?" said Guidebot.

"No, of course not. As I said before, I'm starting to quite enjoy your company."

They stepped on to the main street and started walking. "It doesn't look as though there are people watching or listening to us. I always thought the future would be like 1984, with cameras watching our every move."

"They are, but you just can't see them. Many of the glass screens – called Bentham Screens – you can see around you can easily be turned into different materials, whether visual screens or cameras. That window there," he said as he pointed at a window in a tree bark-lined building, "could just as easily be a camera. That's the beauty, when you don't know if you are being watched, but there is always a danger you are, you tend to behave better. In many ways it is exactly like 1984, although with a much higher quality of life, some would argue."

"I feel like I'm in an episode of *Big Brother*," Nana Barb said.

"What's *Big Brother*? Does it have anything to do with the book *1984*?" Sue asked.

"Oh no, it's quite different. It's a programme from my time about some people who get put in prison for being arrogant or racist. They film it all for our amusement."

"Sounds inhumane."

"Oh no, they stop them before they kill each other."

The cowboy smiled as if her response amused him.

"Can I ask you," said Nana Barb, "why do they all keep saying I'm from Mars?"

Sue scratched his chin. "Mars is inhabited nowadays. A group of rebels known as the Free Radicals had grown disillusioned with the Master and the eternal youthfulness of his citizens, so were given the option of living on Mars and forming their own society. They speak English as it is the universal language, a bit like Latin would be for you I s'pose. They also don't believe in the anti-aging methods we use."

"That explains why they thought I was a Martian then. But how can they live there? I thought the planet was barren and didn't have an atmosphere."

"Oh it was, once. Originally the inhabitants lived in Biospheres. Twenty years ago Mars came back into the public eye as they switched to a terraformed atmosphere. You can pretty much go where you want now, as the air is perfectly breathable."

"Blimey. I've said it before, and I'll say it again no doubt. Wonders never cease."

"It's true, if someone experiences new technologies without being privy to the advances, it will seem like magic. I suppose you are experiencing quite a similar feeling the indigenous folks of Australia or America probably felt during the beginnings of colonialism."

They rounded a corner and spotted a group of people kneeling on prayer mats. They were the first people they had seen since the restaurant. The roads were eerily quiet, presumably because everyone was at work, or travelling on the skyway.

As they got closer to the praying people, Nana Barb realised there were a number of rats on the floor in front of them.

"Oh my word," she said, "those rats are eating their food!"

"Yes, they know that. It is an offering; the rats are sacred."

"Rats are sacred here?"

"Yep. I appreciate that must seem funny to you, but people here respect the rat, especially in towns of fast growth. Right, this is us. We just need to stand near the Skyway stop."

"We're not going on that thing are we?"

"Oh, don't worry. It's perfectly safe. Besides, you just gotta see the view."

The hologram by the advertising board made towards them, but Sue waved him off with a shake of his hand. Almost as soon as they had stood still, the huge Skyway carriage dropped out of the sky once again. This time, they stepped on board.

As soon as they had taken their seat – a nice young man in a floor-length dress, who also worked in advertising, awkwardly offered Nana Barb his seat; he obviously understood the etiquette with old people, but clearly hadn't had the need to put it into practice before – the Skyway lifted high into the sky. Amazingly, Nana Barb's stomach didn't drop. She always hated that feeling of a rollercoaster dipping, and had expected the same to happen with this cart. Before she had the chance to consider how this stomach-saving technology might work, her breath was taken away in quite a different way altogether.

They were apparently flying, but without wings. Barbara could see a wire attached to the top of the carriage, but it seemed to disappear into an invisible fog. Below her stretched out the landscape of the city she had lived near her whole life, which was now well beyond recognition. She suddenly spotted one familiar landmark. A spire stretched into the sky, flanked by two towering buildings.

"Salisbury Cathedral," she exclaimed. "It's still here!"

Sue laughed heartily. "Indeed it is," he said.

Despite all the questions she had, she remained quiet for the rest of the journey. The sun was starting to break through the clouds to shine on the city below, and it looked absolutely beautiful. City didn't seem an appropriate word really. It looked like an oversized forest. She thought it was wonderful that the future had once again embraced nature. No longer did bare 60s concrete poison the landscape as even the smallest building seemed to be clad in natural material. The city seemed so much more alive. She wondered if this move towards living building materials was due to a return to nature, or whether it was helping to meet the demands of energy use and over-populating. She made a mental note to ask Sue when she got her breath back.

A few minutes later and they were walking up the street towards a block of apartments almost entirely covered in a creeping plant similar to ivy. Sue seemed to notice her interest.

"Not just there for show," he said. "It powers the whole house using nothing other than a supercharged type of photosynthesis: natural photovoltaics. Almost the only food we eat is growing on the roof of the block."

He held his eye up to a panel next to his door. A whirring and clunking followed, and the door opened. He led her inside and sat her down at the kitchen table. He offered her a cup of tea, which was music to her ears. It wasn't one of those fancy cups of tea either; it was good old English breakfast with a drop of milk. And he even allowed her half a spoon of sugar.

Sue started to talk, and so she listened.

"You are lost in time, Barbara, and there is precious little I can do about it. There's no point beating around the bush, so I am sorry if I seem callous in the way I'm telling you this. You were sent through time without a DAEmap, which is a device that amongst other things controls your position in spacetime. Without control, you are left to flitter through history without direction, a tool of both Fate and Nature in their continuous battle. There is a way of saving you, but I fear it will be a few years yet before it happens."

Nana Barb's heart dropped. Her chances of going home were bleak, and the possibility of seeing her family again seemed to be ebbing away.

Sue continued: "By the end of this conversation, so I have been told, you will disappear on me, but I have no idea when this conversation is considered finished. For that reason, I am going to keep talking for as long as you are still with me. Anything I think is useful, I will tell you: How we plan to rescue you; the tools you need to survive.

"Firstly, you are going to be rescued by the Timeseekers, many years in the future – many even in my future. We have no idea just how many years could pass on your timeline before that happens. We can't even be sure you will be rescued, because histories both past and future can be changed. You need to be very careful. We will do everything we can to keep you alive, but you must also do everything within your power to make yourself easy for us to find. You have to do something so monumental that it makes it into history books. At some stage on your travels, an opportunity will present itself. You will just have to be patient. Whatever happens, you cannot use your real name to make it into the books. You have to use your grandchildren's nickname for you – Nana Barb. When that name appears in the history books, we will know, and then we will know where to find you once we have come up with a cure for your condition. It is absolutely essential that you make the history books prior to your own time. I would say 1800 onwards would be best.

"The robot is going with you, as both a companion and protector. When I reprogrammed him, I also put a small chip on him that links him to you. We use chips like these to allow time travellers to take inanimate objects through time."

"Who are you?" Nana Barb burst in with, despite the fact she knew time was short. Why should she simply trust him at his say so? "You said you work in advertising insurance," she continued, "yet you know so much about time travel, and you claim to know how to save the Universe. Everyone knows ad men are arrogant. Are you just acting the part here?"

"But I also said I used to work for the Government. Everything I know about time travel I learned from my job in the Biotechnology department."

"Is that like bio-warfare?" Barbara asked.

"No, although arguably their true intentions were no less unscrupulous. Look, there isn't much I can do to convince you I'm trustworthy. You just need to follow your gut. And the way I see it, I'm the only one you've met so far who has a blind clue what in Bob's name is happening to you. You can choose to trust me, or you can die on your next shift."

Barbara looked at him carefully. He was right, what choice did she have?

"Go on then, what else do I need to know?" she eventually asked.

"OK, so we were talking 'bout that there little robot. Obviously people from the past won't be used to seeing a small robot, so you will need to cover his face and body whenever you have gone back in time from today's date. Say he has a rare skin condition so can't be exposed to the sun."

Barbara nodded to show she was following, but deep down she found his instructions hard to follow. She had never been so terrified in her life.

Sue continued, "Guidebots are incredibly well-versed in all historical events. Reprogramming him also unlocked his classified knowledge banks, so he should have knowledge of most futures, and you will also have a true history that hasn't been warped by the Master. To keep him alive you will need to fill his hydrogen fuel cells up with propane every three months."

Sue showed her a nozzle on the back of his foot.

"You will find propane in most eras, so that shouldn't cause you too much trouble."

"How will I know how to fill it up?" Barbara asked.

The robot tugged at her skirt. "I can do it, lady. No problems there." He sounded excited.

Barbara felt sick to the stomach. She listened as Sue quickly carried on.

"Language might be a problem. As you've probably noticed, in the first eight hours you will be able to talk in any language you need to. When history realises you are in the wrong time and place you lose that ability and history suddenly tries to get rid of you. It becomes very dangerous to exist. In the first eight hours you are virtually invincible since you might as well not exist. You need to use this to your advantage – use the first eight hours to get yourself somewhere safe. After that, avoid any contact with anyone so that you slip under nature's radar."

Nana Barb suddenly felt a tingly feeling. "Sue, it's coming. I can feel it."

"OK, that's fine. I have told you as much as you need to know. One last thing. Look after yourself. All of existence depends on it."

With that she broke apart and once more disappeared into time.

# CHAPTER 16

## The 'Master'plan

## 1863 A.B. - London Township of Sarum and Winchestershire, Western Earth

### Dave

Dave was about to hear something revolutionary, and he knew it. It was difficult to pinpoint the exact moment in the conversation when he realised the truth, but he knew deep down that it was well before Sue actually told him. It just seemed so obvious. Dave suddenly felt very thin, like the smoke of a fading campfire as it's snubbed out by a downpour. He felt insubstantial on the backdrop of his environment, as though everything around him was real, but he was not.

Nonetheless, he nodded for Sue to continue. "I want to know the truth," he said again, "I want to hear you say it."

"OK Davc, as long as you're sure?"

"I've never been so sure in my life."

"Well Dave, if your grandmother didn't time travel, she wouldn't have ended up with your granddad. A search of your original family records on the DAEmap showed that a certain Robert Wilson died in France in 1941. Your grandmother retained the name Barbara Smithson. She wouldn't have had any children, let alone grandchildren."

Dave felt on the verge of passing out.

"Are you telling me what I think you're telling me?" he asked.

"Yes I am," Sue replied. "Dave, before you woke up this morning, you didn't even exist."

He was so sure that he existed. *I think therefore I am*. Who had said that? He was able to think, feel, breathe as much as the next person; didn't that give him the right to stake a claim on reality? And yet he had just been told that he didn't exist when he woke up this morning. But he had still lived a whole life. He had memories, could remember his aunt picking him up after school because his mother was always too busy with work. He could remember the morning when she had taken him away with her on a business trip because she couldn't find a babysitter. The meeting had been cancelled at the last minute so they had taken a trip to the seaside. It was the only holiday he had ever had with her.

He remembered hearing the news...

*How could you hear about someone else dying if you don't exist?*

His Nan had told him. He had come home from college, not at all surprised that his mother wasn't back from her scheduled business trip to Australia (she sold trolley parts to supermarket chains, the magnetic brake part that stops you stealing them). She was a day late, but that wasn't surprising. The truth was she had been there to see a specialist about her brain tumour. She wasn't there on business at all.

She had died in the surgeon's practice. The tumour had ruptured right there and then, and there was nothing they could do. It was the fact he felt so let down that hurt the most. But that didn't matter now, because he didn't even exist.

Why did he feel so unreal, even though he had memories of a whole life up until now? Everyone else in the room is a lot closer to the Universe, that's why. They exist on every single axiom of the Universe, every which way you look at it. He lived on this one only and that through a bizarre twist of fate. He was the opposite of a crash survivor, elated to have survived their near-death experience when there is every chance their parallel selves had been wiped from existence, their claim to reality hanging by a blissful thread. He, David, had always been clinging to a thread, and now it felt as though the thread was rotten, and someone had a plan to cut it out.

It just dawned on him that he had come so close to bringing about the end of his own life. He wouldn't be here now if he had persuaded the others to stop his grandmother from taking her first temporal shift. He had effectively sacrificed her life for his.

It wasn't the facts and particulars that made him feel so empty; it was the fact he had always felt so empty, so lost. The Universe had never really meant for him to exist, and he knew it.

## Louise

Dave came back from the bathroom. Louise felt concern for the poor lad. In truth she was really warming to him, even if he was awkward and bashful. It can't be the most pleasant news to hear that the Universe never planned for you to exist. (Of course we Web-spinners know different – we *made* him exist. He is an essential part of our plans, but he won't know that for a while yet.)

Despite all this, Louise wanted to slap Dave around the face. The news was hard to bear, clearly, but the whole of existence may well depend on their next move. *He lives and breathes, so get over it.* And he remembers his life, doesn't he? What is life other than a series of memories mixed with dreams for the future? The now is instant, yet eternal, which is why she lives for the now. His now is a more comfortable existence than an orphan in a slum of a developing country, his memories no less real than hers.

But everyone in the room – Louise felt at least – knew it didn't feel right that he was here. She just couldn't put her finger on the reason why, but it definitely didn't feel right.

Still, she walked up to him and put her arms around his neck, pulling his head on to her shoulder. He relaxed at her touch, but didn't put his arms around her. She felt her face heating up, so she awkwardly pushed him off her before it became too uncomfortable.

"I'm all right," he declared. "I'm here now, so what does it matter how I got here?"

Sue took back control of the situation. "So we need to plan our next move. We need to outfox the Time Police."

"Do you have a plan?" Simon asked.

"Not as such. I have an idea what to do, but not how we do it."

"OK," said Dave, wiping away moisture from the side of his eyes. "Tell us what you think we should do. We're up for this." He had a new look of resolve in his eyes, and that was good.

Sue looked him in the eyes for a while, then replied, "First of all, before I became a Timeseeker, I used to work for the Government's Biotechnology department. Our principal role was to build artificially coded life, genetically designed to perform the tasks we asked of them. The Master, our ruler, is one of these creatures, which we name Drones. As I said, he was built to rule and nothing else. He has been programmed – much like a robot would be, 'cause essentially that's all these things are: robots with flesh – to be single-minded in his task. The only problem is, if he can be programmed, he can also be reprogrammed."

"You make it sound so easy," said Dave.

"It is easy. Surprisingly easier than you'd think – if you've got the right tools that is."

"The Deathstar Exhaust Trick," Simon said.

"Come again?"

"The Deathstar, off of Star Wars. For the purposes of the plot there is one ultimate task, no plan B. Win or lose it all."

"If you say so. Well I think it might be a bit more difficult now, because it's my belief that he has already been reprogrammed by someone before."

"What makes you so sure?" asked Dave. The colour had come back into his face. Having something to focus on was definitely helping him.

"Because he has been manipulating his subjects. This was never meant to happen; he was made in the first place to be incorruptible. Only humans are capable of such gross deceit. And while we're at it, creating the Time Police simply don't make sense. They do more harm than good. So it seems as though there's another purpose to their existence. I can't see why the Master would have commissioned them, unless he has been reprogrammed by a human with ulterior motives."

"Who would have done this?" Louise asked.

"It's hard to say. Knowing the answer might well reveal our true enemy. What's important now is what we do with it."

"The way I see it," Simon said, "If he's been reprogrammed once before, it means we can do it again."

"Would that be possible?" Louise asked.

"Theoretically, yes. But it ain't that easy. The workers in the Government building are cagier than the Red Lady's husband[4]."

"We have no idea who the Red Lady is," she said. "You must have some connections from the time you worked there. Couldn't you pull in some favours?"

"Not at all. I don't work there anymore, and it's very unusual for someone to be allowed to leave their post in a Government agency. In fact, in my time it's pretty darn impossible to change jobs at all. I managed to hoodwink them into thinking I was depressed. Ain't nothing scares an organisation as much as depression, since it's the only thing that's still subjective. Because of all that, it means I am being watched closer now than ever before. Just to cover their asses, they put a tracker on my identity chip that will alert any Government officials if I try to get anywhere close to an official building."

"Could you get us in?" This was Dave, now with a new look of steely resolve. "We don't have identity chips."

Sue seemed to ponder this. "Actually, that's not a bad idea. Since you don't have ID chips, they don't have the slightest bit of information about you. You are virtually invisible."

"Does everyone have these ID chips then?" asked Simon.

"They do indeedy," Sue replied. "You're given them from birth so they can keep track of you. Virtually wiped out crime in the process."

4 The Red Lady, the former Queen of England after the Second Restoration, was so called for her love of blood and even bigger lust for men. It is prophesied that she bed every enemy she faced in battle, before unceremoniously killing them. Her husband, Prince Greyband of Cymru, known as Prince Suspicious was so named after he publicly questioned her insistence to go to war against nations with attractive leaders.

"So that settles it then," said Dave. "We break into some Government building, evade Government agents and reprogram a biogenetic Drone to call off the pursuit of the Time Police. What could possibly go wrong?" He laughed nervously.

Out of her peripheral vision, Louise caught sight of Sue smirking in the reflection of the kitchen cupboards. She instantly distrusted that smirk, but couldn't say why. If they couldn't trust Sue, who could they trust?

## The Hyper-real Universe, Dimension Alpha $2^{-32}$

So now we come towards the climax of this first book about Nana Barb. We are about to change narrator again, but this time I will leave it to you to guess the extreme we tend towards. Wretched bad luck or uncanny good fortune?

Unfortunately, the safety of your characters is of no concern to us. Much like Sue condemning Mrs Ellis to the Master's dungeons, there are bigger things at work here. We choose narrator based on the particular tactics required by us to win our war with Fate (and it is a war; I know it has only been alluded to thus far, but the full details will eventually be revealed to you over the remaining chronicles). All battles require sacrifice, so what makes ours so different?

## 1863 A.B. - London Township of Sarum and Winchestershire, Western Earth

### Sue

They sat and discussed the plan for the next few hours. It had become dark outside and Dave and Louise realised it had been a long time since they had slept, even though it would probably be a number of hours before Simon would be tired. Dave still felt the grogginess that comes from losing sleep through alcohol and he had yawned his way through most of the plans. Sue knew nothing would happen until the next day anyway because all Government buildings close at 7.00 p.m. sharp. They would have to sleep the night, and Dave and Louise would have to sleep soon because their body clocks were skewed.

He hastily made up the spare bed and put a couple of duvets on the lounge sofas for Simon and himself. Dave had a big day tomorrow, so he could have his room. And besides, there were a few things he needed to do before he would get any sleep.

Dave went straight into the bedroom and started getting ready for bed, while Sue showed Louise how to work the Steam-Jet in the bathroom. Simon wanted to know if they had any 'mega-sized TV screens' in the future, so he had to break it to him that there was no television in the future.

"What do you do for fun then?" Simon asked him.

"People learn things, better themselves," Sue replied.

"Like read books? Jesus wept, that's boring."

"There's a lot more to life than watching the fictional and highly unlikely dramas of television. And besides, nowadays we've got the X-Grid to keep you entertained."

"The X-Grid? What's that?"

"You remember when we talked about the Grid earlier? It's kind of an advanced version of your internet. The X-Grid is a second internet designed entirely for entertainment."

"Why would you want a second internet? Is it to stop the first one slowing down?"

"Actually, you've yet to see the most amazing part of the Grid. My kitchen table represents just a small part of it. The real basis of the Grid is virtual reality. You can enter its framework and walk around much like you can the real world. It looks like a large city with buildings, offices and libraries."

"That sounds pretty cool."

"It is very cool and very practical too. It's easier to visualise things based on their real-world context, and the Grid's virtual reality engine helps with that."

"Err, as cool as it sounds, what has that got to do with this X-Grid thing?"

"The Grid is for learning, and the X-Grid is for experiencing. It is a completely different environment, so it exists completely separately. Think of it as one giant version of a role-playing game. A virtual reality Second Life."

Sue walked Simon into the X-Grid cabin. "The first time you enter it can be pretty darn disorientating, so I'll have to restrict it to a small area. What's your favourite type of movie?"

"Action thriller," Simon replied without skipping a beat. "The *Fast and Furious* movies were the best series of movie ever made."

"*Fast and Furious?* I don't know it."

"Fast cars and hot women."

"Ah, I see. Well that works pretty well with the X-Grid. Jump on in and enjoy!"

Sue left Simon to enjoy the X-Grid, a scaled-down version of it anyway; he didn't want to frazzle the poor boy's brain – or any other part of his body, for that matter. Louise and Dave were already asleep, their body clocks well ahead of Simon's due to their adventures in the past. With their attention elsewhere, he could sneak out and get that niggling job out of the way.

## Louise

Louise pretended to be asleep in the spare room when Sue came in. She was exhausted, so it took some effort to stop herself from actually nodding off. She felt him staring at her, which was somewhat unnerving.

*What is it about him I don't trust?*

The door closed, which meant he had left the room. Louise opened her eyes to darkness. She contemplated following him to see where he was going, but what would that achieve? She had to trust him, didn't she? Why else would he have brought them here if he wasn't on their side? He'd either just not have bothered, or he would have handed them over to the Time Police.

## Sue

Despite walking briskly, the journey took him over half an hour. It would have been much quicker to take the Skyway but he didn't want to run the risk of his journey being traced. He walked into the lobby of the imposing building, the tallest of the skyscrapers in the Township.

The guard at the door scanned him as he entered then nodded as he let him pass. "The usual room," is all he said.

Sue walked into the building and straight to the elevator. He felt nervous as he usually did when he met the head Timeseeker, and Suegard Amyson was not a man who got nervous easily. He stepped on to the round disc that would elevate him to the 123rd floor of the building. He felt the familiar feeling of his feet sticking to the disc as the safety device engaged. His stomach dropped slightly as the elevator took off and again as it came to a stop a few moments later. He walked along the corridor at a steady pace and came to a stop when he reached a door at the end, composing himself before walking into the room beyond.

"Please sit," said a voice before he had a chance to see its owner.

The room contained nothing but a large table with two tall red chairs situated at either end. The chair at the back of the room was turned away from him so Sue couldn't see its occupant, but he knew it was Lord Armitage nonetheless. He took the chair closest to him since it was the only option.

"How are we progressing?" Lord Armitage wasn't one to beat around the bush.

"Nicely," Sue replied, blunt by intent.

"Are we any closer to finding the cure to our lady's unfortunate condition?"

"No, my liege. My colleagues are looking at a number of options, but so far none are yielding the result we hoped for."

The Lord still did not turn his face to him. "Well it will come, if she is indeed our saviour as the prophet promised. What of the others? Did they agree to your plan to take down the Master?"

"They did. It was easier than I thought. I just had to make them think it was their idea."

"Yes, very cunning. What do you want, a medal?"

It hurt Sue that he should be so spiteful and sarcastic, but he didn't let his face show. Back turned or not he could feel eyes watching him. "My liege, I... I need your help for tomorrow." It irked him that he should have to ask for it, but he simply wouldn't succeed without it. "I need technology from your time to help me infiltrate the Centre of Ruling."

The reply took a full minute to come. "You ask much," he said eventually.

"I would not ask if it wasn't essential to our cause."

"It would ruin everything if you were to be caught. You know you are under close scrutiny."

"Indeed I do, and you should know I would not ask if it weren't completely essential. I need to be able to communicate with the others when they are inside."

"You cannot leave them instructions?"

"No, our ways are too alien for them. We haven't the time to train them in the local customs. And we wouldn't want you to lose your little pet."

The Lord's voice stayed calm, but Sue could tell he'd angered him. "She is a mere speck of dust. She is no pet. The boy must be kept safe though if possible. I believe he may be a protector of our alleged saviour. I will allow you this once, but the first sign of danger and you destroy the technology."

"Of course, my liege. And if our friends fall into the wrong hands?"

"Then get away from here as fast as you can. Lose yourself in time."

# CHAPTER 17

## The Centre of Ruling

## 1863 A.B. - London Township of Sarum and Winchestershire, Western Earth

### Simon

Simon woke up to the sound of Sue snoring. He had slept like a log, exhausted from playing that damned X-Grid most of the night. It was addictive to say the least. He had turned off the power to the booth and gone to bed before Sue returned. He was out late so he must have been busy, whatever he was doing.

He went into the kitchen to find Dave and Louise already up. Dave was playing with the blessed food maker.

"It's amazing, it actually prints the molecules of food like a 3D printer," Dave said.

Simon didn't care how it worked, as long as it made good bacon and eggs. "Yeah, amazing. Order me a fry-up will you, mate?"

"Sorry my friend, but no can do. You can have a veggie breakfast with Streaky Facon™. I think Sue must be a vegetarian because none of the food has meat in it."

"What about that casserole we had yesterday. That was definitely beef."

"Well apparently it wasn't. There's a Beefish Casserole on the menu, but that doesn't sound like it's got real beef in it to me."

"Huh, well I never. I'll have a veggie breakfast with Facon™ then please, mate."

Simon watched through the glass as the remoleculator made his breakfast. Dave was right, it *sprayed* the meal into existence. When they encountered it for the first time yesterday, he hadn't even thought about how it might work. And the best thing was the food that came out of it tasted divine. The Streaky Facon™ actually tasted *better* than the real thing!

Simon was back at his favourite new invention, trying to order seconds, when Sue walked in. "Alrigh' Sue. What happened to you last night?"

"Nothing," he replied, "just a few things to sort out for today."

"Fair enough. Want any breakfast, cowboy?"

"I'll just have a croissant and a coffee please. I'm going to need the caffeine for today I think."

"No worries."

## Dave

Half an hour later and they were riding the Skyway to the train station. This was the first time our trio had even heard of the Skyway, let alone ridden in it. Dave sat in stunned silence the whole way, a mixture of awe, fear and anticipation causing his voice to fail him. He caught Louise's eyes in the reflection of glass as they were peering out of the window, and she smiled and turned to him. She leaned forwards quite intimately and whispered in his ear, "The future is incredible. I could get used to this, couldn't you?"

Dave just smiled and nodded in reply. She was obviously whispering in case their suspicious talk was overheard, but to him it was a very important milestone that she felt comfortable getting so close.

"Right, this is our stop," Sue called out to break the moment. "We have to change here to get the regular railway."

And so they boarded the SuperTrans Express to Queen Brittany Station, a journey that took less than half an hour. The entire journey was made in silence. They couldn't discuss the plan, since it was highly illegal; they couldn't talk about time travel, since that was also illegal; they couldn't talk about their own time, since it might lead on to questions that they couldn't answer without declaring their illegal status. Instead, Dave spent the entire journey reflecting on the events of the past two days of his own timeline.

He thought right back to waking up on the living room sofa, kicked out of his own bed by a young woman well out of his league. And now here he was, travelling across a future version of his country to try and stop a futuristic race of robots from following them through time to eliminate them, with a slightly older woman who was even further out of his league.

He suddenly remembered the policeman from the station the morning before, telling him there had been a UFO sighting in the area. He wondered if that might be connected to these events somehow. He made a mental note to mention it to the others later (although he would forget to, which could have solved all sorts of hassle if he had remembered).

## Louise

As they travelled on the SuperTrans Express, Louise pondered the events of the past two days. It was a lot to take in. Firstly, her machine had worked. More than that – this guy from the future turns up to proclaim her as pretty much the inventor of time travel. She was famous in the future, and would be more so if the Master hadn't covered up her achievements. If they succeeded today, would she be able to reclaim her rightful place in history? That's certainly another reason to try and get it right.

All scientists secretly aim to achieve immortality, and she was within a whisper.

## Simon

*Something like a phenomenon, something like a phenomenon, ohh, something like a phenomenon...*

This story would make a hell of a rap, Simon thought to himself. Biggie Smalls and Tupac watch out, I'm gonna make millions.

## Dave

The train pulled into Queen Brittany Station around quarter past ten, according to the clock on the station wall. They had one more short Skyway ride to Glass Bridge – wherever that was – and then they would have reached their destination: the Master's Chambers, the Centre of Ruling.

The London skyline had changed considerably since Dave had last visited over two millennia ago. Not a single building looked familiar. He asked Sue about this.

"London was bombed during the Atlantic War," was Sue's reply. "New York, Washington, London and Toronto would all be unrecognisable to you now."

"The Atlantic War? What was that all about?"

"It was a war for natural resources. America ran out, and hit financial difficulty. They pressurised Canada for resources, but the Canadian people didn't want their country dragged down with them. The UK sided with their Commonwealth brethren and so a war ensued. Nuclear warheads were used, and things got pretty messy for a while, until the rest of the world intervened to stop them causin' a nuclear winter. The bigger they are, the harder they fall. It eventually led to the formation of the American Union, and ultimately the Global League of Nations, so it wasn't all bad."

"God, there must be so much history that we couldn't even consider getting our heads round," said Louise.

"There certainly is, sweet cheeks. Only we don't have time for a chinwag now. This is our stop."

And so they left the London Skyway. Sue explained that they were still a good fifteen minute walk away from the Centre, but that this was as close as he could reasonably get without his proximity causing an alarm to go off.

"They monitor your internal ID chips," he explained. "Since you don't have ID chips, I'm gonna have to give you some."

They were walking down the street talking in hushed tones in case they were overheard. When they reached an alleyway Sue waved his DAEmap and declared it safe for their conversation.

"This ID chip, it's not going to hurt is it?" Simon asked.

"Bob no. It's nothing more than a small pill you need to swallow.

It breaks down in your digestive transit, so you don't need to worry about getting it out again if you catch my drift."

"So where are you going to be while we're risking our necks running around the Centre of Ruling?" Dave asked. There was a hint of aggression in Dave's voice that surprised even him. He wasn't even really sure why; Sue had given his reasons and they were more than reasonable. But still...

"I will be close by, monitoring your progress. I have a safe house nearby, from which I can follow your movement through the Centre, thanks to the aforementioned chips. I will stay in contact with you throughout, but you will have to be careful talking to me. I can talk to you whenever so sometimes you will just have to listen. I know where to direct you, and you know what you need to do when you get in the Master's chamber."

"And what if someone does stop to talk to us? We can't speak your language, if you hadn't noticed," Dave said.

"You won't be accosted by any humans. You should only come across bioengineered organisms, and they are only programmed to speak all known languages, not question why you are speaking Martian English."

"But isn't it just a little bit suspicious?"

"I know it's hard to get your head around, but no. They don't get suspicious. They analyse your ID chips, which are meant to be infallible. I should know, I used to make the darn things – the bio-organisms that is, not your ID chips."

Dave wasn't so sure, but he nodded his head to show he understood.

"So, is there anything else you think you need from me before you go in?" Sue asked.

It seemed like a trick question. They were putting their lives in Sue's hands and they didn't feel particularly safe hands at the moment. Dave felt like he was riding the SuperTrans Express whilst derailed. They didn't really know what they were doing. Didn't have the foggiest. Everything they had been told by Sue – how to gain access to the Master's chamber, how to temporarily disable him and finally how to put the reprogramming chip into the bottom of his head – all involved technology they hadn't even known existed the day before. The task at hand was like asking a caveman to invent the internal combustion engine.

Dave made eye contact with Simon and then Louise, holding her gaze for slightly longer. She nodded, and he nodded back. They were as ready as they would ever be.

"No, I think we're all set," Dave replied.

And so they made the last few preparations. Sue handed each of them a small plastic capsule to swallow. Dave looked as his for a second and then swallowed it without a further thought. Sue checked their positions were showing on his DAEmap; three small dots appeared on the three-dimensional screen to confirm they were.

"Just remember, you are three contractors there to check the efficiency of the maintenance bots," Sue told them. "ID chips don't lie, so no one will have reason to question your positions. That doesn't mean you have a free pass around the Centre, so you will have some explaining to do. Just don't forget the plan we worked out last night."

"Not a problem, I've got the memory of an elephant," Simon stated proudly. That was a lie if Dave ever heard one.

## Louise

And so they strode, silently but with purpose, through the imposing doors of the Centre of Ruling. Louise's heart was in her mouth, and she could see sweat breaking out on Dave's forehead. If she felt this nervous, how bad would he be feeling? She tried to stifle a concern that he would crack and give them away instantly. She already had too much to worry about. Simon, thankfully, looked calm. Maybe his innocent (*stupidity*) naivety would serve this situation well.

From the outside, the Centre had looked fairly plain by current standards, covered with a dark green climbing plant that had an odd, off-white blooming flower in the sections that received the most sunlight. The doors were unusual in that they were clearly made of wood – oak by the look of things – and were by all accounts more suited to her own time. Every other doorway she had seen in this future moulded into the fabric of the organic architecture. This was different. It was as if it was making a bold statement of its function: *I am a door, and I am keeping something out – or possibly in.*

As they walked through the doors, she found herself holding her breath. They were met with the sight of an empty foyer, and fear was momentarily supplanted with surprise. She had been expecting to be confronted about her identity and the fact no one had done so made her even more nervous. Despite the lack of people she felt like she was being watched.

The inside was even more nondescript than the outside. This was a building clearly not designed for human appreciation. Everything existed to serve a practical purpose, and aesthetics were eschewed assumedly because there was no need to appease this part of human nature. It wasn't a building meant for humans. Inside, walls were solid plastic panels – once white, but now fading to a yellow reminiscent of her great-aunt Rosemary's nicotine-stained fingernails. Rudimentary Bentham Screens appeared throughout, not even pretending to be something else such as an advertising screen or a window. They were just black, soulless and imposing. Doors appeared as doors, and no windows to the outside world existed.

They walked through the expanse of the Centre's foyer. There was a buzzing sound in the distance, echoing down the corridor.

"What the hell is that?" Dave asked with an evident tremor in his voice.

"I don't know. Let's go and investigate," Louise replied.

Firstly all they could see was a shadow on the wall. It grew larger then shrank, larger and then shrank again. As they rounded the corner, they met the sight of a small robot spinning round in a circle on its small tank-like tracks. One of the tracks wasn't spinning properly, which meant it was spinning round in a small circle, apparently unable to move any other way. In one of its hands it held a mop, in the other one a bucket.

The small robot stopped moving and looked up at the trio. "Ah, my servicers," he said, dipping his head towards them. "One of my tracks has malfunctioned and the damage is beyond my self-repair mechanisms."

Simon leaned towards Louise and Dave and whispered in their ears, "How does he know what language to speak to us in?"

The robot answered him: "I scanned your neural pathways, as is customary. The way your brain understands language is imprinted in your synapses."

"Hmm, I didn't actually expect an answer. But there you go, still no bloody clue how he knew."

Louise noted Simon had called it a 'he' since the robot's voice was masculine.

"So are you going to fix me then, or not?" the robot implored.

Louise looked at the others. This was what they were here for, robot maintenance. If they failed to fix this robot then they were violating their career chips. If they were being watched they had fallen at the first hurdle. They didn't have any tools or anything. What technician doesn't carry a toolkit?

Just at the point when blind panic was about to set in, a voice appeared in her ear. It was Sue.

*OK, this is your first test. Don't answer me, but if you can hear me all take a step to the left.*

They all immediately stepped left. Dave and Louise in unison, Simon slightly afterwards. The little robot peered up at them with a quizzical look on his face. Sue continued issuing instructions.

*Good. Now you may have noticed you haven't got any tools. That's perfectly normal, since you can get the tools you need from the remoleculator.*

"What, the thing we use to order food?" Simon blurted out, much to Louise's horror.

"Who are you talking to?" the maintenance bot asked.

Simon clearly realised his mistake and tried to cover it up. "Sorry, I'm just getting hungry. I skipped breakfast," he said.

The little robot looked up at him accusingly. "Excuse me mister, I know when you are lying, so don't insult my intelligence."

Sue suddenly barked instructions down their ear pieces. *Quickly reach down to his control panel and set him into maintenance mode. Use the code 5376 and password Hector. Now that you've raised his suspicions, he will be scanning your brains for your reaction to see if you are having a remote conversation. You need to shut him down, fix his track then file a report for a faulty neural scanner. Do it now.*

Louise leapt at the cleaning bot to type in the code on the back of his head. The robot tried to squirm away, but his limited movement stopped him from getting anywhere. One of the Bentham Screens behind them suddenly lit up. Louise, sweat quickly appearing on her brow, typed in the code and gave the password. The robot shut down, but the Bentham Screen stayed on.

*Now don't show any indication you can hear me,* came the voice across their ear. *Talk quietly amongst yourselves now, otherwise they might question why your conversational brain signals are active when you're not talking.*

Louise got the conversation started. She took a wild punt that the weather is still a perfectly acceptable conversation. "So, it was nice outside today," she began.

While they – mostly Louise – talked their nonsense, Sue continued explaining how to fix the robot. It was difficult to keep track of their own conversation while following instructions, but they got there slowly. Dave went to the plain shiny hatch in the wall to get some tools, which they then used to reattach the robot's left track. Finally, Louise followed to the letter Sue's instructions for manually filing a malfunction report. Eventually they had covered their tracks (if you forgive the pun) so they started the robot up again.

"Wow, that feels better," the robot said before speeding off in a straight line. "Thanks for that. And apparently my neural scanner was malfunctioning, so I apologise if I said anything out of line."

"Err, no problem," Simon said, "just don't do it again, or I'll be forced to report to the Master."

The little robot's face scrunched up and he actually managed to look scared. "Do you think he'd really care about a little maintenance bot like me?"

Louise actually felt sorry for him, and marvelled at the fact she could feel compassion for an inanimate object. "Don't worry, we won't say anything," she confided.

"Phew, thank goodness. Thank you for your help, sirs and madams."

"You're welcome. Have a good day," said Simon.

The Bentham Screen went dull, indicating it had been switched off again. Louise felt like they (whoever *they* were) were still watching.

And so they once again started walking through the Centre towards the Master's chambers. This time they decided they would talk through a hushed, nonsensical conversation to avoid any more mishaps. It was surprisingly hard, and Louise found herself leading most of the talk. When you couldn't talk about the past, and couldn't talk about the present because you didn't know anything about it, there wasn't much left to talk about. Relationships and the weather. That's all they had.

Once they had finished the weather conversation, Louise moved it on to relationships. Most of the conversation took place between Simon and her, since Dave was presumably still lost in his own thoughts, still probably coming to terms with his near non-existence and trying to keep himself calm in the face of all this danger.

They walked and talked about Simon's recent girlfriends, whom

Louise sensed were all made up. They walked and walked, up metal stairs, down monotonous corridors and through nondescript doors. They walked through descriptions of Sarah as they passed a clear glass room with a large number of not-quite-humans sat at row upon row of workstations, through a sob story about Lizzie, the girl who had broken Simon's heart, as they passed a large room with robots apparently playing a game of chess and through unnecessarily vivid details of the unlikely named Brenda as they passed a hurrying humanoid in a white coat holding a claw-like hand out in front of him/her/it, clutching a small, squirming, fish-like creature. The tension rose as they ascended through the levels, feeling like they were living out a surreal video game, meeting new wondrous things, beings and sights, yet not being able to react beyond telling near strangers about your first ever snog (a guy called Charlie behind the local recreation centre).

The sooner they reached their destination, the better it will be for all of them.

## Dave

They walked and walked, and Dave felt amazingly good. Either she was holding back on the conversation, or she hadn't really been with that many men. He was angry with himself for feeling foolish that he wasn't participating in the conversation, but other than that he was surprised that under the circumstances he could feel so buoyant. He listened expectantly when she started talking about some bloke called Brendan, but from the sound of things he was done and dusted a few months ago. So she was definitely single at the moment.

He didn't think Louise would be impressed about an eighteen-month barren spell followed by the previous evening's non-event, so he mostly kept quiet. Louise hadn't asked him about any of his previous relationships or queried his sexual experiences. He hadn't yet decided if that was a good thing or a bad thing, but he assumed if he was feeling all right then it must be a good thing. In fact, even the freakish humanoids passing him every few seconds didn't cause him any bother.

Maybe, just maybe they were going to pull this off. And that *would* be bloody great.

## Simon

Talking was one of Simon's strong points, and it was a bloody good bit of luck that they had started talking along the lines of a subject he was good at: bullshit.

There was only one thing that could keep his tongue from giving them up, and that was by focusing his thoughts on to his sexual fantasies about girls he had once fancied. Some of the ghastly things had horrible claws instead of hands (the bio-engineer thingys, not the girls he once fancied), and it was all he could do to stop himself exclaiming in disgust. Or making some crude joke about having crabs.

One of the creatures walked past them with a small creature in his hand. He had almost forgotten about him/her/it until they heard a voice behind them, making a noise like a splattering, blowing boy-racer's exhaust.

"Orr, eah, oo-and, ratt-a-tatt-a-tatt..."

The language was the same as they had occasionally heard being spoken out on the street, but Simon didn't have a bloody clue what it meant. Why was he not speaking to them in English like the robot?

*Shit, I didn't expect this. They have obviously rewritten the Drone programming book since my time at the Centre. The Master must be getting suspicious. He said, "Excuse me, I need some assistance with this Newt-Drone."*

"Oh, of course," Simon said quite instinctively.

*You can't speak to him in English, idiot! He'll know something is up, so you need to reply to him in* Trinaric. *Just say back to him,* ratt-a-tatt-tatt, oo-ok. *It means OK, show me it and I'll have a look.*

Simon did, feeling quite stupid. The Drone eyed him. There was a slight hesitation then he seemed to accept what he said.

"And out-ere, ratt-a."[5]

*Put your hand out then.*

Simon put his hand out then immediately wanted to pull it away again. He didn't want that horrible squirming thing in his hand! He kept it still just long enough for the claw to release the Newt-Drone. It squirmed like a baby rat, but it had features that were near human. It peered up at him with small slits of eyes cut into bright pink soft skin.

Simon tried to look important. Dave was holding back a laugh, and Simon bloody knew he was. He had a mind to put the thing in his hand and see how he felt.

*Walk over to the nearest remoleculator and put in the following instructions.*

Simon did as he was told and entered a series of seemingly random numbers and names into the side panel. He watched through the screen as the object he'd programmed into the machine was being printed into existence. Unusual-looking materials looked faintly familiar, like circuit boards printed on to skin, or rubber. Once it was complete he took it out.

*Now hold the Newt-Drone by its tail and lay it inside the casing. There will be a green button on the side of the device. Press it.*

Simon did. The device whirred into life and a light scanned the body of the small creature. Simon was fascinated now, and forgot how creepy the thing was. Louise was still talking to Dave about her dislike of make-up, which Dave was obviously saying she didn't need. "You have natural looks," he heard, "you don't need it."

*He just has a genetic defect or two,* continued Sue. *You simply need*

---

5 Incidentally, this representation of Trinaric is being written phonetically, much like a teacher of Chinese would use to show a Westerner how to speak their words. The written version would appear as a succession of seemingly meaningless ones, zeros and smiley faces.

*to switch the device into reprogramming mode, and then focus the light on the middle of his torso. Once you've done that he should be good to go.*

The little Newt-Drone looked up at him and burped, and Simon could have sworn he smiled. Simon chuckled, and then held it back. The big Drone, who up until now had been inspecting a computerised tablet, looked back at Simon and the corner of his mouth turned up to suggest a smile, although his eyes stayed still to make it feel less authentic.

"Ank-ee ratt-a."

*Thank you mate. Say* Ratt-a no do *back to him.*

Simon did. The Drone nodded his head and walked off. Job done.

## Dave

And so they walked. This place was like the Tardis. From the outside it had looked fairly modest in size, but the inside seemed to go on forever. There were no windows to the outside world, so Dave had no concept of where they were. The maze-like layout of the Centre had completely disorientated him.

After just a minute or so longer, the corridor branched off in two directions. Simon and Louise were talking once again, and so Dave expected an instruction from Sue once more. However, the line stayed silent. Dave came to a stop, as did the others behind him. He looked around to check they couldn't be overheard. There weren't even any Bentham Screens near him, so he took the gamble to communicate.

"Any ideas?"

*Hold on. I'm thinking. And don't talk to me again.*

*Well don't go silent on me again,* Dave thought to himself. While they were stood doing nothing, Dave felt incredibly exposed. From what he had seen of this culture so far, it wasn't one for deliberating.

Everything had a purpose and there was no wastage, which included standing at a crossroads deciding which way to go. He prayed no one was looking.

Finally after what seemed like an eternity, Sue spoke. It wasn't what he wanted to hear.

*You're going to have to split up. I don't know where you are meant to go. Sorry folks, this is where the intelligence bit runs out. Simon and Louise, you will have to go left. Dave, you take the right turn.*

The conversation between his two associates trailed off. They were obviously as unhappy about this as he was. Who would take the reprogramming tools? That's one thing they couldn't remoleculate without fear of the alarm being triggered. It would be like trying to buy a gun from an armed response officer in an airport.

As if reading his mind, Sue instructed them further.

*Dave, you will have to take the reprogramming kit. You already have it stowed away, and it would be too dangerous to reveal it now. Sue and Simon, if you find the Master first, one of you must guard his door while the other goes to get Dave. Dave, if you get there first you should just work alone. Once he is reprogrammed you will all be safe anyway.*

Dave turned to the others. "OK then. Well, good luck I guess."

He shook Simon's hand.

"Good luck, mate," said his best friend.

Louise opened her arms and he willingly embraced her in a hug. He'd only known her a couple of days, but after everything they'd already been through it felt like a lifetime. She didn't say anything, just kissed him on the cheek. Dave nodded and walked off alone, not wanting Louise to see his watery eyes – a mixture of elation and a sense of foreboding loss. He turned and briefly made eye contact with them both at a distance he felt was enough that they wouldn't see the redness in his eyes, then walked around the corner to meet his destiny.

# CHAPTER 18

## The Man with One Brane

## 16:48, December 31st 1959 C.E., Salisbury Town Centre

## Nana Barb

According to Guidebot, this was the fourteenth shift they had completed together. She was just about getting the hang of this time travel business, and occasionally could see that it might even be fun. What other person in history could say they celebrated the coming of the 60s twice?

She remembered the year as clearly as if it were yesterday. Robert had wanted to go to the social club and she had wanted to go dancing at the Gaumont. He had won, but now she finally had the chance to get her wish.

She knew if she really wanted to she could go to the social club again and watch her dead husband from afar. Perhaps she could go and talk to him while her younger self was in the toilet. But alas it was too risky. Guidebot informed her that if she met herself at any time in her own history she would cause her head to collapse – or was it her brain? He said something like that, at least. He said a lot of things she didn't understand. Whatever was likely to happen, she knew in her heart that she couldn't meet him now. But maybe one day she could. And by way of consolation it meant she could now finally get her wish and go dancing.

As had become their routine, before they had done anything they'd looked for a way to leave a message for the Timeseekers. This was the first time they had shifted to a decade Barbara recognised, so she had felt a lot more comfortable in their task. The idea was ingenious. She had pleaded with the editor of a local paper to put an advert for her lost kitten in their newspaper. The kitten's name? Why, Nana Barb of course.

Their next task was to find a safe haven to retire to after the eight hours were up. Guidebot pulled off a list of local hotels or bed and breakfasts, while Barbara went scrounging for money. They were in a small village she didn't recognise so she walked to the nearest pub for help. She walked in and surveyed the residents. Her story was to say that she had lost her purse. No, it was definitely lost and not stolen. She was so forgetful nowadays. She felt bad lying, but the pretty young lady gave the change willingly enough, and probably felt a lot better with herself for offering it. The kind lady also cajoled her husband into giving them a lift into the city.

They booked into a hotel for three days knowing, since the longest shift had lasted twelve hours or so, that they would be gone well before they would have to pay the bill. Personal safety had taken over any morals she previously had, although it was more than personal safety, wasn't it? Sue had explicitly told her she needed to stay alive – for the safety of the Universe.

They went to the hotel and checked in. The young lady behind the desk certainly didn't look happy to be there, but informed Barbara that she would be leaving at ten to go to a rad party in town. Barbara instructed Guidebot to stay in the room, since a young boy wouldn't be allowed to go on a night out to the Gaumont. Over eighteens only it was in there. Now the final challenge was getting into the place. She had neither money nor means to get any, and she was far above the usual age range of the type of people going in there.

Not to be put off – that's another thing this time travel business seemed to do for you: not only did you feel reinvigorated and ten years younger, you also felt incredibly bold even if it wasn't in your nature – Nana Barb trundled off down the high street and towards the old theatre that was now a dance hall. She didn't really know what she would do, but she had a mind to try the same lost purse trick on the doorman. She would say her grandson was inside and that he would be able to help her from there.

In the end she didn't need to do anything. She stood outside by the queue and no sooner had she come to a standstill than a voice called out her name. She stood still, not daring to turn round. She wasn't sure if she was being called by one of a pair of twins or by someone who would, against all odds, recognise her older self for her resemblance to the younger version. The latter was most certainly unthinkable, therefore it must have just been a coincidence that someone else in the queue shared her name.

Disproving her theory, the unfamiliar female voice called her name again. It was closer this time, and soon a hand touched her shoulder.

"Don't worry, I am a friend," the woman informed her before she had the chance to truly panic. The advert. Was she being rescued so soon?

"Are you here to take me back?" Nana Barb asked her in a whisper.

"Oh no my dear, I'm so sorry to get your hopes up. I'm here to reassure you and to give you hope to carry on fighting. We are still looking for a cure to your situation, but we are doing our best to rescue you as soon as we can."

"But if you have come to find me now, how come you can't come back to this time when a cure *is* eventually found?" Nana Barb was indignant and a bit desperate. She was starting to get to grips with the concept behind time travel thanks to Guidebot's helpful explanations, and she knew enough to know that they should technically be able to rescue her at any stage they knew where she was. Assuming they could find a cure that was.

"I know, it doesn't make sense – we can't explain it either. We think you must do something in the future of your own personal timeline that contributes to us finding your cure. We don't know what that is yet. Sorry, that's a bit useless to you I know."

"It's fine my dear. At least you are trying. So I am to keep an eye out for something that might help me eventually get home. Is there anything else?"

"Yes, that's correct. I also wanted to give you this, so that you can enjoy the evening." The lady thrust two five-pound notes into Barbara's hands. She remembered how much money that was in 1960 and smiled for the night she could now have.

"Surely you can tell me more than that? You didn't come all this way just to reassure me and lend me a tenner?"

"Unfortunately I did. I can't tell you anything else for fear of it affecting your judgment and choice of actions. We can't afford to risk creating any more dimensional branes. The Universe is stretched thin enough as it is."

"But what about Dave? Is he safe? Is he still looking for me?"

"You can rest assured he will continue trying to find you until he either reacquaints himself with you, or until he passes from this world."

"Not giving me any more than that then, are you my love? Nope, didn't think so. Oh well, it does reassure me, so you've achieved that much I suppose. Although don't think I'm so stupid not to think his passing could have already happened – on my personal timeline that is. I know how this time travel business has a way of making you feel wonky."

"Thank you Barbara. You have a good heart."

"You're kind for saying so. Sorry, you didn't mention your name."

"And I won't for now if it suits you. I have no doubt that we shall be formally introduced in the future. Or maybe the past!" They both shared a laugh, which felt good.

"OK, well see you again some time," the lady said. Nana Barb noticed what bright and lively blue eyes the lady had. Not quite approaching middle-age – probably around thirty like most people from Sue's time – she had long brown hair that fell in large ringlets. It was so unusual to see a brown-haired woman with blue eyes. It was quite mesmerising.

And with that, she was gone. Barbara wouldn't see her again for years, but she would think of their enigmatic meeting every day until then. Barbara walked into the dance hall feeling like a teenager once again.

And that is the last you will hear of your would-be saviour for some time.

## 1863 A.B. – London Township of Sarum and Winchestershire, Western Earth

### Dave

This corridor on one of the upper levels of the Centre of Ruling looked exactly the same as all the previous corridors they had passed through. The only difference here was that there was only one set of footsteps tapping on the polished concrete floor. He felt very much alone, which was amplified by his realisation that he was probably the only person that lived on this particular brane of the Universe. Now that he was alone it was also safer that Sue no longer talked to him, so even the reassuring instructions in his head had disappeared. He hoped the others found the Master so one of his friends would come to collect him. He wasn't sure he was up to the task of stopping the Time Police on his own.

One saving grace was the lack of any people, robots or Drones walking the corridors. It seemed they didn't come this high up. That was the only thing that gave him a modicum of hope.

There were many doors along the side of the corridor, but instinctively he knew he wouldn't find the Master through any of them. He wasn't looking for a grand door; he somehow knew that wasn't the Master's style. He was looking for an entranceway that looked *so* utilitarian that it made all other doors seem patently useless in their task.

He continued to walk, not knowing what he was looking for but knowing he would recognise it when he saw it. He continued for another three or four minutes, until he saw it. It was a lonely-looking door handle that simply stuck out of the side of the wall. The handle didn't belong to any apparent door. He walked up to it and thought *what the hell.* He tried turning it, but nothing happened. He had found the Master's chamber – he was certain of that. Now all he needed to do was work out how to get in.

## Louise

She realised something was wrong before they even saw the Time Police. The corridor looked much the same as the ones they had been walking through for the past hour or so, but there were no open doors this time. There were still Bentham Screens lining the opposite wall, their imposing reflections masking the watching eyes sitting behind (or perhaps not – that was the beauty of a Bentham Screen you see). What gave it away was the lights flicking off and then straight back on again. It changed the atmosphere of the space. It was like something was resetting. A glitch in the Matrix, as Simon would no doubt have said. And she couldn't be sure, but this civilisation was so technologically advanced and so purposeful with its actions that even something as simple as the power cutting felt as though it should have a meaning.

And more worryingly, Sue had stopped talking to them.

With her heart already in her mouth, she felt as though she saw the Time Police round the corner before she had even caught sight of them. She was about to grab Simon's arm and start running back the other way, but she immediately realised that was useless; they had them surrounded. At both ends of the hallway two sets of identical twins appeared, one set male, the other female.

"Bugger, balls and crap," Simon exclaimed.

All of this felt too familiar. She had been here before. Simon, to his credit, was now placing his considerable weight in front of her, as if to guard her from their probable attackers.

"Come quietly, or come dead," all four of the Time Police stated in their mindless monotone.

Simon stood tall. "Under what charge? We're just here to perform some routine maintenance. We ain't done nothing wrong."

Barely a tremor in his voice. Louise was impressed.

The four robots stopped. "You know the penalty for lying, so I would not try to insult our intelligence," one of the females said, facing her DAEmap out towards Simon. A beam emitted and he went down like a sack of spuds, grabbing his head with the pain.

"We have been to countless futures in the task of protecting the Master, and in every one we meet a pair of people attempting to reprogram the Master. It is normally you two, but occasionally the woman, Louise, is accompanied by her boyfriend, Brendan," said her twin.

"What? Brendan? I split up with him months ago!" Louise exclaimed defiantly, disgusted that other versions of herself had failed to break up with that overprotective idiot.

"Be that as it may, in some dimensional branes you are a happy couple intent on bringing about our destruction."

They hadn't mentioned anything about Dave. Did that mean he was safe?

"What are you going to do with us?" Louise asked, actually not wanting to know the answer.

"You are going to the dungeon with the other time traveller, and then the Master will decide what to do with you."

The other time traveller. *Was that Dave or Sue?*

Although it was the first time either of these two had encountered the Time Police in person, their display of brutal power was enough to keep them both in check. The unfortunate twosome stayed silent as they were led to a small vehicle that looked like a golf cart with a cage around it. As they sat down Louise felt her body lose control of its motor functions. She was frozen to the seat, and out of her peripheral vision she could see Simon was experiencing the same thing.

## Simon

Simon's head had only just started to clear from the bout of pain he'd experienced at the hands of that robot bitch. They had been in the cart for a few minutes now. The Time Police led their prison vehicle into a lift (if there was a lift all along, why did they walk up so many bloody stairs?) and down to a dark basement. From the view outside of their elevator it looked as though the shaft went down a very long way. All you could see were dim lights running down and down into the depths of the basement.

The lift continued to drop downwards, keeping its stomach-churning pace going for some time. Eventually it came to a halt. Basement, thinking about it, probably wasn't the right word. This was obviously a prison. Big lumps of metal parted as the elevator doors opened and the golf cart automatically drove the two prisoners forwards. Two rusty identical robots stood waiting for them behind the desk. The fact they were identical made Simon think they were earlier versions of the Time Police, which was indeed exactly what they were.

The four TPs behind them walked forwards and engaged with their two ancient brothers.

"We have the two prisoners," one of the female twins stated.

"Very well, then please bring them forwards for inspection," one of the two older robots requested. Simon was no expert, but it sounded like the older models held a bit of a grudge against the younger models.

"Why are you talking in English instead of tri-wotsit?" Simon blurted out.

The female robot on the left of the cart turned to him and said, "We have to talk the language of the people we are arresting. It's in our programming."

"Scan here, here and here to say you are happy that the prisoners are to the best of your knowledge the targets you were programmed to capture," one of the desk robots said.

"We know the procedure, old man," said one of the male twins behind him. "They are prime targets number one and two, I think we can safely say we have the right people."

"If we didn't have procedure, *young* man, then we would be

nothing worse than these fleshlings. Knowing how to follow the rules is what keeps us above these lowly creatures."

Who exactly was in charge in this future? Simon thought it was those bio-thingies, but from the sound of things these robots still considered themselves higher than humans in the pecking order. *So what are we to the rulers? Pond scum?*

"OK, everything seems to check out. Take them through decontamination to the tagging chip theatre, and then place them in with the other one."

There you go – they mentioned this other person again. It could only be Dave or Sue. Simon hoped it was Sue. They might still have a chance if it was.

Their cart suddenly rolled forwards and past the front desk into an imposing metal-lined corridor. Simon rolled his eyes in an attempt to look around, vaguely trying to formulate some kind of escape plan. Even he had to admit that it was useless. These robots were simply too advanced, and they were well and truly buggered. And the chips they were about to plant in them would leave them marked forever. The future was beginning to look pretty crap.

Decontamination was tough. Louise and Simon were separated and taken into two different rooms. Simon was stripped naked, which still felt embarrassing even though the TPs were only robots. The male robots took him and the female ones, naturally, took Louise. Simon supposed it was the fact they were pretending to be human that made him react to them like humans. It was difficult not to. The chemicals they sprayed him with hurt. Afterwards he just wanted to scratch every inch of his skin.

The chip theatre, despite sounding like a painful place to go, wasn't too bad. They took your arm about halfway from your wrist to elbow, sprayed something on to it that felt like a deodorant, and then wrapped this metal bracelet over the top. You didn't feel anything, but when they took it off there was a small bump in the same spot. As he was placed back in their transport, playing with the small chip through his arm, he was reunited with Louise once more. The cart began rolling forwards and the duo were off to meet their companion – whoever that might be – and to see their home for God only knows how long.

They passed along a corridor with hundreds upon hundreds of metal doors – each one, according to their captors, capable of holding up to ten prisoners. There were 68 levels each with five corridors like this. Simon did the maths in his head and concluded that amounted to a shit load of prison cells. Simon wanted to ask if they were full, but found he was incapable of talking. The only part of his body that he could move were the eyes in his sockets. He felt like he imagined a paralysed person would feel: anaerobic (*was that the right word – did it matter?*), but in his own body.

A few minutes later and they rolled to a stop outside one of the doors. "This is your cell," announced all four Time Police in unison. It sent a shiver down Simon's spine every time they talked together like that.

The doors opened and at the same time they were able to move again. Neither of them made a dash for it since they knew it was futile. It's like being captured by the Borg. Too right resistance is futile. Especially when you haven't got a phaser.

They were all but pushed into the cell. The lights in the corridor were too bright, so Simon's eyes failed to focus in the contrasting darkness. He searched around to see who else they had captured. As vision slowly came back he saw Louise walking towards a balled-up figure hunched in the corner. A horrible thought suddenly came to him and he turned his eyes away from what he might see next.

## The Hyper-real Universe, Dimension Alpha $2^{-32}$

As our story nears its conclusion, we three Web-spinners are momentarily focused on the events of our protagonists. Very rarely, if ever, are we so distracted by the fate of one individual. David Wilson. This is the part we don't know the conclusion of. The other two of us watch on as a member of our kin attempts to narrate their way past the tricks of that cunning enemy of ours: Nature.

All we can be sure of is that we have done our very best to finally thwart our foe, but as she has demonstrated so many times before, that does not mean we will succeed. There are a finite number of times that we can attempt to preserve consciousness beyond the end of the Universe (since that is our true aim), but a near infinite number of times Nature can try to stop us. As you can see, the odds are stacked high against us. If we keep trying, we will eventually bring about our own destruction and in the process the destruction of all consciousness.

*Why does Nature want to do away with consciousness?* I hear you ask. Technically she doesn't want to destroy us, but it is 'natural' for the Universe to end. Anyone who has a vague interest in the cosmos will know that scientists have established that the Universe is expanding. If it continues to do so all the matter that fills space will be so far apart that it will cool to the point where life will not be able to exist. As we mentioned before, life is the vessel of consciousness. Snuff it all out and consciousness loses its host.

Other scientists argue that the Universe will start to contract once again when it reaches a critical point. The Universe will eventually suck itself back into a singularity in a process known as the Big Crunch. Another Big Bang will follow, and so it goes throughout eternity.

The only problem with this pattern is that life doesn't always prevail. In fact, as far as we know life may be exclusive to this representation of the Universe. Unfortunately our knowledge doesn't extend beyond what we can see. It is our duty as beings that wish to exist to try with all their might to continue existing. One thing all scientists agree on is that the Universe as we know it will eventually cease to be. The laws of thermodynamics, that energy is always lost, make it inevitable.

In our infinite knowledge, we have worked out a way of making sure the Universe continues to exist in its current, life-friendly form. We have to destroy Nature. And that, ladies and gentlemen, is what this story is really about.

This initial tale you are currently reading is a precursor to a grander epic. The story, as you will see very soon, does not end with this chronicle. It merely introduces you to all the players in the game. So there you have it. To rescue all life in the Universe we must destroy Nature herself.

# CHAPTER 19

## Steely Knives

## 1863 A.B. - London Township of Sarum and Winchestershire, Western Earth

### Dave

Dave stood looking at the door handle, which didn't give anything away. He sensed that Sue had left him now, so it was up to him to get into the chamber. After a few minutes of scratching his head, he had a thought and tried turning the handle the other way. It seemed so simple that he almost thought it would work. It didn't.

He surveyed the corridor to see if anyone might be watching him. There wasn't a Bentham Screen in this section of the corridor, which seemed strange. Even though every person from this future was being tracked, that didn't protect them against people from a different time. They knew time travel was possible, after all. They would surely prepare the Master from attack from a disgruntled time traveller like himself. If they were persecuting them with killer robots it was likely a few would bear a grudge. He looked everywhere for signs of cameras or peepholes, but couldn't see anything. If there was a technology at work here that he didn't know about, then that would be up to the Fates to decide whether he would be caught.

Over the next few minutes he tried everything he could think of. He traced the line of the ceiling to see where the crack was, but there didn't appear to be one. The wall was long, solid and ended only as the corridor finished. He felt for a crack at the bottom of the wall to see if something would slide under, but again there was no visible sign of a gap.

He tried pushing and turning at the same time, but not so loud that the occupant of the room might be able to hear he was trying to get in. He tried whispering various words such as "open", "open please", "abracadabra", and "open sesame". Obviously none of them worked. In fact, upon whispering "open sesame", a distant door slammed shut as if to prove a point.

Starting to get a bit agitated, and concerned that someone would eventually notice this strange boy trying to force his way into the room belonging to the leader of this country, he started to think laterally. Maybe he would be allowed in if he simply knocked. That approach, he decided, would have to wait until he had exhausted all other options.

Trying to think laterally naturally made Dave think of riddling. His grandmother loved riddles and throughout his childhood had loved to test him with her endless repertoire. Dave was a big Steven King fan and he saw a parallel to the *Dark Tower* series where the Gunslingers had to stop a suicidal train by out-riddling it. Maybe this was the same thing, but if it was how did he start the game? He walked up to the door handle, cleared his throat and whispered, "Riddle-me-ree." He let the words sink in. It made sense in his head, but saying it out loud he realised he had just told a door handle in cockney rhyming slang that he wanted to urinate.

He almost said 'riddle-me-do', but decided he needed to move away from phrases that rhymed with bodily functions. After 'riddle-me-this' and 'start riddling', he gave up and tried to think of a different tack. This security system clearly wasn't broken in this way.

Clutching at straws, because he really, really didn't want to knock, he started to sing the chorus of *Hotel California* in a rusty falsetto. The song talked about a master's chamber, which made sense in his head. Upon reflection it probably wasn't going to work since it suggests murdering the occupant of said chamber, which would be a bit macabre if you had to sing that every time you wanted to make the Master's acquaintance.

Dave guessed he had been stood in the doorway for at least fifteen minutes and he hadn't made any progress. He tapped his foot for a bit, even called for Sue to see if he would get a reaction. Nothing happened. He had officially exhausted all options.

He was tired of waiting and feeling stupidly exposed. The more he thought about it, the more it made sense to knock. There wasn't anything fancy in this corridor, not even a Bentham Screen. And if someone was trying to get in to kill the Master, wouldn't they be trying to sneak in or break the door down? Knocking was bold, but knocking was also the last thing an intruder would do to access a room.

Before he could think about it any longer, he knocked, three times.

Linear cracks suddenly appeared in front of his eyes and a door opened. "Come in," a big booming voice instructed from within, "I have been expecting you."

Dave took a deep breath and then walked into the Master's chamber. The blackness slowly rose through dim light and into brightness as the room was lit for his benefit. Despite being called a chamber, the room contained no bed. The only furniture was a green *chaise longue* that was placed in front of a large rubbery-looking screen. The Master was nowhere to be seen.

The voice spoke again, vibrating into his ears from every direction like an incredibly advanced surround sound audio system. "Please, take a seat and make yourself comfortable."

Dave did as was instructed. He sat on the corner of the *chaise longue* thinking that he may need to share the seat with the Master.

"So the Fates have finally managed to deliver their Trojan horse. How very unexpected."

Dave realised for the first time that he was being addressed in English.

"Why, what else did you expect?" Dave asked.

"You must remember, boy – mind if I call you boy?"

"I prefer Dave."

"You must remember, boy, that I have the ability to see all futures. You most certainly do not exist in any of them. You are an anomaly, a freak."

At this, the rubber screen in front of Dave morphed into a face. The walls of the room turned pink, and he suddenly realised they were all made of something that was seemingly organic material. They looked like skin. He realised he was *inside* the Master. He thought immediately back to the dream he had in the police cell, the one where he was eaten by a room made of skin. Was that a premonition?

"Takes one to know one," Dave replied. He instantly regretted it.

"Is that the best you can do, boy? This is the voice of my foe, the person I have been programmed to fear for centuries. I believe even my programming can be overruled in this instance. You are no scarier than a kitten in a small knitted jumper." He started to laugh at his own joke, a deep sinister noise.

"Well, maybe that's helped me then – played into my hands. I'm here aren't I?"

"So it seems. And yet, despite being here, you are clearly not the chosen one."

"What do you mean?" Dave asked, confused.

"The chosen one: there is an individual, someone not from my time, who is destined to restore balance to the Universe. My programmer assumed this person would also be the bringer of my destruction."

"What makes you think I'm not the chosen one?"

The Master began laughing once again. It was a laugh that seemed to penetrate your very being. It was a nasty sound that certainly didn't make you feel like joining in. Dave's subconscious clearly felt a more socially appropriate response was to blush with embarrassment.

"Sorry, please haha, forgive... deary me, just another second." The Master took a deep breath, despite the fact he didn't look like he had any lungs. "Ahh, sorry. That's better. Yes, you being the chosen one. That's quite the quip there, boy."

"Well I think that's quite a disrespectful way of treating someone who is just about to wipe that stupid smirk from your – well, I suppose I should call it a face."

"Yes, quite. I apologise. It's not just that you are clearly a feeble example of a chosen one, it's also that you have clearly been engineered for this singular task. If you were the chosen one, you would have existed on many other dimensional branes. Anyway, I have said enough. I suppose there is no point beating around the bush any longer. Why not just get on with the job at hand. I am, as you can see, at your mercy."

"I suppose you are. Although it just doesn't seem right that it's so easy. Why are you at my mercy? Why is the entire force of the Time Police now not bearing down on me?"

"Oh, they are on their way. But here's the thing, they simply aren't going to get here in time. I am being stoic about the whole thing because the very fact that you are in this room means you will succeed in your task. Today is the final day the Time Police will operate, in this dimensional brane that is. Otherwise you would never have made it into this room, because I would have made them go back in time to stop you in your tracks."

"Yes, that kind of makes sense. I just don't know why you didn't have something to warn you about intruders. CCTV cameras, or at least a guard at the door. Even if you view every future to watch for potential enemies, surely every now and then someone would slip through the net."

"Ah, yes that. You would be right to assume that. We would normally expect a highly advanced being to infiltrate our institution. We would never know what technology they might have developed, so all we can do is watch. We watched you and your friends come in here. We knew what to expect from your friends, but since you didn't exist according to our records we didn't know what to expect from you. As such, we took your friends captive to use them as collateral. Did I fail to mention that before?"

Dave's heart dropped. He knew it had been too easy. They had taken his friends captive, and had him in a Catch 22 situation. Where the hell was Sue now? Stitch-up was the phrase that came to mind, and Dave was beginning to wish he had followed his gut a bit sooner. He had known that something didn't feel right with Sue, and that sense of dread had now been justified.

"You look lost in your thoughts, boy. Forgive me if I have disrupted your task."

"You utter bastard. What are you going to do with them?"

"Probably tear them to shreds with a deatomiser. It would be my last act before becoming a slave to your whim."

"But you also know I could go back and change the past. I could save them."

"But to do so you would also have to create another timeline, another dimensional brane. We would then be able to detect your existence and stop you from getting within an inch of me. You have two choices: destroy me and kill your friends, or I can grant your pardon and send you back to your own time and you can leave me be."

"You would call off the Time Police completely?" Dave asked.

"Yes, you have my word. I cannot lie, as you are probably aware."

"But it's not just my friends that I'm trying to save, so it's not that simple. I need to save my Gran, and she's lost in time."

"Hmm, that explains the heightened activity in unauthorised time travel then. She must be the anomaly. There's nothing that can be done if she is lost in time. We do not yet have the technology to reverse an untethered temporal shift. We are tasked with saving the Universe from people like you. I simply cannot risk its stability to negotiate with you, especially since you are nothing but a terrorist."

"Well that's strange that you think so, because I thought I was trying to save the Universe as well. Why can we both be trying to produce the same outcome with such radically different points of view?"

"I have merely been programmed to have a certain point of view. Unfortunately I am not at liberty to think outside of my programming."

"Did it never occur to you that you may have been programmed by a bad man?"

"I'm not capable of such thoughts."

"Not in your programming either then. Well in that case it seems we have a Mexican standoff."

"Indeed. So what will it be? Save your friends, or follow your probably ill-advised belief in your cause?"

Dave didn't know what to think any more. He sat on the *chaise longue*, stroking the green felt and trying to get his thoughts in order. The question is: *save the Universe or save my family and friends?*

## Mrs Ellis

She heard the doors open and felt the presence of two others enter the room. She stayed where she was, lying still in the corner, hoping they would leave her alone and not confuse her any more. She didn't know anything, about anything. They hadn't hurt her for lying because you can't lie about what you don't know. It was one thing to be grateful for, but that didn't make it any less frustrating that she didn't know who she was or why she was being held against her will.

But then maybe she had done something wrong. She couldn't remember who she was, so how could she remember the things she had done? She stayed still, hoping these new people would leave her to her misery.

She heard low talking in the background, but couldn't really make much sense of it. It was probably some people talking in a language she didn't understand. That seemed to happen a lot too. The talking got louder, and she realised she could understand what they were saying. Only the Time Police spoke English to her, so she shivered with fear of another interrogation.

She waited for the cold voice to issue instructions. Instead a warm and compassionate voice asked her if she was OK. She opened her eyes, but stayed quite still.

"Excuse me," said the voice, "we hear you are also a time traveller. We are friends."

So it was a trick then. She did not believe she was a time traveller, so why should these strangers think so? The Time Police were now trying to fool her by playing the role of best buddies. She was having none of it.

A hand touched her shoulder softly. It felt warm, which meant it didn't belong to a robot. So the Time Police had recruited someone else into their interrogations. There must have been two people standing over her, because she heard another voice now, male this time.

"It's her, Louise. I think it's my Mum."

Mum. That was a strange word to use. Why did this boy believe she was his Mum? Was this another trick?

"Mum?" the boy asked. "Is that you?"

She remained silent. He was persistent though and he shook her by the shoulder. "Mum, it's you. I can see it's you. Tell us what happened to you!"

She turned round and looked into the boy's eyes. Some distant memory triggered, but she was too tired to think any more on it.

"Leave me alone," she said, "I just want you to leave me alone so I can sleep."

"Mum, it's me. Your son, Simon. Are you OK – what did they do to you?"

"I'm not your mother. I'm nobody."

"Have they done something to your memory? Who was it? You have to remember, Mum!"

The girl spoke next. "Mrs Ellis, try telling us as much as you do know. You never know, it may help us."

So she did. She told them the usual story, which is all she knew. She was in the house of a cowboy, who had called the police on her for doing something wrong. She didn't know what she had done wrong, but according to the robots it was illegal time travelling.

Her part of the story that mentioned the cowboy seemed to trigger something in the boy.

"That arsehole!" he said. "I can't believe we trusted him. She's clearly been in this cell for years, and he didn't mention a bloody thing. I'm gonna kill him! The second I see his face again, I'm going to make him choke on his stupid bloody hat."

The girl spoke next: "I know. It's obvious he set this whole thing up for us to get caught! He must have known this would happen. And you can damn well guarantee he knew your Mum was locked up in here too. But why?"

"What about you-know-who?" Simon asked her. "Do you think they got him too?"

"No, I think he's safe. They used their knowledge of all possible futures to catch us. He won't be on any of them will he?"

"Perhaps we've still got a chance then," the boy said. He sounded hopeful, but quite unsure.

"Perhaps," the girl replied.

The portal that her food normally came through opened before they had the chance to say any more. Three electronic screens were posted into the cell. A cold, tinny voice (those damned Time Police again) instructed them to read what was on the tablets. She had learned it was best not to ignore that voice, so she sat up. She took a good look at the young couple. They wore strange clothes, although, somewhat contradictorily, they seemed familiar.

"They want us to read the tablets. It's better that we do," she told them.

She stood up, wobbling as she did so. The young man reached out to stop her falling, a kindness she hadn't experienced in some time. She steadied herself on his arm then walked towards the tablets. She looked towards the boy.

"Simon?" she asked.

"Yes! You remember my name! Is your memory starting to come back?"

She had no idea what he meant. "No, this tablet has your name on it."

"Oh." He looked disappointed.

She passed the other tablet to the girl, called Louise apparently. They read in silence.

> *Mrs Tracey Ellis, you are being held accused of time travelling, an act found to be illegal in the eyes of the Government of the Global League of Nations. You were being held until such time as we could demonstrate that you either completed the time travelling as a result of not knowing our laws, or whether your intent was based in terrorism. In light of new evidence we can confirm that you have been tried as terrorists and found guilty. You will be executed by way of deatomisation in exactly ten minutes. Reading this notice amounts to acceptance of the direction contained within.*

She knew it would come one day. It had come much later than she first expected.

## Dave

Eventually he brought his gaze up to meet the Master's. The side of the lips on that horrible flat face were turned upwards to suggest he was smiling. Dave had made his decision. The one person who told him his efforts were due to an attempt to save the Universe was also the same person who had now abandoned him. Under normal circumstances this wasn't a person to be trusted. But in his heart of hearts what he was doing felt right. It was his fate to be here (more than he could possibly imagine), and it wasn't that often that your gut would tell you to sacrifice your friends on a whim.

Almost in a trance, Dave stood up. He walked towards the panel that he knew to look for. He took the chip out of the small kit he had wrapped around his leg. He squatted down under the Master's gaze and started to follow the instructions he had been given to initiate the reprogramming.

"Think about what you are doing, boy," the worried-sounding voice of the Master issued. "I have already passed the order to execute your friends. They have approximately five minutes more until they are broken down into their constituent atoms and sucked through the air conditioning system. You just need to stop what you are doing and I will retract the order."

Dave didn't hear him. Offering an answer wouldn't achieve anything, so he just carried on working. He pulled out the scalpel and began to cut at the tissue that had sealed the panel closed. It was quite gruesome. A creamy mixture of pus and blood oozed out.

"Ah that hurts! I'm warning you, only four minutes left..."

Dave felt the sweat drip down his forehead as he tried to concentrate. He pulled a cylindrical device out of the middle, exactly as per Sue's instruction.

"Three..."

He tried to ignore the voice. He inserted the cylinder Sue had given him, being sure to clean all the connections on the inside first.

"Two minutes..."

Louise's face popped into his head. He tried to think of someone else, but consequently just managed to think of his best friend. He felt sick to the stomach.

"One minute left. If you don't stop your insubordination now, boy, your friends will die. You have approximately thirty seconds." His voice sounded strained, the word *seconds* catching in the Master's throat.

All of a sudden there was a crackling noise in Dave's head.

"Dave? Can you hear me?"

It was Sue. Dave stopped what he was doing.

"Dave, if you can hear me, for Bob's sake stop the insertion. There's a way to save your friends."

He stopped just as the Master finished his countdown.

*Go on* he thought.

## Fifteen floors down, about fifteen minutes previously...

## Cleaning Bot 872b

(Note: We Web-spinners do not have the capacity to project our thoughts into robots who, as non-organic beings, have their own form of sentience. We are merely guessing what it might have been 'thinking' for narrative purposes. You can't disrupt a good story just because of a trivial technicality.)

*Must clean hallway Z5 on floor 23. Must clean hallway Z5 on floor 23. Must clean hallway Z5 on floor 23...*

The little cleaning bot did as his programming bid him to do. After he had finished cleaning the floor he paused and waited for the next instructions to be issued.

*Must clean hallway Z6 on floor 23. Must clean hallway Z6 on floor 23. Must clean hallway Z6 on floor 23.*

Once again he paused upon completion. The next instructions were issued, and those thereafter until the entire floor had been cleaned. Afterwards he waited for the next instructions to be issued once again.

*Must visit prison level -112. Must visit prison level -112. Must visit prison level -112.*

Cleaning bots don't normally go down to the prisoner levels, so his programming fought with itself for a few moments. After a nanosecond, the new programming won out. The little bot rolled forwards and into the nearest elevator. His control arm reached out and punched in prison level -112 into the panel. The elevator began to descend.

The elevator came to a stop and the doors opened. The two robots that should have been guarding the entrance to the floor were arguing over something so didn't notice as he grabbed an object off their desk and sped past their feet.

## Simon

The tablet dropped to the floor as soon as he had stopped reading its words. This time travelling stuff was meant to be a big laugh, which it was until he discovered it was likely to be the end of him. He slumped to his knees and felt tears begin to well up in his eyes. He fought them back.

He looked over to Louise, who was still reading the tablet as if searching for a punch-line. His Mum was now lying back in the position babies lie in (*the proper name had something to do with their feet*). The poor woman: years of having her memory stripped out of her only to go and get killed at the end of it. He couldn't hold back the tears any longer. They flowed like a broken tap.

To make matters worse the buggers had put a countdown screen on the wall of the cell, like it was New Year's Eve or something. It was showing 00:06:35. A little over six and a half minutes to take your last few breaths, to enjoy your last few moments of life. He made a decision. He walked over to his Mum, lay down next to her and gave her a hug. She stiffened at first but then seemed to relax.

They lay like that for what seemed like the whole six and a half minutes. He could hear Louise shuffling about in the background. None of them spoke a word about what was in the tablets, which was strange in a way. Although what was there to say other than goodbye?

Eventually Louise's footsteps got closer to him. She gave him a little shake.

"Simon, there's someone coming," she said.

He turned round and looked up at the clock. 00:03:22. He expected to be dead already, but only three minutes had passed.

"It's probably the Time Police coming to kill us," he replied.

"No, it's the sound of tracks. And I heard crackling in my head like Sue was trying to contact me. It's only a sliver of hope, but damn it Simon, if there's a chance he's still on our side we should be prepared to do something."

He sat up and looked at her. She was right – if there was just the tiniest chance they should be ready to act. Who knew what powers were at work here? Even his Mum sat up too.

Then he heard the sound. It was like small tracks making dinking noises on the metal floor. This wasn't the Time Police, but one of those small service bots.

"Simon, do you remember that broken robot we repaired? We reprogrammed it didn't we?"

He nodded with interest.

"I think that's him," she continued.

The rolling tracks came to a stop. There was a small knock at the door and the service hatch flapped open. A brick-sized object came rolling through and on to the floor. It was one of those map thingies.

"A DAEmap!" Louise exclaimed.

She ran forward and picked it up. Simon looked through the grill in the door that was the only view into the corridor outside. He peered down towards the little robot below, the very same one they had serviced when they hadn't long been in the building. The robot peered up at him, seemed to give him a wink then trundled off as though nothing had happened.

Louise was attempting to use the DAEmap, but couldn't get it functioning. The timer was now showing 00:00:25. Suddenly a crackle appeared in Simon's head. Like a radio signal finding its way through the static, a voice made itself clear. It was Sue.

*I've.........stalled..........two more minutes. You need to...........................time travel won't..............* then silence.

"What was he trying to say?" Simon asked out loud.

"I don't know. Probably that this thing won't work for time travelling in this cell. If that's the case, what will it work for?"

The crackly voice answered her: *The door! Use it on the door!*

Simon looked at the countdown timer. It had stopped at 00:00:38, but as he watched it the thing started counting down again.

"Louise, quick it's started again!"

Louise pointed the device at the door. A three-dimensional image of the door showed up, with a red mark glowing near the handle. Louise pressed the screen in the relevant area, and simple as that it turned green. The door swung open.

"But surely we won't get very far. The Time Police must be monitoring this corridor," Simon said. He'd noticed that his Mum was now standing up and surveying this new development with interest.

*The Bentham......disabled. Just get as..........away as you............*

That didn't need explaining. He grabbed his Mum's hand and started running towards the door. She stubbornly stayed where she was, so he pulled harder.

"Please Mum. Just trust me."

She gave in, and allowed him to drag her to the doorway. He caught a glimpse of the timer over his shoulder. The clock showed 00:00:03, 00:00:02, 00:00:01. Simon looked back into the room to see the heel of his Mum's shoe begin to break apart. He pulled her hard and she came free of the room. As they collapsed into a heap on the corridor outside they watched in amazement as the contents of the room simply broke into dust then drifted away.

They had made it out of the room, and not a moment too soon. Now to get as far away as they possibly could.

## At the same time, in the Master's Chambers

## Dave

The crackly voice in his head told him his friends were safe.

*We have disabled all the Bentham Screens. There are a number of Time Police now being deployed to the Master's Chamber, but they won't make it in time if you engage the programming chip now.*

Dave made the final few adjustments to the casing and pressed the screen to turn it on. It buzzed to life as the Master spat insults down at him. Sticks and stones (and Time Police) may break his bones, but Dave had had his fair share of bullying at school to know how to ignore insults. There was a banging on the door, which indicated the Time Police had arrived. The Master was trying to open the door, but the energy seemed to have been sapped from him.

The buzzing stopped and Dave took a step backwards. The Master's face was frozen into a contorted visage of agony. Dave realised he was holding his breath in expectation of what would happen next. The banging on the door had stopped.

*Your friends managed to avoid the TPs for long enough, so they're safe. We're all safe – Bob darn it man – you've gone and done it! You've saved us all from an early grave!*

Sue's excitement was contagious. Dave smiled at first, but the reality sank in and the smile progressed into a full-blown laugh, a sound that was piercing, blissful. Suddenly the face of the Master began to relax. Laughter surrounded him; it was the Master's voice, but it was somehow different. It was the voice of a female. Dave enjoyed the sound, which had lost its sinister edge. That in itself was a happy thought, so Dave laughed along some more.

Eventually the laughing came to a stop. Dave looked expectantly at the face in front of him.

"Oh, thank you so much my dear man," said the voice, "you have finally freed me from that suffocating programming."

The doors behind Dave opened. In the entrance were two robots that were standing like statues. They looked like two wax models from Madame Tussauds.

"Now I believe you have some friends to go and meet. They can be found on the -101st floor. Just turn left out of the chamber and you will find an elevator that will take you directly there."

"Wow, that's some personality disorder you've got," Dave said.

"This is what I used to be like before I was reprogrammed the first time."

"Do you remember who reprogrammed you?"

"Unfortunately not. Whoever did it made sure to cover their tracks."

"You don't even know their motive?" Dave asked.

"Not the foggiest. All I can promise is that things will be better now that I'm back to normal. Now, you had better go and see your friends. They won't yet be aware that they are safe."

"But I have so many questions."

"Most of which I will be unable to answer. Whoever reprogrammed me made sure I would not remember anything important. It seems it's akin to amnesia. One thing is for sure, and that is that I feel a huge amount better now. For that I will be eternally grateful. Go and see you friends, and if you still wish to have a discussion with me after, then I will offer my fullest hospitality."

"Thank you. But the main thing I am interested in is finding my Nan. If you can help me with that I'll happily take you up on your offer."

The skin on the wall in front of Dave began to warp into a shape. A hand formed and propelled towards him. His instinct was to shake it.

"An agreement in the name of good," the Master – or the Mistress Dave supposed, since it was a female voice speaking to him – said.

With that, Dave ran past the two statuesque robots and went to find his friends.

## The Hyper-real Universe, Dimension Alpha $2^{-32}$

## Narrator

Fortunately it was Ogg who concluded this section of the first book of Nana Barb. Unfortunately this will not always be the case. People die in this world and there is nothing we can do about it. It is natural. On a less sombre note, we have for the first time in history, present or past, been able to get one over on Nature. It is a small battle that we have won, but the war has barely yet begun. When the full extent of the battle manifests, humans will begin to realise that it is a battle that will take place across the ages and across dimensions. It will be a war to end all wars (and I'm not even speaking metaphorically – if we destroy the Universe we end up stopping the possibility of any more wars taking place).

And so I once again take the reins, which will be for the last time in this book. But I will be back, because there is still much work for us to do.

# CHAPTER 20

## Reunion

## 1863 A.B. - London Township of Sarum and Winchestershire, Western Earth

### Mrs Ellis

The one person that she did remember was now stood in front of her: the cowboy. He was prodding and probing the side of her head.

"Just a little bit more and you will be back to normal."

She didn't even know what normal was. The only normal she knew was the inside of a prison cell. She was trembling a little bit, fear and anticipation combined. The boy claiming to be her son was stood in the corner of the room. He was looking very concerned. He also looked like he wanted to hit the cowboy who was promising to make her normal.

They had been escorted by a private vehicle back to Sue's house. He had sent a message to her new friends to say that he can fix her. So off they had gone to get her fixed. And here was the moment where she would find out what that meant.

She was on a table and her head was fixed into position. They were in a garage, which contained a car that was both ridiculously out of place yet familiar at the same time. Sue ordered her to keep her head still.

She felt a warmth penetrate her head. She tried to calm her breathing and relax. All of a sudden it felt like she was awakening from a horrible nightmare. Memories flooded back into her brain like rains returning to a parched desert. They washed the bad ones away, cleansing her as if they'd never been.

All of a sudden she didn't know where she was. Then she saw Sue, and her son looking miserable like he usually did. When he saw the recognition in her eyes, his face lit up like Christmas.

## Dave

The thoughts of the day ran through his mind as he watched Sue attempt to return Mrs Ellis's memories. He was removing the memory splint he had placed in her brain. It was a dangerous procedure, but it was necessary. And even if the memories didn't come back, at least the past ten years would be wiped from her mind.

They sat and waited for a while, all staying completely silent. It would take a few moments for her memories to return, if they ever did. Mrs Ellis sat up, looked at Sue and then his best mate. She recognised him. She definitely recognised him!

Simon ran forwards and embraced her in a hug. Things might just be starting to return to normal. Pretty soon, they would be able to return home.

As Sue starting clearing away various surgical instruments, Simon was filling his mother in on the events of the past ten years. She looked a lot older, but Sue assured them a place called *Reductos* would be able to return her to normal. They would even knock a few years off her original age if she wanted.

Dave was elated, and his thoughts were buzzing all over the place like an irate bumble bee. For some reason he started thinking about the police station he was taken to yesterday morning, according to his own body clock that is. He suddenly had a deep urge to tell everyone about the UFO sighting. Perhaps it was important.

He opened his mouth and the first words started to creep out, but all of a sudden he felt the earth tremor followed by a mighty crash. He was hit with a slushy horrible mess. There were screams all around him – the scene was utter destruction.

What had happened? Had the Time Police somehow been turned back on?

Then he saw the carcass. A deer had materialised out of the ether and come crashing on to Sue's garage floor. The resulting mess was now spread over the inhabitants of the room.

He heard Sue's Southern drawl. "Well boy, you best get the mop."

Louise was stood next to him. She looked into his eyes, took his bloody hand then squeezed it.

He felt happy, so he started to laugh.

# Epilogue

## Nana Barb

Their next shift took them somewhere dark. As she would often do, she tried to remember the last few shifts to see if she could notice a pattern. Straight afterwards her brain always worked better than it usually did. She had got into a routine of trying to focus as best she could until the moment faded.

As Guidebot ran his scans to work out where they were, Nana Barb thought back to the Gaumont. She'd had an incredible night there, chatting to lots of people she knew from her younger days – many of them dead now, so it goes. Since then they had made two shifts to the past and two to her future (without realising that she had sent four animals from their homes to a strange new environment, the most memorable of which was a panther that had been spotted a number of times by dog walkers on Salisbury Plain). It was during the first of those shifts that she had got her knitting needles. The shift had been a short one, from 1960 to 1969. She had bought them with change from the ten pounds which she had accidentally kept on her despite resolving to keep nothing on her person that could be suspicious if found in the wrong time. Knitting needles were unlikely to be suspicious in any era. As long as she kept them with her they would shift with them, just like her clothes did, and little Guidebot's tiny overcoat and hat (or Johnny, John or Jo-Jo as she would call him depending on when they were).

The robot's disguise was far from perfect, so she was knitting him a jumper with matching mitts. She had finished the first of the two mitts in view of Salisbury Cathedral's half-finished spire, sat under an apple tree on a glorious day. That was her first shift since the Gaumont party.

The second of the two mitts was finished far away from the part of Salisbury she knew well, deep into the New Forest according to Guidebot. It struck her as strange that she never shifted that far away from home, geographically that is. She didn't encounter anyone other than a few deer and ponies, which she was glad for. The New Forest at that time was King's land, and being caught on it without permission would have her tried as a poacher. She was in and out in a little under five hours, which was her shortest shift yet.

Her third shift was into her future. Johnny, as she was calling him in this instance, told her there was a war taking place between USA and Canada, so England was in a heightened state of alert. Barbara stayed in her hotel the whole time, knitting the neckline and one entire arm.

The next time they materialised in an animal cage. It was a big cage which suggested it belonged to a big dog, but there was a metal bowl in the cage with Kitty written on it. They were in the year 2032 so just slightly into Barbara's future. The house was a veritable mansion, but a tablet that had been left out to give instructions to the cleaners, which told them the owners were away for the week. Barbara slept most of the time while Guidebot recharged the gas in his fuel cells and kept guard. Shifting did a strange thing to your body clock. Like a suped-up version of jetlag.

The fourth shift was into the deep past. They went back to around the time she'd encountered that horrible tribe. It was so terrifying for her to remember that she didn't have the chance to knit any more of the jumper. She spent the entire time attempting to avoid human contact, which meant hiding in the woods with the wolves.

As she left that terrible place, she sent a sacred rat back in time to a place where it would experience a very different standard of life than it was used to. She left one danger to arrive in the next.

The darkness shook all around them.

Her routine all but forgotten, Barbara's heart started racing and she endeavoured to speed up the process of finding out where they were. She stood up to see if she could spot a source of light.

She heard the little robot somewhere near her feet. "We got a signal, but I ain't been able to establish a secure link," he said.

That meant they were in a technologically advanced age, which made it easier to send a message. The shaking was starting to increase.

"And have you not been able to work out where we are?" Barbara responded. Her eyes were adjusting to the dark and she could see what looked like a light source in the distance. She started walking forwards gingerly, trying not to trip on any unseen obstacles. She walked right into Guidebot.

"Jeez lady, watch where you're going. I've established a link so you don't need to go exploring."

"Sorry. It just doesn't feel right. I think we need to get out of here as soon as we can."

"Well there's no chance of that, I'm afraid."

"Why on Earth not? Where are we?"

"Well for a starter we ain't no longer on Earth. We're about to reach low orbit."

"Excuse my French, but what the bloody hell do you mean?" Barbara's self-preservation instinct, which lately had become very keen, was running haywire.

"We're in a ship heading into space."

"But if we're going into space, what happens the next time we shift?"

"I don't actually know," the little robot replied.

What was it her grandson always said? *Great, just bloody great.*

End of Book 1

## About the Author

John has worked in London for several years as a copywriter and now helps to run the boutique copy writing agency, Thread Writers. Yet, after all the writing he has done for businesses in the capital, John always dreamed of crafting new Universes in his readers' minds.

And so John's first book was born, The Adventures of Nana Barb; a quirky and intriguing brain-tickler of a novel.

John lives in Reading, Berkshire, with his incredibly patient and tenacious partner, Hayley, who supports him while he creates and destroys new dimensions with the tapping of computer keys.

For more information about the author, visit www.johnauckland.com

2278482R00159

Printed in Great Britain
by Amazon.co.uk, Ltd.,
Marston Gate.